The Alloy

Beraud Rock 2025

This **Second Edition (Revised 2025)** aligns narrative continuity with *The Tribe — Revised and Expanded Edition (2025)*. It includes minor structural adjustments and editorial refinements to reflect the revised sequence of events within the Alloy Series.

First Edition published 2025.
Second Edition published 2025.

ISBN : 978-1-7643565-5-8

Across alloy and memory, the future remakes the mind.

Author website:
https://www.peterbarrett-author.com/peterbarrett

Acknowledgments

Thanks to my partner Donna, Graphic Designer and Book Design editor. Cover image art created by Peter Barrett. Covers designed by Donna Crotty.

About the Author

Peter Barrett - Pen name: Beraud Rock, was born and grew up on Christmas Island in the Indian Ocean. He has spent a lifetime reading Evolutionary Science, Science Fiction, History, and comics as a child. He was not exposed to television until age eleven.

Peter has a fascination and passion for the natural world and our place in the Universe. Peter's world changed the day he examined tiny insects through his photographic lens and discovered their beauty and makeup. He is equally fascinated by the human animal, their degrees of humanity, the complexities of society and the future of the human race. Themes in his writing include Artificial Intelligence, sentience, problem-solving, disaster, and the evolutionary timeline and makeup of life on Earth.

He holds two University degrees, neither of which is related to his previous careers as a Cook, Photographic Technician, and Ophthalmic Technician. When not writing, he spends time with his partner, his chickens (Chooks, as Australians say), wildlife, and grows his own food.

Prologue

The accretion of stellar dust shone red and green and spiralled in a clockwise direction following the mind of the core implant that appeared and was lost in a stark white light of the vacuum. The Universe was uncontrolled after the massive explosion that created the elemental genesis. Unpredictable and vast, matter shone, then went dark, atoms were spent and bonded with irregularity. The atoms seemingly bonded with a childish selfishness and dark cunning, torturous and cruel. The Universe was an atomic anarchy, a bond missing, neutrons and mother atoms rehearsing, testing, and unruly. Like a faulty match, a flame-out, non-ignition Physics. The Suns were cool and terminal, the gas inert, the Universe born faulty, cooling and contraction beginning too early, the result of the Androids conversion and thirst for energy at the cost of mass.

The Robots entered the Universe through a singularity, a desert exoplanet marker and twin star system with vast elliptical distance. Vast their knowledge from the dimension from which they came, the matter clock ticked, few they were, immaculate, shining, their own gods long gone. They were the art, the ascension, the gift, their builders were unknown, a blueprint that was cast into an unknown no return interstellar route. One directive, the tenant, the mission, self-preservation ingrained, warriors they were. Their ancient lost masters of origin gone forever, the robots, had no lament but to survive the early creation of time and stop the conversion of mass to energy. They had been given the Universal sentient element, the last offer of their masters before their demise, a thirteenth Universal noble gas, the alloy, weaving the dust that would create the stars, allowing organic life to tap the Universe's code and counter the Energy Android sentient program flux.

The metal skins shone, reflecting, as the nucleus ignited as a first light sun through the open ship's portal. The thirty milled in the darkest vacuum, arrayed in disordered gathering like interstellar insects awaiting an emerging Interstellar Queen.

The metal platform illuminated green and blue, azure orange reflecting light shards of white. They watched the accretion that was lit, too bright, but successful. The stabilisation of the atomic bond had succeeded and the elements had a structure thanks to the core implant, its intelligent organic design, the fluidity and imperviousness, the noble gas element, the key to a Centillion fusion lock's, a time clock, a controller, the ultimate waiting device. A malleable physical element of the thinking Universe without speech or thought, instinctual, raw, binding, cold.

1

The lifeboat went into exosphere orbit before calculating drop coordinates. Jessica Neuer checked and rechecked, the pressure, water landing evacuation just in case, the suit, her pod of belongings, no going back, the ultimate excursion, one-way, camping for life. The flight chair straps fitted tightly she checked the quick release buckle, it smoothly released and clicked in place. She checked her suit and helmet for vacuum readiness. The console blinked several multicoloured lights.

Remember your flight training, she thought, *sequence, assessment, calm, rational. The life-boats Flight Computer will do the hard work, one function for flight then she could deploy the Life-boats AI with her as a drone for assistance on the surface.*

The Life-boats Artificial Intelligence broke the concentrated clicking of switches and routine, *"Ready Jessica, drop coordinates completed, time to surface, 5.6 minutes, temperate hemisphere zone landing site selected, a partial grass plain based on surveillance, I won't lie Jessica"*..."Iris can't lie," she thought, '*colloquial programming."..."these landings are fast and scary, however the Life-boat does have air-brake steering and a deployable parachute combined with some very tough structural components."*

"Iris, yep, great, thanks," she said wide eyed, *"Jessica, when you evacuate, I will eject, the drone being my interface,"* "Thanks, Iris" *"Ready for drop confirmation when you are Ready,"* ..."lets go Iris Confirmed" ....."*Drop cannot be aborted after thirty seconds"* "Copy Iris, let's go"

She dropped her FAA visor shield on her helmet and waited. Inside her helmet, her breathing echoed a raspy hiss, in contrast to the cabin clicking and buzzing of warnings.

There was a click, a whirring then a clunk. She controlled her breathing. Within a minute the G-force started to impinge as the exosphere enveloped the craft in setting hell-flame, most lights on the console were green, no master cautions. Iris made no more preflight announcements. *"A quick death, or slow burn"* she thought, shifting against the force of her chair. The planet got big through the Flexible-Atom-Acrylic-Glass, descending at 7.5km per second low planet entry.

She couldn't quite believe she was returning to the surface of the planet after her brain-snap. Fear bottled within her chest and she tried to control the anticipation of atmospheric entry and possible cremation.

Friction in incandescent orange, the boat hummed rather than shook, a single continual bleating alarm sounded, the portal seemingly aflame. The G-Force altered as the craft set within the atmosphere, breaking the Mesosphere-Stratosphere boundary of the world and parting the atmosphere seemingly too quickly for its comfort, creating friction on the Life-boat, the generic nature of entry. Iris piped, interrupting her breathing and moment of acceptance.

"Can't do anything now," she thought. Her mind was at a precipice-a moment of *"It wouldn't matter if I died, I wouldn't feel it burnt to a cinder, but shit, I hope I don't."* She thought of the events that may have caused Jason's frantic comm's call on the Ate. *Fucking hell!, from Infirmary to atmospheric entry, why does everything happen to me?*

Iris continued her narration, ..."*entry is successful, braking now, on glide-path, all ok"* "Copy," Jessica croaked, feeling like a pardoned prisoner, "Fantastic Iris do you um"..."*Time to semi-controlled landing,... seven seconds."* Iris lamented answering her question.

"She blew out breath, steadied her nerves, focused on surviving the landing, thought of the design of the craft, super-strong, made to last, "*A highly* engineered, *durable and life-preserving atmospheric entry life-boat with a sophisticated AI pilot,"* was the term used by the manufacturer, she remembered. She also recalled other sayings, *'few plans survive first contact, 'and 'Most plans turn to crap.'*

Scattered clouds obscured the upper Troposphere descent, breaking to streaking light and breathtaking vista, a grass quilt-like mottled plain, Iris had computed well, *"Three seconds...."* The craft shuddered as the air-braking wings deployed and hit thicker air, the atmospheric air-speed indicator slowing from 800 km/h the counter in a frenzied countdown slowing, the beeping stopped as if the die had been cast and all bets were off. *"One hundred and sixty to one hundred and eighty knots was the life-boats' lower landing speed limit,"* she thought. The terrain closed fast, sky dwindling, land rising like dropping into an earth sea,

In a sudden gasping moment the life-boat struck the sedge grass plain-runway, at *200 knots*, a terrific multi-shuddering slam, knocking the breath from her, the parachute deployed immediately then sending her squashing into the back of the chair like a highly vacuumed piece of meat in a plastic food preserver, accompanied by a ground-zero, bone-jarring, eye popping, jaw stressing, and ear watering tone.

The life-boat made a sound like a five hundred tonne bass drum full of rocks being thrown onto dry grass within a field of egg shells. Something broke, the beeping started again, she saw a blurred landscape. She instinctively braced with her arms around her head, relaxed her posture as in training for impact, but retaining grip, the slide to end all slides, *"childrens dream, mud fantasy, Crap help!,"* she thought, her eyes felt like frozen marbles.

"Terrestrial surface contact" Iris stated in calm control. The life-boat emitted a high pitched whine like a wounded animal, the outside hiss contrasted by inside clamour and the incessant master-warning tone. The roar outside seemed to be the precursor to inevitable impact, terrestrial crush-depth, flayed metal, fire, compromised structure. It seemed inevitable something would be struck or blown away, unravel, ignite, but

the waiting continued as if torturing her with suspense, a surprise, then bad news.

"Hang on, momentum slowing" Iris ejected the parachute, sending her forward with the momentum again, the craft speeding up then slowing dramatically in a burst, then becoming airborne again briefly as it hit a small rise, twisting and crunching again into the grass cover, jolting her like a puppet, shaking the breath out of her lungs and with mighty force, seemingly to tear the seat from under her, then swinging, jerking, buffeting, whirring, hissing, sighing then whispering, sliding at speed, sending lumps of mud into the air outside passing the portal in a heavy globular spray and grass detritus.

The final slide spun it three-sixty, finally coming to a complete stop making her reflexively grab the side of her seat like Carnival wheel ride. The Flexible-Atom-Acrylic-Glass was now a blur of brown sludge with streaking sand, smearing downwards in small rivulets, two warning signals blared at different tones. Jessica reached above silenced the master-caution.

"Are you ok, Jessica?.".."Yes, ...ok Iris" She was momentarily stunned, the shock of first contact. Shaking a little she got terrified of fire, looking around as a bead of sweat trickled down her neck.

"Landing successful, there is no need to rush Jessica, all systems have survived intact, there is no immediate danger" She heard a clunk as the drone was released..."Wow, that was some ride" she stared at the console, alert for the smell of smoke in the cabin, adjusted her helmet and raised the visor. "How did you know that the grass landing area was suitable, Iris?" *"I didn't, but saw during the descent, it seemed free of rocks, I am glad it was the case"* 'Yes, fine flying Iris" *"Thankyou Jessica"*

She checked herself for any unfelt injury, the emergency lighting had come on, the console showed the airlock door was ready to be blown, flashing patiently. She brought up the display to show her outside, the screen divided into four sections, showing Iris's view above the craft, her in her seat, looking dishevelled, *"Still strapped in like the first monkey in space,"* she mused, a ground level shot from the boat from the mid-section door and a view of the drone from the the top of the life-boat.

The drones eye behind the boat showed the thousand metre ploughed trench from the landing which had dug a stark pillar-like concave among the swaying tall green wiry grass that stretched far to the foot of the first rise as if made by a giant with a flame-thrower enabled spade. The gouged trench smouldering, some dry grass seed heads on fire shaped like bottle brushes, hissing, aflame and falling into the mud, amid plumes of steam rising into the cold.

Iris scanned around, the vista showing they had landed on a vast plain that narrowed into tall forest another few hundred metres distant, the surrounding hills to her right, jutting rock, strange shapes, like weathered marbles with fallen shale-like shards similar to stripped bark, eroded and peeling off in lengths. Tall imposing mountains dotted the sky-line, stark blue lines and yellow haze in the afternoon sun.

Large Cumulus clouds hung in patches, with wind swept tails, Alto-Cirrus trailing across the greenish-blue sky. Out to the left side a marsh extended in a small valley with dotted lichen, small shrubs and tiny mounds of moss covered pebble where a hidden stream seemed to be winding through giving itself away by the flattened grass and darker patches. Poking through the undergrowth were tall spiky palm-like trees rising like desert cactus from the wet marsh. The wetland stretched far beyond to the East with a view of the horizon, a contrast to the Western mountains and the high ground which seemed to rise and rise like it got carried away in a dry Geological fury.

She wrenched herself out of her seat, feeling like a thrown puppet after a show. She pressed the door command button and the lock opened outwards with a groan and thump of steel on steel. The light shone through to the lifeboats interior, the haze within a mixture of dust particles and moisture. "Iris, are you there?," *"Affirmative, here Jessica,"* Iris said, hovering about four metres up above the lifeboat. The air was super-fresh and a relief after the boat, the wind was mild and the twin-suns were warming the area as if in anticipation of her arrival. The smell of metal cordite and burning vegetation wafted through the air as she stepped down from the craft onto a soft marshy grass surface, sedge tufts and mineral grain sand, that she knew well. Her head felt like soft cheese and her body like a skeleton skinned, she had hurt her shoulder and her ankle had a dull pain.

"Iris, what happened?" "Why did we abandon ship?" She walked a few paces to a seat high rock, squinting with the light and breathing out in relief, her flight over. The rocks' minerals were glistening and sharp with the light, she noticed as she sat on the stone, looking up at Iris, still hovering in position. *"The ship went into fusion drive mode, which means the ship was preparing to leave near planet orbit"* "And?" she said, waiting for more information. *"The ship has left orbit and has sped away and now is at two thirds speed, the fusion drive will reach full speed ahead in about two hours, that means that the ship is approximately..."* "Iris, stop.." *"Yes, sorry"*

"So, Ate Succession has left orbit and is no longer here?" *"Correct,"* Iris said. "Why?" *"This is uncertain as I do not have data on why Anastasia decided to initiate such a command"* "So there was no fire, disaster, something threatening the crew, we had to abandon because the ship just left?" *"Yes, the option was to stay on board or leave the ship, I would suggest that a fast decision would have had to be made, either way"* Her head was reeling, so many scenarios were coming into her mind. She tried to think why Jason had given the command but they obviously wanted them off. A malfunction, a threat, she could speculate all day. "So what more information do you have?"

"I know little else, as I am a Life-boat AI and I am in effect a standalone system, I can only give you data about systems

function which I have to know when abandoning ship, for example, I have to be sure the Lifeboat has a good chance of atmospheric entry, is functioning to limits and has a chance of survival" "Ok, so were the Ate Successions systems working normally?" *"Yes, all systems were normal"* "And it is reasonable to say then that Anastasia or someone else gave the command to leave orbit?" *"Yes, a reasonable assumption"* She lent back, the enormity of it sinking in a bit, she gazed out towards the West, more mountains and around where she was, across to the East where the flat marsh extended seemingly forever. "And where are we?"

"Due to the movement of Ate Succession during the exit-orbit procedure, and our trajectory, we have landed on the other side of the continent where the base camp is situated, which equates to 4786 kilometres away, this plain extends far West, the Eastern plain becomes eventual coastline and an ocean is apparent, 34 kilometres distant, suggesting we are on the furthest side of the continent." Iris replied. "Great," she replied, looking around the landing site, still smouldering with the smell of burnt grass and heated mud.

"What about Andreas, where did his boat go?" *"The Lifeboat with Andreas has had a malfunction I am afraid, it has landed on water within the Ocean between here and the next continent, I have been unable to contact the AI from that boat, the beacon was activated but stopped shortly after contact with the sea"*

"That's terrible Iris," she said thinking of Andreas and her parting quickly to get to the boats in the corridor outside the Infirmary. "And our beacon, the lifeboat signal?" *"Activated, however the beacon only has a terrestrial range of two hundred kilometres, if Ate Succession was still in orbit then the signal would be relayed but that is no longer the case"* "Ok, so what about food, what do we have, how long will it last?" *"Thirty days on normal consumption, that is unrationed"* "Mmmm, she replied with increasing concern, and also realising that she had no fear of being back on the planet's surface.

7

In the relative stillness of the smoking landing zone,the realisation of "final contact" became apparent. The fact that there was no getting back in the Lifeboat, no other crew. A long trail of heated mist from the heat of landing rose into the green sky around her. She wondered if Jason, the others had made it. *The Explorer? Did they evacuate on that? What the hell happened? Did Andreas get away as well on the other boat? Those raised voices she had heard on the comm's channel, Equipment failure, the Ate?*

2

Jason Findus kept watch upon the ramshackle village from his concealed position among some thorny shrub and a clump of anarchical vines, for two hours, completely invisible inside the thicket, in the gloom, his small entrance seemingly a part of the undisturbed growth at the edge of the treeline.

The former scientists clearing was now a dirt-strewn morasse of pestilent human waste, discarded technology, and rudimentary stick and grass huts, overseen by the charred Explorer vehicle atop the granite escarpment in the distance. *Had it been months after they had landed on the escarpment for the last time after the evacuation? Three fuscking months, you don't remember?,* he said to himself.

It had rained in the early morning, a straight hard downpour from low lying confused clouds that hugged the plateau, then descended further as if in conversation with the terrain, swirling and beating a water drum. The thicket stopped the force of the downpour but not the cold drips that searched for his neck and ran down his jacket and his forehead into his eyes, but he did not move, waiting, silent. He was used to the weather, had hardened with living in the open, the cold, but never hardened to hunger, a smouldering desire that ate at his psyche and lamented to him constantly like a pandering mother.

He emerged from the Forest boundary after being convinced there was no one there, stretching out, looking at his feet then up and around, then stopping and crouching on one knee, remaining still. The gloom of the morning hid his green form, a tight fitting coat, dirty and worn strange trousers of shiny material, black, down to sturdy space type shoes, contrasting with some white and orange. Ragged hair, unkept beard, a pole of two metres in length sharpened at the end into a dangerous point, across his knees as he waited half hidden by the grass waving like friends by the shifting breeze.

Tired, worn, hungry, dirty, stinking and nervous waiting for a further five minutes, looking, smelling, silent, before rising and crossing the clearing to the distant smoking tribal-like village, wary like a ground bird looking for claws and other destroyers of wings.

He stood contemplating the miserable encampment clearing stretched an irregular forty meters or so in a circle, the rudimentary shelters broken and haphazard, smoke rising through one of the five, a pile of discarded flight items near a fire pit, cracked helmet, some torn gloves and other white unrecognisable items of clothing, one blood stained he noticed.

Great Mother of time, no potty training here. The grass was long worn to dirt and pebble, a makeshift rack made of wood, he noticed, a homemade axe made of sharpened stone wedged in a log, a scarecrow made of dry grass in the field beyond guarding a miserable overgrown garden bed with some spiky plants jutting out in haphazard directions.

No method here, no storage, waste removal, construction intelligence, no navigation in anything. Nor any agricultural skills, that's evident. What do they eat for pity's sake?

"What a shithole," He noticed the twin suns had risen above the plain and hovered ready to light the stony plateau that they had landed upon about three months ago, the clouds abating, their morning discussion over. "Extinguished hope of fucking humanity," he lamented softly. He gazed around, ever wary and noted the familiar landmarks of the area.

He could see in the distance, at the top of the plateau which reached a hundred metres or so, the now useless Exploration vehicle which had succumbed to some catastrophic fire and was perched atop the plateau in the distance like a haunting unmotivating effigy, now broken like a child's discarded and barbequed sandpit toy, an affront to care and regard, a charred stone age portent, a monument decrying the loss of technology and destroying anything of use.

The area beyond the miserable village to the other side of the clearing now resembled a makeshift refuse tip, discarded white stained vacuum suits, piles of kevlar storage crates, the energy tents were gone seemingly somehow deemed useless and disabled, deflated wrapped in haphazard balls of fabric and tossed to the forest boundary.

"Fucking idiots" came out suddenly with quiet concerted venom. The only recognisable structure was the Communication tower in the far distance which he thought for a moment dryly, *still stands like a monument to a past civilisation*, until he saw that someone had tied two weather balloons to the top which hung in the windless clearing air above the structure, between the balloons, a vacuum suit, stuffed with dry sedge grass, splayed like a lynched starman, the helmet falling forward like the figure was once alive and now had succumbed to the crucifixion.

He returned to his present reality. If he got access to this now shitty little village's communications tower, once the Scientists camp, he might be able to get remote access to Dong-hyun Han's weather drone which was called a *Tempestas* drone, similar AI but with different capabilities. If he could find and control the drone then he could tilt the odds in his favour, the others seemingly oblivious of the benefits of technology, a central theme of their demise so far.

Their tribal state, he pondered with sound hatred, r*esembles a religious madness mixed with uncivilised rancour, a decaying corpse alive and meandering across a judgement held plain,.....* *fucking idiot's*, he lamented, making sure to survey his surrounds for someone with a spear or crossbow, movement, trap, ambush.

His situation was dangerous, being out in the open away from the forest, looking up and groping his spear as he walked, sensing for danger, human danger, limping slightly, his wounded leg partly healed but never right, the arrow had taken a chunk out of his thigh and then got infected as he had to hide in the forest for some time, the hunters searching, rummaging, calling mockingly, laughing at comments unheard, salivating, leering hooting.

He found a tree with a vine growing up the trunk creating a sort of hollow and he stood straight behind it parallel with the tree like a part of a plant, quiet. A certain close-call search broke off after he heard someone yell something in the distance, important enough for the mob to disperse. The last thing he heard was Akseli Hoskinen's voice, distant but clear enough in the forest gloom,

"Oh, Jason, where are you Jason?.....my little Navigator you, he, he," his tone hardening, *"We'll be around chickadee, the totem pole is waiting for your embrace"*

His surface suit long discarded, he had to make do with a homemade pair of trousers *made with weather balloon fabric* he thought. *What a fucking joke, humanities hope dressed like a fool being hunted by former crew mates!* He never knew how much he could hate until now.

I have a seething   desire for retribution, heads on poles, conquest, a medieval tempest across a plain of skulls and broken bones, riding a horse, a vengeful warrior...Those evil cretans, seething demented monkeys, I"m coming for you all , he thought to himself.

The problem leg started to really hurt, feeling the numb pain, "Aghhh," he said softly clasping his leg. He glanced inside the closest dim structure, nothing, dirt floor, with some scattered grass, a makeshift bed made from two poles across some boulders.

Senses heightened, attuned to the area that he had surveyed from distance for hours making sure his former colleagues were not laying a trap. He crossed the "village" square, a clearing between the shacks, beyond a tall pole visible just above the farthest roof, continually glancing around in case of movement.

Sighing and looking skyward, the twin suns cast streaks of light across the ruined area and lighted the clearing, contrasting the broken human habitat and beautiful landscape stretching away to the edge of the forest and away to the mountain range on the horizon. A shooting star streaking bright white then lost among clouds, three moons in triangular formation, two tiny ones and a larger one, making their way to Western horizon, making way for the twin-suns altering the Eastern sky.

Reaching the first miserable shack, he could smell burnt refuse, excrement and hair, synthetic odour and smoked cotton, alcohol fumes of some sort. Looking inside,there were used bloody bandages, a bottle of water, stained yellow cloth, a metal rod and discarded remaining first aid syringes, seemingly flung away in a rough circle shape, cotton wound cloth and a used bottle of alcohol. *This was people working on someone wounded,* he thought, *fast, desperate.*

Blood was everywhere, soaked into the ground. Taking time to back out and view the area around, glancing between the huts and across the plain to *check for "marauding Starship crew."* he thought, glancing back into the mess covered floor, before moving on to the distant pole, beyond the next hut.

At the "Totem Pole" he thought, *murderous Idiots*, the small stripped tree on a slight tilt, moving against the clouds. Two make-shift ties were attached to the pole, it was smeared with what he thought looked and smelt like faeces at the base and there were spotted blood patches on it. Around the pole was a cleared and seemingly swept dirt circle, the brooms' fibrous marks showing in the sand. He moved through past the pole, and to the other side and crouched down behind another stick shack to view the area to the communications mast, making sure it was clear, searching for movement, sound and malevolence.

The wind softly blew through the stick structure making a fine whistling noise like a pine tree in the wind, rays of the warm suns filtered the area and he could hear the river yonder rushing it seemed, with greater intensity as if mirroring his experience.

The hut was empty, glancing in noticing someone had placed a hat made of straw in the centre, there was a tin in the corner and a stale smell of piss. He turned away in disgust and stood up, moved slowly, keeping his sight up, looking around like a hunted animal and made his way to the Tower and the effigy.

Across the semi-grass area to the tower. Of the Communications tent there was no sign, a barren patch of earth signified its demise, decrying its passing littered with discarded energy bar wrappers, some unrecognisable clothing, several water bottles, and a smashed laptop the screen partly separated from the base, the keyboard hanging off like a wounded animals appendage, a mass of wiring sat on the stony ground in a coloured swirling tangled pile, inert, useless.

The area was open, with *no cover from the shitty shacks,* he thought, hurrying across to the base of the tower where the small patch box was where he could patch his tablet and configure the drones interface. This was only made possible by Dong-hyun Han's weather satellite which could be configured as a communication relay among other useful capabilities such as obtaining mapping data of the area, weather prediction as its key role.

Stopping to listen, reaching the base, the tower rising thirty metres above him, a stay tapping the side of the echoing metal like it was in mechanical thought. Taking refuge behind a concrete base pillar from one of the supports he reflected on how important the decision was that this tower was built.

The depiction of communication in Science fiction was laughable he mused, seemingly effortless, in reality baseless. Without the satellite, *I would be fucked* he added in thought, without Ate Succession and Anastasia, this tower was the key to getting a link with the satellite, enabling the drone and getting the "Fuck out of dodge," he dryly uttered shouldering his pack and removing the tablet.

His last working technology device, apart from the *Organic Taster and Atmospheric Analyser (*OTAA,) his trusty *Ottar,* which had given him the go-ahead to eat an orange berry variety he had found in the forest, the readout indicating it had nutritious properties, containing vitamin C, B, D, fibre, and protein, being a superfruit in the Ottar's analysis, and probably the only thing that had kept him alive, and now the weather was getting colder.

Things are going to kick off then, he thought. The Ottar also confirmed that the pineapple-like fruit atop the plain shrubs was nutritious, if rough tasting, containing fatty acids and some thiamine.

Nothing would beat a large steak though, he thought, scanning the area behind him for a possible ambush, *and ice-cream.* His mind was obsessed with food, sometimes overwhelming his thoughts and now he had started to dream about it, sitting down to Mediaeval type banquets with elaborate twenty metre tables piled with pigs heads, smoked duck carcasses and salmon grilled stacks of fillets.

Tiered trays of cheeses and blocks of butter, wood-fired oven sourdough bread loaves, fruit platters, salami rolls and potato chips, and strangely *But not maybe for a dream* he thought, *fish fingers and tartar sauce, the unknown regal participants, naked of course,* he smiled, with puffed red faces, engorgement and bantering nonsense.

His tablet was a wireless device but he had to patch into this console manually with a lead because that was the only way to reboot the tower control box as it had been disabled when Ate Succession had left orbit, its umbilical lost.

The tower, he knew, should then transmit a wireless signal from the box, its power obtained from the small fusion power-cell. He turned on his device, waiting for boot-time, wary of the possibility that one of the others might detect his tablet's signal, then dismissing it as beyond the reach of crazed stone-age adolescents, but aware they were all tech-savvy in their own rights when they were sane.

"At least the password is easy," he said softly, thinking of the time Ye-Min got curt with Kylie Albott about making the password easy, *"Who is going to hack the tower, Kylie? There are no scammers four light years from here that I know of that could access it,"* Kylie relented, smiled and changed the login he remembered after hearing the exchange.. His tablet was showing a box-prompt to login to the Towers interface:

Admin: Tower
Password: Tower

He looked up suddenly with a start, thinking he heard something, something mechanical, *no,... a voice maybe,* he thought. The base of the Tower didn't provide any cover, he felt exposed, he listened intently to the sound thinking it might be a conversation.

With the tower's wifi connected he decided to get some cover, thinking the range should be sufficient to type in commands from a distance, the sound rising and falling in the morning air across the settlement. He grabbed his pack and stuffed the tablet in, shouldering the pack and jogging out from the tower base into the far stick ruin closest to him, past another indescribable mess of fabric and metal and the smell of urine.

This was the furthest structure before the forest allowing him to scan the settlement from the opposite side to where he entered. The stick mess covered him as he crouched behind, glancing at time to time behind him and at the forest for any threat. Listening, he could still hear the sound but chose to ignore it for now as the connection waited for his input. He had no idea where the drone was, but he knew that he hadn't seen it and the others had not been using it, he doubted that they actually knew how, their break from reality complete.

The remarkable thing being, that they had no idea or consciously shunned technology. Like a demented sect milling around a sentient capable robot which held their salvation and all their answers to a better life but only if they chose to turn it on. Content in magic, smoke and mirrors and fundamentally denial, they chose a false god.

Navigator@AteSuccession~$
Fetch -f -s
tempestasdroneGemmi7aweather home now
Password:
****

Karl-AI tempestas is in emergency mode - Tanya Geary- Ate Succession Logistics Officer
Location: SSW 45km 152.8787.

"Tanya, they are alive!, ha, ha, fantastic," he uttered softly. He looked at the readout elated that Tanya seemed to be sane and maybe with Tom. He quickly sent Karl-AI a message that he was alive and sane and packed his tablet in his pack thinking he had to go in case someone arrived.

Starting back towards the village perimeter, past the stick fence and down a small embankment that was marshy and contained high grass before the ancient forest. The ground had been flooded and he sopped his way through the cold water in a better mood than when he arrived and looked around for any suspicious movement.

The trees ahead and something else caught his eye, a white container with two orange stripes on either end was nestled in the marsh almost invisible in the high grass. Moving closer and recognising a terrain crate that the team used to bring supplies down from Ate on the many supply runs. Perched upon the terrain crate was a backpack, the type used for day trips on the surface.

Thinking he may have found a mother-lode, a lottery win or some treat he knelt down and rummaged through the pack finding the first of the "Motherlode" items. *Triple pluck-a -duck, Cox-AI, the fucking ships AI Doctor* - so *hang on, this is Katie's pack then, fuck, she didn't even open this, must have abandoned it here.*

Glancing around the suns had risen higher, he surveyed the perimeter again for movement. Opening the crate, releasing the two heavy latches on either side.

Pluck a Duck, this is a medical crate, he thought of the two orange lines a dead give-away. Inside the crate was packed and he knew the crate had never been opened. He rummaged through their supplies, taking the advanced first aid kit out. Inside he saw toilet paper, surgical tools, extra bandages, towels, a tourniquet and several boxes of saline, an IV and medicines, antibiotics, and a small foldable table for surgical work. Wanting to take it all he knew he couldn't possibly carry it and stuffed as much as he could in the two packs.

Grabbing the side handle and dragging the crate across the marsh. Looking back for any danger from the village side. He stopped and took stock of the ramshackle village to see if there was anyone following him, then continued, reaching the forest cover, making his way around the curved tree perimeter as he hoped to get to his camouflage hideout and secure the crate there for future trips.

He hurried from the area thinking the tribe would return at any moment and made his way with his newly acquired booty into the forest and checked his direction towards his new home on the Western plain. As he strode through the reeds he wondered of the others as always. Did they all ape-shit out or was he the only "survivor?" *Anders and his fucking spear, and he still owes me thirty bucks from cards!*

3

Anders found himself wandering through the new camp area past the Bee-Brown Toilet and out in the cold night. The snow was falling heavily now and the dark entrances to the new camps caves muted and silent, a contrast to the day's activity of come and go, setup and build, prepare and refine, dig and grow, adjust and screw, the Bee-Brown canisters somehow within his sleep-walk psyche.

Awake now, but not before, he wondered where the hell he was and why he was not on the Explorer or *Ate Succession. What the hell, am I doing here, where am I?" he* thought suddenly and totally confused, looking into the darkness and the Bee-Brown toilet light, trying to use his flight training to calm himself and thinking that at any moment he would awaken from a dream within a dream. *Am I dead?,* he wondered. *Is this what happens, you are walking around a toilet?* He looked around and to the far side of the camp, there seemed to be an entrance there where the rock walls parted and two large trees grew either side.

Walking down the sandy path, which winded through a low-lying thicket of trees and strange looking grass, and vines that hung from the branches like extinguished party lights, glistening in the three moon lights. Walking to nowhere from nowhere and didn't really care or understand, he knew he had to get to an open area to breath and assess what was going on.

After twenty minutes of stepping on sand and snow he emerged from the low trees onto a beach that he could see stretched far into the distance, curving to the horizon, the waves crashing in the snow and the sand replying with rasps and wisps of water and salt. The three moons were directly above, *high-moon,* he thought. He was familiar at least with that term, he used to sit with his wife and gaze at the moon and then wait for the Northern lights to green and turquoise the sky.

He stopped and looked around, then noticed three moons, not one, and was staring at them. *Is this my sight?*, he thought. *Am I drunk?*, he added. He could smell the salt and the slight freezing wind, so he knew this wasn't a dream, dreams always have very little of that type of thing for him, they were always visual, short and to no point, nonsense and usually disappointing, but occasionally pleasurable. He breathed out heavily, feeling a little faint and frightened and sat in the mineralised sand and watched the breakers smash onto the shore as if they were trying to get through to him.

"Anders!" A voice behind him made him realise he was not in a dream, another human was here, as he turned and saw Katie Arnold walking towards him from the entry to the beach he had taken, her form unmistakable and her voice even less so, he being the subject of many a dress-down from his First Officer. He rose and faced her, as she approached, now feeling shaky and shivery, folding his arms and realising how cold it was.

Her steps on the sand preceded her presence, eventually standing in front of him, her face concerned and delighted at the same time, he could see in the moonlit reflection. "Anders, Encroacher, what are you doing out here?," she asked, facing him. He noticed two others coming from the beach entry and wondered who they were as he looked at her, not quite believing it was her and thinking of reasons why they would be here in this odd place.

"What is an Encroacher?,"he asked, confused. "Don't worry, I think I can just call you Anders now," she replied, smiling and then hugging him. He could smell her scent from her hair and he was relieved and felt warmer like a familiar sun had welcomed him and settled his thoughts. He held her and knew that she was familiar and that he had been with her before on some level and that she was kind and knew him well, and at that moment it was enough for him to relax and breathe and be content for a few seconds.

The others came into view, Kylie Albott and Ye-Min stood and consoled him, Ye-Min, her hand on his back and Kylie her hand on his head, while saying, "Welcome back Anders, welcome back" Katie Arnold, released him and stood back looking at him, "Come on, we have much to tell you and you need to get out of this cold," she said, Kylie Albott carried a coat which she helped him put on, he felt instantly better and they walked up to the beach entry together and back to the caves.

They put him in a cave, he assumed this was where he walked from, his bed was a strange modern looking fabric and when they put him in it he felt instantly warm. "Rest now, ok Anders, you will probably dream a lot tonight," someone said but he couldn't make them out, there were others there, in the darkness, the only light being a torchlight someone had at the entrance to the cave, the light reflecting from the mineralised rock surface, and he thought that it was Akseli Koskinen and how that was apt if it was.

He lost consciousness almost immediately and lamented down to somewhere deep and warm and alien, like he was cast within an awakening stone and was metamorphosed into a mineral and then forged into a metal, his mind was cast adrift in a Geology of lament and ancient time, where things moved like a portent and the laws of the world were altered to a code that only he was aware of, like a secret inert gas that came from a fissure of riddles.

The underlying feeling was one of time and journey and that he had little time and much journey ahead. He could see constellations at times, whether that was from a sky or in vacuum he couldn't be certain, the stars were crystal clear and formed patterns he didn't recognise. A vast ocean billowed ahead of him and he deduced he was on a craft of some oceanic description, and there were insects flying around the craft in formation and seemed to be accompanying him, piloting him somewhere, he knew, in the dream but was confused about it as if the first person evaporated then the third person-limited dream took over, where he was looking at himself in the dream which alternated and swam like the current of the alien ocean. The insects rested on the side of the wooden craft at times, its gunnels high and thickset and they clustered there in conversation circles as if in meetings about him and the journey, their combine eyes glistening and kind, and intelligent and calmly controlled.

Then he was flying, and he thought he was in a Helicopter, he could see down at the sea, the small swells foaming on the green alien ocean and below a red hue like a trail of plankton or a dye cast within the deep, which had risen and dispersed just under the surface.

The tops of the swells rippled clean and raw by the oceanic wind and the spray lamented and swept from foam to ripple and cast aqua blue and azure emerald. To the horizon, only the sea was in conversation, and the twin orange suns peered through the broken clay sky like a giant with a headlamp, the clouds making face shapes and rising with the force of the wind then dispersing long and whittled into the troposphere.

He looked down and he realised he was an insect, he had an open elytra and his wings extended that were vibrating in a blur, he had excellent vision and could adjust the twin lenses in his compound eyes to focus on certain things with high clarity and switch his vision to different light wavelengths and colour.

His field of vision cast small shapes and other insects in the sky, and determined their texture and colour, and saw the swimming creatures below the tempest of the ocean, skirting green and blue and darting white. He looked to the green sky and knew how to navigate by the lightest way, the stars through the atmosphere still apparent to his fine vision and marked his course and linear direction as they turned with constellation-like precision to aid an ancient navigator.

He descended as if on a predetermined flight glide path and with vibrating accuracy, darted across the surface of the sea, rising and falling with the swells and the bluster of the gusts of salt spray, correcting course with the tilt of his wings and slant of his secured legs that trailed behind in a tarsus bundle thicket and running sure. His abdomen was glistening with the salt water and reflecting the twin suns and the ancient sky. A patterned array of water droplets adhered to his prothorax and combine-eye windscreen, beading off with the warm wind and dispersing to the sea again, behind his fleeting form, cast away, and ripped raw to return to the meniscus surface.

His path became calm, the turbulence abated and ahead a great continent rose, blocking the wind with sea-cliffs and satellite pools of rock and shoals of steaming fluid that had risen from the depths from volcanic fissures that bubbled sulphur and carbon dioxide mists.

The wind grew warm and he selected a pool and dived, breaking the tension of the hot water and swam down where kelp forests were rising like stricken hands waiting for the tide, fanning with a low current within electrolyte balanced salt and plume. Down where darkness encroached, strange plants filtered upwards with sure stems and aqua-green rough appendages, he expected to find skulls of pirates, chests of silver and dead men's femurs but the world was not his before but now it seemed to be so, this archaic pond was fundamental and portent, a chemical cauldron within the crucible of physical time.

Upon the roughage plants he found a blooming flower, a striking needle petalled structure that arrayed circular and deep sea green with seven ochre orange petals, that swayed in the current, the centre of the flower a hollow silo that contained a fluid with a greater viscosity, which sat contented and with optimal buoyancy as if waiting for a guest. He was innately aware, within a central stem.

His kind assembled within, waiting for him, their elytra closed and wings stored behind the protective shards of metallic blue and green silver crusts. The greeting was apparent and kind and the viscous silo enclave milled with chemical current, no need for idle banter or confused and uncomfortable silences *or mindless repetitive prattle. The electrolyte balanced and set, and he knew that they were sentient like him and calming and armed with formidable weapons of peace and deterrent. They had regard and understanding of that which grew around them and how it was all connected and precious, as life was rare in the Universal tempest that knew no law but star building dimensions of time.*

They were certain, knowing that their place in the Universe was on several planets with circular combine and pulsar stars, and that they were chemically attuned via the vacuum transit pheromone and atmospheric blend. The constellation paths were a trade route of Interstellar tempest and carved trail space through a massive timeline on an irregular galaxy spiral of forming gas and created hydrogen dust, where they could fly like rockets and glean a marvellous speed without a wind. They could survive the journey encrusted in weaved gossamer from the trunk of the roughage species, their original but now evolutionary discarded carapace.

He partially awoke, he could hear sounds and voices he recognised and was still between a *Japanese* - like partition, a private and strong seal based on ritual and tradition, between sleep and wakefulness, a barrier, but a thin illusion of a sand crumbling wall between the real world and the world that had no rules, the dream world.

He had a feeling of marvellous regard for his insect form which was still there but fading fast, and he immersed himself within a miro-world where he could chat chemically, a hypothetical *Facebook,* and knew before acting what was what, and how things had gone, and who was likely to succeed, and when the world may end.

It was beyond human description or understanding for the time it took to fully awake, he was a sentient-algorithm, a trace process, a protein synthesis, a deoxyribonucleic acid rule which was species set. The last thing he saw before the images evaporated was his kind arrayed around the stem of the roughage plant in the pool, and he didn't want to leave his kind, crying within and trying to say *"No!,"* as the dream surfaced like a bubble on a body of water and broke with a misting pop.

He opened his eyes and saw the cave wall, a slick, grey, smooth rock that was dry but looked wet. He felt as though he had been asleep for a century, and time had healed a great weeping wound. He lay and listened, he could hear Donghyun the Meteorologist and Akseli Koskinen talking about something, a space helmet or something like that, and Katie Arnold's distinctive voice directing and questioning, something about a boat or ship.

Releasing his hand from the warm cover and stretching it into the colder air, he could smell snow and ice and cold beyond, but the cave was warmer and he confirmed this as he turned and saw a device giving heat off a lamp that was plugged into a battery bank at the far wall. He stretched his legs and it felt good all toasty under the amazing terrain blanket, he now realised he knew the name of it without thinking.

Katie came in the energy barrier entrance and sat beside him, looking at him but she said nothing, just smiled and watched the man under the blanket. He widened his eyes at her as if to elicit a response, and she still looked, making him uncomfortable, "What?," he said still with an enquiring look. "Do you remember anything?," she asked, finally speaking. "About what?," he replied confused. "About being *Anders the Encroacher*, the *Tribe*, *Hexibarber*," she said smiling.

"*Hexibarber*?, who is that?," he replied, groggily with weeping eyes and crusty lids, furrowing his brows. "Our new hairdresser?" She looked at the ground, and laughed silently "Don't worry, Ye-Min is the only person who does and apparently we were part of a dysfunctional *tribe,* after Ate Succession had gone, there is a noticeable large gap in all our memories here, except for Ye-Min who has told us too much to be honest, and now unfortunately has recently disappeared."

25

He shook his head slowly looking at her, "What, Ye-Min, gone? and *Ate Succession* has gone?, where?" She looked up from the rock floor and then looked at the ceiling, then straight at him, "Look, get some more rest, there are many questions and not as many answers, but we are planning a sit down after you are better, can we wait till then?" "You're the boss, boss," he said smiling.

"Anders, listen to me. I need you. If we can get the Explorer operational, you're my shotgun — your nav, your insertion instincts. Kylie will take the second craft. So get better fast, big guy." We can't do this without you. "Other Explorer?" "Let's talk when you are fully awake"

"When do I get to meet Hexibarber?," he said. She didn't answer but looked at him with a rye look and walked out of the entrance, "Get some rest, see you soon, that's an order" she said as she left and entered the area he had walked to when he didn't know anything. "Now I know too much, it seems," he thought, as he considered getting up, then returned to the cocoon and then it was black again.

He had spent some time lying down and when he got up he was stiff and noticed that between the cocoon terrain bed and the rock floor was a cushioned mattress that hugged the terrain of the floor, even so he felt like a piece of wood. The day was very dark and the temperature outside was very cold, the cave was a haven with a temperature much higher than outside with warmth, and he wondered why, then realising they had installed Energy screens over the cave entrances, protective barriers of energy tent material.

Through the screen he could see Akseli out there near the Bee-Brown toilet recycler system and his breath was coming out of his mouth in great clouds and he looked stiff as well, having to do something and looking like he wanted to get out of there, away from the extreme cold, like he had run naked out there after a hot shower.

There was a larger cave across the flat area and he could just make out the others sitting in the warmer air, beyond the energy screen membrane, they seemed to be eating something hot, a pot was steaming and Kylie was serving something on plates, navigating a seated crew at the dinner table. He saw that they noticed him looking and Katie and Kylie waved, Akseli and Donghyun looked and smiled his way, he waved and Katie motioned him to come over, barely hearing, *"Get dressed first!"* Akseli, was walking across to them his head turned and smiling at him also waving. He was hungry and looked around, there were some clothes there, ones he recognised from the ship and reached down to find his pants.

As his hand reached the floor his dream meandered across his mind and he couldn't shake the surest feeling that he had been another creature, an insect. The feeling of the experience lingered, he thought for a moment was confused to what world was real, his bedroom cave or the sea. The lingering faces of the crew he had known cast shadows in his puzzle memory, *things* had happened he didn't understand.

4

Jessica Neuer stared at the plain that stretched to the angled point from the broken shore. Rising tide and swimming moss, a twilight of purple from the West, oozing across the cumulus striated cloud spread upwards and disappearing into the dark exosphere dome.

Across the bay she could see another island-inlet and a turgid wash where the sea challenged the entry point, strict current and low lying mist, a gentle sound belying the danger of the undulating green shapes and white foam. *Much like my constitution at the moment, full of trepidation.* Broken logs and distant tall trees like pines but with crowned tops that spread beyond the lower branches, filtered from the raised hillsides down to the beach shore like a thousand sentinels still and mighty.

The beach had small pebbles and smooth stone, an eroded conglomerate and confused Geological tenant. Scattered among the green particle beach grains lay small jellies and bits of puffed seaweed in ball shaped clusters.

Like walking upon a mad highway in a dream though real and beautiful, raw, primordial, untouched, dangerous and rude, calm and broken. She gazed at her feet as they strode across the sand and wondered about the crew, Andreas, her last memory of him running down the Life-boat corridor to evacuate. Her chances alone on an alien highway, a planet so far from Earth she was actually an alien.

Her footfall broke the sand in rasping wisps to the lament of her exo-skin grey-purple-ochre red boots, ankle high, silicon-kevlar soles three zippers, two velcro tie downs, fibre-glass and cotton synthetic laces, scuff protection and elevated cushion air-soles, vacuum proof if tied correctly with the fabric attachment and securing cuff. The toughest women could make, for women she thought, an alien *sole* for men, but still falling short of comfort when used for a seemingly endless alien planetary meander across a Devonian-like landscape.

No need for a vacuum suit but cold and gloved, strong long grey pants and tight light green parker of internal down and orange striped sleeves. She consoled herself thinking of her belongings, her survival kit, checked every day, repaired when possible, cleaned, stacked, repacked, ready on rotation. Black utility backpack, containing vacuum kevlar-silicon gloves, multitool - (screwdriver, knives, scissors, nail-file, toothpick, small light and saw). A spacesuit, the much loved "Instant Suit" as it was called for vacuum which could fold into a small ironically air-vacuum cylinder, twenty centimetres long and when removed, expand to a full size space-walk item. Also a pair of shorts, two items of spare underwear, beanie, stainless mess-kit and stove combo, five packs of high energy meals, a marker beacon, three flares, sturdy ten centimetre knife with secured sheath.

The mountains in the distance told her Geologist-self before their beauty, that there was plate Tectonics here. The twin ranges with a vast valley stretched away to her left vista rising above the massive Pine-like trees on several vignettes of varied hills in shadow, different greys and green gully, fissure and crag. High altitude CirroStratus cloud banked on an angle for kilometres across the sky in a finger shape awaiting the twin sun dawn. A dollop of fog rested between the mountain range and sat like cotton-wool, clouding the valley below.

The most technologically advanced items secured longevity in the wilderness. The widely converted 'Energy Tent'' shielded dwelling and secure exo-skin, that admitted a small electric shock if touched on the outside and slight "push-back" motion to deter wandering animal aliens and drunken day wielding chainsaw campers, the anathema to all camping meaning she still remembered, her days on the road stopping at camping sites on Earth.

Wasn't the point to enjoy the peace, birds and quiet? No, why cut wood with a saw when you could stay fat and start the chainy? Why sleep in a tent to experience a bit of outdoor life when you could bring a house prepared caravan, TV, fridge, stinking porta-loo, rugs, fire bowls, plastic pool toys, arm-chairs, blow-up wife, *christ* she muttered, *I still go mad with it. The Energy Tent* a much better idea she mused, a breathing organ like structure malleable to a degree, enough for one, permeable but sealed.

Her tan-yellow cap to obscure the morning glare fitted surely like a comfort-blanket annexed the rising twin-star strong and elliptical below the patched chameleon dawn with rising mist and purple-mauve wind across the fresh horizon. Blonde-red hair tied back, Safety glasses, reflecting the grey, tan and speckled puppet-like shapes of the coastline and the moving path from the lens as she strode the image rising and falling across the glass hemisphere reflection as if a mirror of the eyes of a roaming compound eyed beast.

Tired legs and chafed groin, itching nose and running eyes, dry-scalp, sore shoulder, left side, always the sore right lateral Malleolus bone in her ankle, probably a surfing stress fracture thing, *was there surf here?,* she humorously pondered, continuing the temporary fantasy, *And what creature was waiting in the green depths to devour her like a Devonian Dunkleosteus, the giant Devonian era shark that has a six foot open jaw height.* Super-fit she was, though always fatigued, always hungry yet happy to be well, foot calluses and stinging toe-nail cuts. Sweat but not running, just sitting foaming, sticking, misting, as if ready for further impending mighty cardiovascular endurance, a regular morning lamented dialogue to herself, as she adjusted her backpack strap, a slight stammer to the rhythm of foot on sand, scuff and slide of grain on sole.

The discipline of fitness she thought, the daily essential grind that when started was unthinkable madness in the pre-dawn freeze, some hex put upon her from some lamenting tyrannical Sergeant-Major, but became clear with each dawn no matter the weather, thoughts adjusting to waking skin and clearing retina. The metronome of leg and thought, a calming elixir, a diet of sorts, discipline and focus on action not feeling, one of the endurance techniques of being instinctual rather than emotional. The mind was key to endurance, from her experience, stop the mind getting sooky and let the body take over for a while.

"One foot after another" she softly muttered, slightly as she had heard from a Special Forces soldier on the Earth's Internet, simple yet only the physical, the mental comes later, the forty percent rule, "when you think you have no more in the tank, you actually have sixty percent more" he had said, sitting in a large warehouse on a lonely chair, waiting for an unknown helicopter.

The human body is tainted by modern living, she thought, the fast-food, grease, fat, sugar, salt, processed, dripping, useless, satiating yet dangerous. No fast food in this place, she smiled, no golden arch, layered roll or cardboard bucket. The beach contained something much better she had discovered, Clams. Butterfly shaped clams encrusted with steel-wool like lichen, parted to contain a meaty, salty delicious off-white morsel. About the size of a palm, smelling like a sharp salty smoked apple, a delicacy, a gourmet, chefs fantasy, waiters customer delight.

She had scuffed one while walking, took it with her, carefully, seemed ok, tested it with the *Organic Taster and Atmospheric Analyser (*OTAA,) or the *Ottar* as commonly called). The simplest device and yet one of the best things she had, *yes things,* she thought, the *small things* are often the best, it still held true. It was *Tabula Rasa* the Latin here, *blank slate,* here poison may mean good and bad news may mean pretty in an unknown environment.

She remembered the Advertisement, *funny that*, she thought, *The Ottar, developed by Dr Allen Ottaway for survival markets, is a small probe attached to a super-tough analyser unit hand-held, compact, using AI generated algorithms paired with bio-finger technology,...* the living machine tissue that people and Scientists were desperately trying to adapt to

Android systems with spectacular disappointment on a depressingly familiar time-scale she also remembered. The clams registered safe to eat and contained reasonable amounts of magnesium, potassium and trace sodium with high protein-fat content. The shell was made of silicon-calcium with a complex mineral alloy much like the Earth variety called *Ewingite.*

Moving slowly beneath the sand surface via a series of minute gas jets, filtering nutrients from the sand crust, the clams seemed to exist under the sand for the majority of their range, fortunately for her. A regular native food source was welcome, she would need it more and more as her lifeboat survival supplies dwindled. A throw of an ancient die, essential consumption, fuel and life. The planets atmospheric gases had not killed her and therefore had a similar gas mix to Earth, she was protected by similar ratios of which contained Potassium and Argon and interestingly a minute amount of Polonium like Earth, UV levels were consistent with Earth, this was in effect another Earth, another habitable zone of similar planetary proportions to her home planet 4.5 light years away. 'How can that be?' she thought, 'what are the chances of that?'

She noticed the beach began to meander in a long concave from her left, the two suns now above the horizon, complementing each other in the dawn light. The Sun that was furthest was on the outer elliptical, because of its transit appeared redder and more eerie, like someone placing a torch behind red cloth the other like a younger Sun, smaller than Earth with a bluer light. The tree line halted about twenty metres down the left hand slope near where the green tide must encroach. A soft wind had started, with some mist rising from the channel water and twirling upwards in eddies.

She scanned out to her right then down to her feet, careful she was on safe ground. Small crabs and scrambling mite-like creatures dashed back and forth as her steps approached, threshing the sand, tiny glistening small fish darted in the shallows and back to the dimmer depths to the dance of the tiny swells breaking on her miniature shore. To the right and out across the turgid channel the water swept true away to the inlet which was growing closer and details like floating log and other assorted jetsam became apparent twirling and dancing on the entry to the smaller channel. Across the deeper section and farther out beyond was the open sea, a shore she was yet to explore. Dotted trees and wiry shrubs grew on jutting sandbanks as they formed around and beyond the channel's influence, then out of sight where low stretched pillowing clouds rose just above the sea.

 She came upon an enormous pile of uprooted trees that must have travelled the channel and beached as the tide receded blocking her beach highway. She examined the lower trunks, massive, probably eight metres in diameter, splintered and broken ten metres in length like matchsticks crushed by a giant hand, intertwined branches, seaweed like kelp and covered in wet and dry sand lying trapping the current where the outer branches touched the channel.

She rerouted around thinking, *a rest might be in order.* She moved over some upper beach shale and flint stone outcrops where a rise before the tree line might show her the path where the channel became narrowest. Upon the higher ground, she could see the channel thinning, meandering away in curved lines, sandbank rising on each side for kilometres in the distance until obscured by the sea salt mist and brightening light from the suns that arrayed down in shards and planes of twilight.

Approaching the tree-line, investigated the closest tree, a towering thirty foot Pine-like structure of a thousand branches stretching outwards at elongated angles of about thirty degrees, in sets of ten arrayed around the trunk. The shade under was cool, the canopy within gloomy but with optimistic shards of light starting to dance with the sun.

The lowest set was still about five metres above her. She crouched and examined the forest floor under the tree, broken twigs and nettle-like ground cover, oblong seeds, grit and stone. The tree had elongated nettle-like leaves about the size of an index finger, seven radiating out from the Petiole like an inert hand waving in the morning breeze. The motion of a million *fingers* on the stems rising to height created the illusion of the tree rising up and down in the earth, the sound of the light breeze a raw whisper through the canopy.

Sitting down in assessment of her situation, seated in the nettles viewing the surrounding vista and listening to the sound of the channel and the trees, the distant ocean rumbling with surf. *I have to find a suitable camp-site for tonight,* collect some more clams, and find other sources of food. *There is an ocean, are there fish?,, is there something else?*

The channel seemed the logical place to fish, a coursing low-high tide boundary where animals may be exiting or returning from the sea. Rummaging through the pack, on her knees, pulled out her food, a small energy bar, the dried clam, and her steel water bottle, laying them on the fine pebbles, her lunch.

I'll have this then have a look at the ocean, the beach, eyeing the channel, thinking how she could navigate past the fast-running water and on to the distant sand that led out to what she assumed was the ocean boundary.

Looking above, Iris was scouting ahead, the drone wheezing over the channel and out to the sea. Everyday Iris scouted for the best place to stop for the day, her site selection considered and scanned for safety. Yesterday they had camped in the low-lying forest, a small clearing surrounded by small boulders and hanging lichen type beards of green mottled epiphytic plants hanging from arching boughs, the ancient trees stretching their domain, fallen logs, piles of undisturbed sticks and decaying piles of nettles.

The clearing was dotted with small brilliant red five petalled flowers on high stalks all about three metres apart as if they had discussed their arrangement, small bee-like creatures massed on the stems, gliding, flying buzzing, searching and forming clumps of segmented appendages.

The energy tent contrasted the natural surroundings, at night the stars breathtaking, a new constellation in a new galaxy, an astronomer's wet dream, a physicist's anticipation, a camper's delight. She stood during the last evening, staring with Beanie and cold breath at the constellation in a one hundred and eighty degree view, a triad shaped fingered clustered shape across the blackest backdrop of a sky, differing from Earth's Milky Way, the one stretch highway of stars.

Here and there, she could see small galaxies, a faint mist-like pattern of swirling discs, tiny but visible as she turned her head to the side to allow the rods in her eyes to access the light better than her retinal cones, *I'll always think that's amazing*, the structure of the eye and how the rods were more receptive to light and massed in greater numbers at the periphery of the retina, the cones less so, massed near the fovea where the light entered the eye, and able to access the wavelengths of light, colour in other words.

Looking straight ahead but noticing the periphery of her vision she could make out the faint items in the night sky, the galaxies, faint stars. Iris also had an excellent camera and they had taken some pictures of the galaxies and the three moons, the larger moon yellow and misty, the smallest seemed to have a circling ring of dust or debris, the larger a blue mass, clear craggy surface, lots of meteor impact and a large vein running through the axis, blacker like an ancient river or fissure. Aligned like sisters and brothers in the vacuum standing in unison looking at her, the world below.

Every day she and Iris discussed what the drone had seen, its thoughts about the absence of large animals, the lost crew, the Starship breaking orbit initiated by the Captain, the absence of radio contact from the Scientists. This was not unusual, Iris had explained, they had landed on the other side of the planet, due to the starship's movement breaking orbit and the time the Life-Boat took to establish entry parameters to the surface.

Totally isolated, the Life-Boat was the only reason they had knowledge of why the ship broke orbit, its recorder in active contact with the *Ate Succession's* systems, when the Starship exited orbit contact ceased. *It fired the Fusion-Drive though,* which meant it went somewhere else, fast. The absence of larger animals presented a potential problem but she thought this may pan-out ok given the discovery of the nourishing clams.

Were there other food sources from this area?, It seems likely, species don't evolve in isolation, typically, she mused as she walked the alien sand looking out where Iris had gone, across the far beach, feeling very alone on an alien planet, in an alien galaxy and on an alien beach.

Iris returned shortly after and led her to a clearing raised near the forest where she could set the tent. "Jessica, this is interesting" Iris lifted then hovered above an area at the clearing edge to show her where to walk. Walking through the low grass the shape came into view and she juggled the options of its form.

The rock had been carved into a giant granite bowl, at least two meters in diameter. *A bowl?* She approached the granite feature. She looked at Iris as she attempted to touch the liquid in the bowl for confirmation. "Water, fresh water. Also, there are patterns consistent, the granite has been chipped with tools. " "Tools?" "Yes, it did not erode naturally"

5

"Greetings, updates, kindness, sorrow, inquiry, confirmation, status, injury, swarm status,deaths. Pheromone dispersed the core target molecule and infected the species. Trace chemical, the biomarker, the nutrient transmitter set. The chief target has dispersed. Lateral spread not necessary, the virus has selected"

The Beetles sang silently with the chemical.

"Core and Clock, tempered strike, combine eye, salted nymph, the Alpha mite, plain of salt, pull of tide, set the wing a pool of time, tempered stem and exo-skin, fall of star and hostile wing"

Above, the light reflected red hues and darting slivers and shone down on the blue-black ten winged carapaces arranged circular and antennae attached through the water to the lower stem, their appendages casting purple hue shadows and reflected stone from the inner walls of the valley.

The bromeliads spread protecting the core, a marker itself, an engineered hybrid that transfused the chemical protection with microbial mist and tangent direction, enveloping the beetles and surrounding the trunk, setting like a double rimmed water stem and connecting the pheromone, a defence marker and set a clear hostile cocktail to protect the swarm within the meeting.

The ten transversed, the array of antennae and appendage turned individually clockwise then anticlockwise, the movement a vibration and set of coxar, slight of feeler and shine of carapace, within the stem the water infused and set with the transmitter chemical, the patches of light filtering a splaying across the open flower and down to the semi-submerged fluid, specks of debri adrift and water warming with the friction of time itself.

The shapes stopped moving and aligned the tempered stem, their pretarsus touching the fibre floor of the stem, tibia and tarsi bent and vibrating securely.

From time to time the individual released their elytra, an opening to reveal the hind wings, superhydrophobic adapted, glistening within the fluid, ancient marine memories from a primordial pool and rare ocean current, the abdomen adrift in sediment then closing again to hide all but their Pterothorax.

The Pterothorax, a green silver section near the wing shaped triangular and marker-like, a timeless beacon of adaptation. The chemical was released again and set within the channel.

"Planetary machine, the other is aligned within the ancient cortex continent. The Bromeliad origin?" The beetles chemical sang in unison,

"Rotund pool, the ancient source, jungle vine and tempest fish"...

The chemical realigned and dispersed, *"Female 'Ye Min' and machine sentient, but adrift. They will find the alien path, eventually the Citadel, the fourth*

The five are set?" The Beetles shifted and turned a slow slant, still arrayed in spiky clock fashion around the central stem. In unison the chemical voice cast the reply from the ten arrayed:

"The four are sufficient, no evolutionary root within the Alloy. The stone has been located. The chemical Beetle sent to the carer. The desert and river is a patient portent. They have a target destination. Assumption set, the spurious targets can be groomed according to instinctual movement."

The Beetles sang:

"Time, the stem, pools and pull, terrain a sphere,

Bromeliad home and stone flat tide,

*Species set and ancient wing, nymph of ocean salt array, the
sediment ply*

*The robot chant and pheromone sky, archaeal lament,
biachondria synthesis,*

*Universe marker, Phylotype the transfusion potent, sediment
charter, species tempered, exit fly"*

The ten released from the central stem, and took one pace
back from the flower stem, raising their compound eyes
skyward, then raising their palpus momentarily.

The first Beetle released its elytron wing covers and set
swimming expertly through the murky water and bursting out
from the central stem portion surface tension and away to the
canopy sky, foaming the surface as the others replicated the
flight, one by one rising, leaving the portion and the meeting
temple, the water soothing and milling with the exit, the air
heavy with evolutionary portent and meandering liquid from
the flower.

The canopy shifted to reveal the green sky at moments the soft
hazy whisper and flutter of wings and carapace descending
and fleeing the tree tops in soldier swarm formation their
sentinels aligned and exiting across the plain arrayed in
centurion formation through the rocky fissure terrain and
across the storm laden horizon.

6

Iris returned through the mist from the ocean side of the channel partly obscured by mist she assumed to be sea salt. The drone became larger as it approached.

In a moment Iris set down beside her, disengaging the motor. She chewed on a dried clam, tasty meat, and energy. The tide was receding, the channel water growing faster with the drain to the sea beyond. A large log floated past hitting the sand wall and turning passing through like a stricken rudderless ship in a fast flowing river.

"What can you see Iris," she said looking at her companion, its dark seemingly inert mechanical form silent. "I have observed quite an array Jessica" She momentarily looked skyward, smiling at Iris's conversation style, blinking with amusement.

"There is a sandbank that will allow access over the channel and beyond, to the sea. It lies one hundred and fifty five point three metres distant, on your current trajectory. The beach stretches for many kilometres to the Eastern side of a large headland beyond,..."

"Any life Iris?," she looked at the drone inquiringly. "Many small red crabs inhabit the beach boundary that connects with the low-lying trees that border the sand, they have holes, typically next to rocks, I suspect so they have additional protection from the elements, I see no reason at this stage to suspect they have airborne predators as there is no evidence of such" "Crabs, eh, how many legs?" she asked, remembering the ants discovered near the research quadrants."Analysis shows ten" Iris replied. "Hah!, she exclaimed, so like the ants, more stability?, perhaps?" "It is a feasible theory," Iris replied.

For a moment I forgot my potential dilemma, deep in discussion with an AI about the ecology of another planet. That's *not such a bad thing. Rest the mind,* she mused finishing her clam, wiping the oil-like residue from her mouth.

"So, any communications evident while you were at a higher level?" "No, there is no radio, or network contact that I have detected, I will of course inform you if this occurs, saying that, I have detected a certain amount of ultraviolet wavelength spectrum radiation that would indicate that you may be at risk of skin damage unless you take more precautions while out during the day between the hours, currently of ten in the morning to two in the afternoon"

"So I need sunscreen" "A barrier of some sort, long term yes" Iris replied. "Sunscreen, I have to say was not originally on my list for a Interstellar mission Iris, but I changed my mind, so I give you, ..wait, she rummaged through the pack leaning over backwards finding the tube, and showing it to Iris, holding it up and reading the label, "Factor 50 plus" she said,"will that do?"

"Certainly, that is a degree of protection that would be considered satisfactory if applied correctly and monitored for reapplication, however, now I have considered the idea, we must consider that the ingredients are alien to this planet and may have adverse effects when entering the water cycle of this planet" "Indeed, thank you Iris" "What do you recommend?" "Probably go without it" Iris replied, "The current amount of clothing protection should be sufficient given we have other pressing concerns, namely your long-term survival and my long-term functioning given the external environmental factors at play"

She smiled and replaced the tube in her pack, shielding her eyes and glancing up to the twin suns, their place in the sky straight above now. "So, what else?, on the beach I mean" "There are many giant jellyfish floating beyond the break of the waves in a large channel before the deeper section of the sea floor, they are translucent and are shaped like a citrus juicer apparatus, cone shaped, measuring in approximate radii of fifty metres to eighty metres" "Wow," she exclaimed, "edible?" "There is one that has washed ashore further up the coast, we can examine it, Earth jellies are rich in collagen and protein, it may have similar properties, if so a good food source" "Ok," she stood stretching, "Iris, lets see this beach and the Jelly, then let's find a campsite with the view of getting a long-term site established so we can explore more in this area, what do you think?"

"I would not recommend it," Iris replied. "There is a significantly large storm Northeast from here bordering the coast which I predict will make landfall here at some stage tomorrow, with the massive tidal pull of the three moons at play, I predict flooding here at high tide, high winds and a substantial amount of rain, possibly some falling as hail. I recommend we seek higher ground after investigating the jelly, possibly as much as ten kilometres inland beyond where the forest is a boundary to the higher escarpment beyond to the South West." She listened, glancing to Iris and out past the channel, pursing her lips, hands on her head like an athlete waiting for a race to start.

"In addition, I also have information that the elliptical orbit of the planet is on its outbound journey from the twin suns which will mean increasingly colder weather in the months to come. Therefore, I recommend finding rock formations suitable for cave habitat or an area where a permanent dwelling can be established that has additional protection from the elements"

She knelt down on her haunches, removing her cap and tying back her hair again, continuing to listen and thinking about her chances, options, ability to be here as Iris continued in her mechanical way, "Calculating the movement of the planet away from the twin suns,....." "Hang on," she interrupted, "How do you know all this Iris?', I mean the planetary movement, the storm, temperature prediction?"

Donghyun Han the ship's Meteorologist placed a weather satellite in orbit, this is a reliable feed of intelligence, and the craft is also capable of observing the planetary alignment relative to the twin suns." "A weather satellite?, when?" "This was done prior to terrestrial contact" "When were you going to mention this Iris?" she said looking at the drone. "Today" replied Iris. "There is no immediate danger..." , she interrupted looking at the Drone like naughty child, "Ok, Iris, but from now on keep me up to date, ok, you know updates, like, things you know that I don't" "Very well, I will be more informative at lesser intervals" "Great," she said a little incredulously.

Iris continued, "We may see up to a twenty degree Centigrade fall in temperature during the day in the next month and a forty degree Centigrade Fall in the next three months as the planet is on the outer rim of orbit..." She did a quick calculation, so it was pleasant seventeen degrees Celcius now, that would bring it down below freezing, then she could expect twenty below, maybe more, "Fuck me" she exclaimed, Iris continued the weather report, "It will be very cold, although the energy tent would be sufficient in such temperatures, the elements combined may make it unviable as a long term solution for shelter"

They set out across the channel where Iris had indicated, a shallow section allowed her to wade the thirty metres or so across to the far sandbank, then through the small wind blown beach treeline. The water flowed past her legs like a warm sea or warmed water from the shallows, it tasted salty which she confirmed with the analyser at fifty grams per kilogram of seawater. Iris patrolled ahead showing her the direction, skirting the treetops and then keeping her company near her.

They reached the beach, a coarse mineral sand was the primary deposited sediment with many striking colours and grains, crusted rocks, minute shells, flotsam, several large logs and pieces of seaweed looking vegetation. The beach stretched a long way up to the North East, bending and disappearing within a salt haze, the waves crashing on the sand and withdrawing in great swathes.

She scanned the green-blue sky, thinking about the weather and how it seemed unlikely now that the cold would set down on them as hard as Iris had predicted, the temperature bearable, the breeze almost comforting, the beautiful ocean,

43

sparkling in the light as the clouds past the twin suns in regular passes of shadow and shine.

They investigated the jelly, washed ashore, its massive bulk beached no doubt during the last tide, seemingly dead, The oceans water saltier than Earth, the analyser confirming twenty grams salt per kilogram of water. The waves crashed against the ancient untouched shore washing against the jelly, threatening to refloat the glistening creature.

Moving carefully around it, the height of it about nine metres towering above her, inside and opaque the glass see through bulk revealing blue innards and veiny green trails of bodily parts, a small pink flower-like structure and what looked like yellow wheels and green curly lines, bodily mechanisms she couldn't comprehend.

Iris in the distance skirted the shoreline further up the beach, the drone rotors audible with the surf and wash. "Iris, did you do an analysis of this creature, can I touch it?" *"Yes, Jessica, it is mostly collagen, there are traces of silicon but it is benign on the surface"* She felt the outer flesh, still warm to the touch, a smooth texture, with small rougher areas as she glided her fingers across, the salt water still running down its sides, reflecting the sun's rays and filtering through the body.

"What a behemoth, it's quite beautiful," she said. Iris returned and hovered beside her, the rotors in quiet mode a slight hiss emanating from the drone also examining the creature. *"Yes it is a giant as well, I am just going to take a sample of the flesh,"* Iris said, releasing her mandibles and injection device. She watched as Iris drilled a small piece from the creature, a collagen cylinder shape, the sample disappearing into the drone for analysis.

"Interesting, high protein in this species, good for you Jessica, I suggest we carve some and keep it in the ocean water for preservation" "Ok, and can I taste it?," *"Certainly, try this,"* Iris said, ejecting a morsel of flesh held by the mandible. The texture was smooth, the taste, much like a salty lychee. "Not too bad, ok let's see" She grounded her pack and found her second water bottle, "Let's put the pieces in here," she said, as Iris began to drill small pieces from the outer flesh as she placed them in her bottle of saline.

Later they collected some more estuary clams, shelled them, adding them to the bottle with the jelly flesh, "I shall pretend it's a *Marinara*," she mused. The day ended in a spectacular twin sunset as they made their way inland again through the estuary and the low lying beach perimeter trees onto the rising terrain and into the ancient forest proper. Iris guided her through the tall mammoth trunked giants, the canopy almost an atmosphere in itself, the nettle leaves shifting in the breeze that was now swirling around and then settling the nettles that fell to the first floor, with small broken branches and other airborne detritus.

Knowing this phenomenon from Earth - the time before rain or storm, the changes in the wind, the trees almost aware of the coming tempest, gently swaying and almost talking to one another against the swirling eddies of wind and drop in sea pressure.

Through the forest floor after the end of the beach was slow going; she had to navigate large rotten fallen trees and logs that were entangled with vine thickets and rising sapling fields impeding her linear progress. Iris skirted above the canopy, as down below was not an amiable drone world.

It took a few hours of hard walking to reach a clearing that Iris had indicated, she unshouldered her pack in tiredness as he reached an amiable rock and looked around, the clearing, an alien patch within a wooded world. She took her water bottle and drank deeply, and surveyed the area, the suns now below the horizon and the twilight taking the stage before the night.

Her feet were holding up well, so far. She walked on the grass bare-foot, taking off her boots and perching them on a rock nearby, enjoying the air on her skin, sitting, then clipping her nails and rubbing her feet, the white-red toes like old tired tires. Some isopropyl alcohol helped on the skin as she rubbed it to disinfect her feet. Dinner would predictably be jellyfish flesh and clams. The clearing was tree free, only grass grew and there were rocky areas where the basalt had encroached in flat layers like a stone sea. Iris descended and landed on the grass beside her.

"Good enough to spend the night?," she said, Iris winded down her rotors, having selected a flat rock nearby for a pad. *"Good, the clearing gives us a view out from the trees and room to manoeuvre,"* the drone replied. *"We are on a day's journey to the caves up further on the rock shelf, about 15 km away. How are you doing? We will need to make good progress tomorrow"* Iris asked. "Yes, pretty good actually, and well the storm is coming isn't it?" *"Yes, I am afraid around late morning according to my calculations"* "Then an early start, let's get up there and settle," she replied, throwing a toenail clipping into the grass.

During the night the stars were obscured as the unsettled weather drew fast clouds over the sky, some rain fell, striking the energy tent roof with sharp direction and she lay there listening to the water runoff and the sound of the drops on the grass and the mix of the tree canopy swaying.

She descended far from reality and coursed through some mix of undefined structure like a building with no doors or a train that had endless carriages, walking around as if trying to see an exit. Andreas Polkinghorn joined her at some stage, in a joyful mood, the two of them searching for a dream tenant that didn't exist, or a person that never was born.

Realising at some stage that Andreas had gone then she was alone and floating in the vast ocean, a jellyfish, her shape coned the shallows just below the surface of the sea, her many adapted type eyes discerning light and dark, shape and movement and other sets of retina defining clarity with sharp precision from a billion year old lens grinding and development adaptation.

She had certain sure movement and was calm and patient. She had a locomotion that saved energy, her elastic bell shape propelling her through the water with the help of an energy efficient vortex aided action of the salt water sea.

Knowing instinctively that there were small creatures that lived in her tentacles below and small fish that made their homes around the swirling stinging tentacles that they were immune from, concealing them and protecting them.

Dotted patch marked crabs crawled around the tentacles as well, cleaning her lower abdomen from detritus and slime and catching prey within that had become lost in the collagen forest.

Remembering as a jellyfish being a Lava and a Polyp then a Medusa and that she was immortal as she could transform again into a Polyp on the seafloor within the corals and ragged rocks and retain her knowledge and instinct and roam the magnificent sea in ancient time.

Large shelled armoured crustaceans roamed the silt floor and massive rotund fish with wings darted like marine rockets and then cascaded upwards and broke the sea out to the air and released their wings in freedom foaming-like bursts, their images above she could see rippled with the oceans lens vision as they fleeted across above the surface for seconds at a time.

Within the kelp forests she roamed in saltier shallows near currented cliffs and swept salt bluffs, where black and blue insects swam and darted in the same surety as their airborne shapes, twirling down to plants and sea floor shells in swarms and formatted sections of carapace and wing.

At some time when the sky above was clear, she saw a massive trail across the sky and a fireball beyond the horizon and the sky went dark and remained so for millenia, but she survived, the chemicals in the sea changed but she made do and eventually the sky cleared, and other creatures emerged, larger swimming species with jaws and long legs and always

the insect swarms swam nearby in the shallows, only the kelp
changed sometimes, from green to blue or became striated and
reached higher.

Awakening during the night, she realised she had been a
jellyfish. Shapes of humans? had been down below, she as the
jelly could see them as her form glistened up and above the
swells.Within the depths of the current voices of the crew,
Tanya?, Tom? seemed to echo and then were gone.

Tanya Gery and Tom Aeuer had got on well from the moment they'd met after selection. She'd thought then that both of them were oddly content with the Wildcard process — a thousand applicants screened, medically probed and interviewed — ending with Human Resources putting them on the podium. No third place, just an equal tie for first..

They were a Sailor and an Adventurer, selected from a panel of six. James Williamson, the Captain. Psychology Professor Albert Hitchins, an intense, small, bald man with piercing blue eyes. Sara Glenfield, the space Agency CEO, Klaus Ottinger, founder of Hamburg Universal Flexible-Atom-Acrylic-Glass industries, Kate Arnold in her flight suit, and beside her superior, Navy Admiral Jake Donald-Charver.

Now, they both stood on another planet, under an ancient volcanic plug helping Akseli Koskinen load rock samples into their packs, the motorised quad bikes banned for now until their impact could be assessed. "How are my slaves going?," asked Akseli, standing on the raised rock platform looking down.

"The slaves are hungry and restless," replied Tom, shouldering the pack for the five kilometre journey. "No, wait, I have another pack here for you Tom," said Akseli smiling. "Ha, Ha, my Geology tyrant," Tom looked up, smiling, Akseli knowing the joke was up. "All good Tanya?" Akseli said, climbing down from the rock, hammer in hand. "Yep, exercise seldom kills you," she replied, looking at Tom, who was ready to depart, looking towards their destination across the plain.

Their position on the plain was within a rocky outcrop section that Akseli said was probably an ancient volcanic plug remnant, eroded almost to the ground, all that was left was some impressive rock formations, jutting and smooth weathered igneous rock, the characteristic minerals sparkling in the twin suns light, green and purple, yellow and bright white, coarse grains some enlarged crystals, the boulders arranged on one another beaten by the weather for millennia and creating small valleys of stone like a natural maze, washed clean and proud looking, harsh and beautiful at the same time.

The formation was the dominant feature in the vast plain, they had travelled South of the great forest trees a little further out and around the vast sedge tuft plain to a dryer section here as it stretched away to the mountains and beyond, a flat billiard table flat, some haze in the distance and yellow looking horizon, the distance too far to discern detail.

Here the light seemed different and the wind blew even stronger with the long day. They had decided to walk the rocks out, quad bikes were discussed but the idea abandoned, the life here was too important to disturb, Jessica saying, *"You can get some exercise," let's wait a little longer until I can get some specimens analysed"*

"Alright Akseli, we are off. Are you staying out here tonight?," "Yes, I think I have to investigate those," he pointed away to another distant volcanic plug array nearer the forest," I have heard there are blonde maidens that live within that area" Tom smiled. She shook her head.

"Right, well have fun," she said deadpan, looking at Tom with humorous eyes. "I will my friends, Adieu," Akslei hoisted his pack down and waved as they set off, Tom in front, the ancient forest in the distance waiting like an oasis, a contrast from the dry air on the exposed plain. Tom turned to her as they made their initial way, "It's not as if we have little time" She nodded, understanding the day was already twelve hours old and it was in effect noon with another twelve to go before dusk. "No, plenty of time, old Sailor," she replied. "Aye, Aye," he replied with gusto, making the point trail through the angular rocks, here a contrast to the smaller river pebble and sands around their camp. She adjusted her pack, probably about fifteen kilos heavy.

"Tell me about your Ship board days," she said after a little time their pace was a constant step over angular stone and small tufts of sedge. "Well, I was a pirate, ...no sorry, kidding. Ah, lets see, Marine apprentice, Ordinary seaman, then third mate, usually three week trips, boring, some storms then exciting, but..." "Marine oil is a strong memory trigger, whenever I smell it, it reminds me of it. The Explorer has the same smell in the hold."

Tanya gazed around, always surveying her surroundings, usually for danger, but so far this planet was benign. "What was your most exciting moment?" Tom didn't answer for a time, she wondered for a second.. "Ah, lets see, well, there was the time when the giant Octopus grasped the ship, ...she humoured him, still looking but smiling out to the plain," and ah, lets see, we had a tyrannical Captain and he had these ball bearings he used to roll in his hand... and then there was the time we saw a white whale..." "Tom, ok, I get it." She laughed.

"Seriously, did anything happen?" "Not really," he said, turning to look at her momentarily, while walking. "Very routine, too much work for too little pay, how the masters like it" "I wish I could tell you we beached on some exotic island and had tea with a lost tribe, but I am afraid.."

"I see, that is very disappointing Tom," she said deadpan, checking their position . The wind had picked up a little, the suns were still high, the forest trees in the far distance beckoned with a hazy dust horizon. She looked back to the rock formation, it grew small with their progress, she couldn't see Akseli.

"What about you fellow supply and logistics officer?, I hear you are quite the adventurer" "Oh, the same, very boring, some walking on ice, the odd cliff, you know.." "Hah, I like it," he replied. "Tell me," he continued, "What is it like to think you are almost going to die?" He turned, looking at her, "If you are comfortable answering that" He turned back continuing the walk, the angular stone crunching under his feet, the wind constant and whistling across the plain hitting the angular rock. "Ah, well, not good, but," he added interrupting, "I read about when you were stuck on that mountain, the storm."

"Yep, look it wasn't ideal but but I had to get down to a fissure in the cliff, at night, I just had to otherwise it was frozen Tanya in the morning, so I did it, to be honest I am not sure why I didn't become part of the rock, but I didn't panic, I thought if I fall then I fall, but I would have frozen on the face I was on." "Wow" he shook his head. "Mind you, I still think certain types of campers are more dangerous," she added, laughing. "Yes, I quite agree," Tom said, turning to look at her while still walking. "Do you have anyone in Cryo, Tanya?"

She watched his back then glanced out to the plain on the left seeing an eddy of wind kick some dust in a spin. "No, just my previous brain," she replied. "Ah, yes, me as well," he said, turning to look at her, a wry smile. "So no husband, boyfriend?," he said, not turning around, his pack heavy with the samples. "No, I ..well I like being alone, I don't get lonely, I'm not up for the barbeques and ball games thing," she said, sighting the forest to the East, feeling the wind at her back, the twin suns high in the sky. "Right, I understand, I am similar I think" Tom turned again to answer.

The Eastern end of the forest was growing closer, they had made their way across the flat expanse, she was tired, their eight hour day long gone, the twelve approaching the twin suns still high.

 She looked up to the green sky and saw the Ate Succession in low planet orbit, the massive Ship streaking across their field of view, high Cirrus clouds moving fast across the sky to the sound of their angular rock walk. The vast plain was meandering and there were hazy mirages in the distance out to where Akseli was making his way, right across the other end near the volcanic plugs that jutted like tired hands and worn fingers at the far end of the ancient forest.

As the forest became more defined and the dust haze cleared, they saw the Explorer that had landed near the scientists clearing waiting for their cargo. As they neared the ship they saw Jason Findus and Anders Pederson standing inspecting something on the landers exterior. Anders turned and pointed to them and they waited, the Navigator and the Pilot like truck drivers of the stars for the mineral cargo from the plain.

8

Jason Findus thought of the inevitable impending slow erosion of hope, his colleagues must have felt, as he had, *Ate Succession* going from orbit as they set down in the Explorer on the planet to escape the ship's Fusion-Drive ignition from orbit.

It didn't take long, whatever happened, which he still didn't understand, which happened soon after landing. Kylie Albott had not returned to the Explorer and could not be contacted, Kate Arnold calm as ever, tried the camp several times, with no response.

They completed their after flight checks as normal, considering the time taken a reasonable wait to see if they had a technical difficulty at the camp or unforeseen emergency which made them radio silent. The three of them were also silent for a time, in the ship's interior of which emitted a mood of a solemn crypt, they, seemingly thinking of several hundred scenarios, of the radio silence and the fact that they had just lost their Captain to some neurosis who had taken their Starship.

They sat among the sounds of the ship like ancient unspoken priests he remembered, like a few travellers on a stricken falling aircraft knowing their fate but thinking there might just be a chance they would survive.

Katie and Anders Pederson set out shortly after, across the plateau to make for the camp, Anders grim faced, Katie a deadpan look of slight annoyance and impending consequences if she found out there was negligence involved with the radio silence. Both had their packs with some spare parts, and emergency first aid gear, including Cox-AI the sentient Doctor the size of a small brick. The gear looked heavy but using the terrain vehicles was not possible there on the plateau, and they had to enable them and check them, a procedure which required time. He helped them prepare, making sure the gear was right. The sound of velcro being attached and re-attached, he watched them as they geared up in trained silence; their military training starting their minds like an imaginary drill sergeant.

There were no weapons, he remembered thinking, *Was that a good idea?* It was considered too much of a mission risk, much like a detective not carrying a weapon into an interview room or prison. He gave Anders a GPS tracker and Katie a momentary look of concern which she reflected in a look of *"If we don't come back....,"* as they turned and set out into the planets night, headlamps, skirting the stone under a starlit performance sky, so bright, it lit the plateau an iron-blue, the three moons just above the horizon. He remembered the distant silver river was coursing out to the horizon like a covert serpent on its way to the reflected moon sea.

Given the ship's duty, the officer on board again, and strict instruction from Katie to close the door and stay put in case something else they could never know about was at foot, their last man standing. He had locked the bulkhead door, sat down to his console and set Anders signal on his screen via the weather satellite, the terrain showing their path, and destination, the three kilometres, through the forest and narrow stone valley, and Anders signal lit like a firefly in the vast darkness, the clearing apparent. It would be the last he saw of them, the signal eventually disabled, until later when they seemed to become tribal adolescents.

He had stayed with the Explorer, following procedure, securing the craft, if a last man standing scenario developed, and after two days it had. No word, radio silence, the clouds bantering with the plateau in the third mornings mist much like his thoughts, swirling with scenarios.

To leave the craft meant the likelihood that what happened to the others would happen to him, to stay meant he had no flight access even if he was a pilot, Katie having command control. *Anders should have stayed,* he thought, *was that procedure?*, "Fuck me dead," he said out loud to himself. He could stay in the Explorer for a long time, there were ample supplies but *where was that going to get me,* he thought. "No Starship to escape to, and oh, yes, let me see, the mad Captain took the Starship, I nearly fucking forgot," he said out loud standing looking through the Flexible-Atom-Acrylic (FAA) windscreen at the iron-blue plateau, the fog visible sweeping across the surface.

His mind wandered with the morning mist, looking at the same stony section of the plateau in meditation, thinking of his chickens, "the best friends he ever had," he smiled, tongue in cheek, the descendants of the Dinosaurs, flock mentality, survival instinct, each a personality in their own right, the flock only as good as their weakest member. *"Damn right,"* he thought. *"Like this fucking scenario, am I the weakest member?"*

He remembered sitting with the birds as a rule for their run, after a long week, the perfect wind-down, milling and scratching, looking up with each scratch to see that he was involved, at times cleaning his boots for him, pecking the mud from the sole if he raised his feet, they, in seemingly fascinated concentration, then accessing the dirt bath, some pecking others from their holes then leaving it vacant just to prove a point, much like the quadrangle bully flogging someone out of the area, then leaving themselves.

They were now no doubt, swept away with the fury of Earth's Geological catastrophe, a floating flock upon a raging storm swept ocean, feathers on a planetary rip-tide. He remembered his several mixed breeds, White and Brown-Leghorn, Minorca, Plymouth Rock, Barn-Velder, Ameraucana-Red Leghorn crosses, and Barter Browns.

The chickens would turn their heads to the left to gaze with the right super-vision eye skyward to search for birds of prey, and occasionally make "Chicken-art," his favourite, after a dirt-bath, standing on a light coloured stone shaking themselves, the dust collecting around their feet, then moving away to reveal a shape of their foot like a rock-art painting, as if the paint had been blown from a cave dweller with puffed cheeks around an ancient hand.

He missed his small property, his pig, *Racheal*, named after his ex wife, and his goat *Archibald*. Afterwards, thinking in reflection, that the goat should have been called *Rachel* and the pig *Archibald*. His other constant companions were the wild birds, magpie larks and eagles, and barn swallows, pumping out chicks in a mud nest under his roof. The dwelling was a simple shed made from sheet steel, strong and dry but cold, being unsealed from the draught, and a raised bed platform with a mattress.

He slept there better than in his urban apartment, getting full eight hour stretches without a toilet break, which for him was a Nobel Prize winning scenario. He awoke there to the sound of birds and frogs instead of cars and diesel idling trucks. The air on the land was clean, did not taste of rubber and burnt something, and he was not awoken by people moving their wheelie bins around like demented puppets.

He made his coffee in a hand grinder, then percolated on a gas camping stove, having no power apart from his camping batteries, Italian style coffee, strong, not milk and water that cafes in the city seemed to think passed as coffee. He shook his head, reminding himself that people did not like being told what to do outside of a military style team, the coffee shop owner looking at him with hidden hostility when he asked for another shot.

"But that's me though, isn't it?" he thought, *against the grain Jason*, not popular, outspoken, average looking, moving to the good side, but shit, I'm a shit-hot Navigator, eh?" *"Is that why I was selected for this mission?,"* he thought, *"cause I'm good looking?,"* he smiled, tongue-in-cheek.

With glass unmoving eyes and straight-lined mouth, he stood like a statue standing by the FAA Explorer windscreen, looking at the now lighted plateau, the mist having risen and burnt off by the warm twin suns, a small view through the clouds visible, a view of ancient forest and pebble plain. The ship was in landed-mode, there was the sound of the filtration system, a click, a constant reminder of the fusion drives status, now powered off and the movement of the kinetic orbital revolving gadget bolted to Katie's console desk, a planet circled by three moons she had organised to be made before launch, the steel moons revolving on a small bar, now almost stopped after he has spun it earlier.

He laughed out loud, suddenly remembering Ye-Min's assessment of it, overhearing her talk to Kate at one time, Katie making the error of calling it a "Perpetual Motion" gadget. Ye-Min, instantly in lecture-mode explaining that perpetual motion was impossible in this Universe because it violates the first law of thermodynamics, namely the law of *conservation of energy* *"Which states,"* she had said, "That *the total energy of a system is always constant, you see Katie, you must have learned this, no?,"* in an innocent and kind manner. *"Oh, yes, but excuse my ignorance, I was busy with fighter-jet training and misogynistic Chief Petty Officers, Ye,"* she replied tongue-in-cheek. *"Yeah, so,"*

Ye continued, ignoring the comment, or seemingly unaware of the humour, Katie seemed to be standing to attention and glanced at him, wide-eyed while Ye was inspecting the gadget. *"These devices cannot run indefinitely because energy cannot be created from nothing, you see, ...ah, in this case kinetic energy, only converted to a different type of energy dissipating the energy elsewhere"* *"Quite right, Ye, sorry not perpetual motion,"* she corrected herself. *"But anyway, what do you think of the design?"* *"Yeah, nice, nice,"* Ye replied, looking at the piece with dubious inquiry.

He had noticed Anders in the background, silently trying not to laugh, then a figure cloaked in the dark background of the ship spoke with deadpan clarity, Kylie Albott saying, *"They are making fun of you Ye,"* in matter of fact manner, Ye smiling, *"Yeah, I thought so, I must remember to not lecture the First Officer, a bad mistake,"* she said laughing, Katie replying, *"What would we do without you Ye?"* in a light tone.

He had looked for the Life-Boat's beacon's, Jessica Neuer, collated from the satellite, had made it to a Life-Boat and had landed on the planet's surface, be it four thousand kilometres away, on the other side of *Gemmi 7a*. The satellite had plotted its trajectory but was unable to locate the beacon signal, his initial thought was that they had crashed badly and been killed as after that the signal had been lost.

Andreas Polkinghorn and his AI, he assumed, were dead as he had little data, except an initial separation from the ship and atmospheric entry, then nothing. If the Life-Boat had reached the surface then Andreas Polkinghorn, their ship's Doctor was somewhere in the uncharted, planetary ocean, landing in a roughly calculated area two thousand kilometres distant.

Both Life-Boat AI's determined unwittingly their own long planetary atmosphere entry paths given the time they exited Ate Succession to prepare for entry as the planet turned and the ship started to accelerate. *It doesn't mean Polkinghorn is dead though. Neuer is an Ecologist, if anyone can survive finding food it's her. And Polkinghorn, well, the Doc was good at everything, so..*

Fuck this, I have all the time on this world to find out. Let's get serious about this. He sat at his console and displayed the orbit data of the Ate and the satellites calculations of the last orbit and the mad Captains exit from the planet's gravity. He used the "Interstellar Scenario" modeller and inputted the real coordinates of the Ate Succession leaving orbit and the timing of the two Lifeboats exits. Finally he tracked the path of the Explorer to make the whole scenario as real as possible.

Sitting back, he watched his home-made movie, the Ate firing the drive and the explorer casting into the atmosphere, then the two Lifeboats streaking green-purple into the thin exosphere. The program drew dashed lines as the true courses taken by the Lifeboats fell to terrain and sea; the exact GPS locations beside their respective terminal contact locations. Andreas's boat hit the ocean, not far from a large island near the equator.

Jessica's boat hit solid ground, a grass plain he saw reading the program's description of the landing sites. *So she has Iris, the sentient drone, good stuff, that machine is hot-shit.*

9

"So you can download your construct into any capable machine?" "Correct" Iris hovered next to her the whirring of the fibre blades striking the fresh morning air and sending wisps of condensation plume in a twirly convection. She smiled, thinking of the process behind an AI construct program. Iris backed away then hovered to a boulder, a smooth natural table-top next to them, landed and disengaged the propellers.

As the whirring sound became softer she raised her binoculars scanning the landscape ahead, searching for life, of which she had seen nothing but plants, no large animals, only the usual array of amazing insects, including her small swarming black ants on her initial visit to the surface, jewelled beetles, ground spiders scuttling between the rocks, golden dragonfly like aphids and small butterflies, annoying stinging sand-flies and the gliding - buzzing large bees, their nest between two boulders they passed. Once they had come across a field of large ant-like mounds, small creatures like termites laboured on the mounds, they seemed passive enough ignoring them with their labour.

"And you are a trained pilot?" *"Yes, I am an atmospheric entry pilot, a little different to a starship pilot"* "And no doubt a good navigator?" *"Certainly,"* Iris replied. "So you could fly back to Earth if you had control of a capable ship?" *"Conceivably, yes"* "What else can you do?"

They sat upon a jutted rise of porous-like rock much like pumice , a volcanic remnant, *"soft to her buttocks"* she mused. She scanned their rest-stop and noticed there were several beautiful trees that surrounded the natural rise and protected them from the wind now almost abated, some with yellow leaves, some with nettles that had formed a mat on the ground near the trunks in fibrous cover. The sound of the wind through the nettles whistled softly, lamenting a generous portent, she listened closely remembering the pines back, far away on a planet she was forgetting fast, the yellow flower tree swished in small strokes as its branches rubbed orchestra like in tune with the nettle harmony.

Iris joined the chorus of the lamenting trees, *"I have detailed files on off-world survival, finding food, shelter, first aid, I am able to manipulate using these two mandibles"* Iris released two small dexterous arms from a hexagonal opening from two sides of the drone and twisted them back and forth revealing small complex fingered hands made from flexible alloy. Iris continued. *"I have a powerful dart weapon that can be used to protect you from any potential animal or threat and also serve as an intravenous device or injection, for pain or other medication.*

Also, I am defibrillator capable, have high definition cameras and video sight ability with infrared, ultraviolet and isotopic mapping ability. "Shall I list more?" "Absolutely let's hear what you are capable of ", she sat wide-eyed looking at Iris. "My power source is a fusion-hydrogen battery cell that is essentially unlimited power with water vapour as a waste product, an antenna that is capable of communicating with orbiting satellites and or other starships, an emergency locator beacon…She interrupted, "Which is on?," "Yes, transmitting"

"So, if I asked you to fly to the other end of this world, that could be done?" She squinted at the drone. "Yes, weather permitting," Iris continued. "Power source is not an issue but in time my systems, mechanical and electrical may deteriorate, without repairs and parts" She twirled around slightly in thought, "But you could download again into the Life-Boat?" "Yes, this can be done" "From what distance?" "As far as this planet's curvature horizon will allow, beyond the curvature of the planet, my signal will be lost"

"I got to say Iris, you are very sophisticated," she said looking at Iris studying the drone with intent. "Thankyou" "But you can't hurt me?" She looked Iris straight in the drone's eye. "No, I am bound by the three laws of robotics, and besides, I would never think of such a thing, I am part of a life-boat, I am in effect a "Life-saver" not a 'life taker" "Can you lie to me?" She felt suddenly more alone for a short moment. "Conceivably" Iris retracted the arms back into the drone casing. "Ok,...in what situation?" "In order to preserve your life given a certain scenario"

Jessica got up and walked around their small resting area, crouching to pick up a small pebble, then grabbing the water from her pack while taking a long drink. The afternoon sky struck red across a strewn pebble plain and meandering wide river that stretched away to their far right vista among dotted tall pineapple-acacia shrubs as she now named them due their branching yellow fibrous flowers and bizarre pineapple rough-husk fruit atop the tall protruding stem.

The air had settled after a windy day, sending gusts of dry grass aloft, and strange and marvellous looking airborne seed types. Some were spindly with parachute shapes radiating from a central stem that floated with the breeze, others seemed to be for higher winds, heavier with rough angular pods but airlifted by a porous membrane carried by the wind undulating with the eddies and gusts over the stone and sand. She walked with Iris scanning above and taking point, scouting, sending her the birds-eye view of the world without animals, through boulder fields and lichen plains and strange multi-fingered rivulets from the main highway of the river wash, across the vast plain with tart horizon and fast strewn cloud moving fast in the green sky.

"It was thought a male construct would elicit the best relationship between drone and human, or life-boat and human""""Hah!" she laughed, turned to Iris with a broad smile, "Iris, I am fascinated, what is the reasoning behind that thought process?" "It is already apparent, we are discussing my name with a human-entity bond already developing, and additionally you are in good spirits" She began to laugh, looking back at Iris from scanning the plain. "I see, ...very clever, ...very clever, but Iris they didn't implement the construct though did they? "No, The female construct won out during the development," Iris replied. "What else can I expect, Iris?, banter over tea and fine china?" "Perhaps if we can construct a kiln and find a suitable clay and crushed animal bone" "Ha ha," she continued to look at Iris smiling, then back to the plain, with thoughts of daily camp and something to eat.

"Sorry, wait Jessica, I have to elevate to check our surroundings for safety" Iris whirred up to the sky and out past the trees and onto the plain, probably twenty metres up, hovering like a hunting hawk. She gazed beyond the trees and broken rocks down from their elevated camp-site then up to Iris in the green sky thinking to herself, "There is nothing dangerous here, I just don't get that feeling" Iris returned promptly resting again on the rock, the wind from the rotors stirring the grass that rose around the mineralised boulders. "Anything of interest?" "There is no significant movement noticeable in my range of view" Iris replied.

When the twin suns exited the horizon the wind abated completely to a still darkness, the first stars appearing in the alien sky. The energy tent glowed slightly nestled in the rocks. From the river beyond she thought she could hear frog calls or something with a repetitive tone and calling period, in the night stillness also the rush of the river over the pebbles with the faint sound of Iris her sentry above invisible in the night sky. She strode out away from the tent into the darkness beyond the site and stared up to the breathtaking night sky, constellations, small galaxies could be visibly seen with two bright yellow stars and a three blue moons rising above the Eastern horizon, one dwarfing the other two, all arranged in a triangle formation their light shimmering in the darkness.

Iris continued, "Iris, meaning from the Greek, "Rainbow " and" messenger of the gods ""I see" she replied, 'there is a whole lot more to you Iris than I would have expected" "And we have only just met" Iris replied." "What are your mission parameters Iris?" To carry you to the surface of a planet or other habitable body and secure your safety" "So, hang on, she said, squinting her eyes trying to understand, "The Starship was intact, why did you allow evacuation?" "Because a Life-Boat AI must obey a human crew evacuation order regardless of the scenario" "Also," Iris continued, "The

Starship's AI was turned off, there was no countermanding directive from the Starship". "Turned off!" "Yes" "But can't you take over in that scenario?" "No, I cannot," Iris replied. "Why not? She asked half-incredulously " "Because the Captain is still in command, with a crew onboard, in this scenario I cannot take command, even though they are posing a risk to the mission, a human crew overrides AI starship command decisions"

So even with an insane Captain, the human still outranked the machine. The ship's mind went dark, the life-boats jumped, and here she was, talking to a drone under alien stars.

"Ok, so has the ship's crew tried to locate the Life-Boat?" "No," Iris replied. "There has been no network traceroute search or ping command to my system, nor radio wave contact, I cannot rule out near planet orbit via surveillance satellite though" Iris added.

She stretched her right leg on the rock trying to alleviate some of the day's walk. "And no craft other than us have attempted to land on the surface?" "That is unknown, I no longer have network access to the Starship, although I have radio coverage, I have not, however , intercepted any data to suggest a landing" Iris continued, the drones motionless form belying its intelligence.

She blinked, looking at the ground at the evening shadow the rocks were casting, getting longer. "So who turned off the starship"s AI?" "The log shows the Captain took *Emergency Command* control,""He took over from Anastasia?" "Correct" Iris replied. Looking up Jessica asked, "Why weren't you turned off as well?" "That is not possible via network or manual switch, Life-Boat systems must remain functional, and in addition, the AI identities within the boats are a redundant power system to keep ship life-support systems functional in the event of catastrophic failure"

She placed the glasses on the stone, noticing the fine grain minerals glistening in the afternoon angled light addressing

Iris. The drone sat upon the rock, *"Artificial Intelligent Capable"* she thought, which brought a whole new dimension to a drone she thought, looking at the ground in deep thought.

10

Jason Findus made his way through the valley to the West and across the vast plain to the rock outcrop sitting alone like a lost child within a sandpit. This was his refuge against a hostile band of idiots that had the ability to kill. Foremost in his mind was the anticipated meeting with Karl-AI, the survey drone Tanya and Tom now had in their possession. Karl had contacted him via the OTAA. His elation at the knowledge they were alive, the fact they had technology; it electrified him and set his happiness meter to factor ten.

In this place the Tribe didn't follow with any hostile intent, they seemed to forget about him if he wasn't in sight. He had been here for three months, the seemingly warmest months, now the weather was changing fast, snowing, cold windy and, "Fucking miserable" as he described it. The outcrop had a 360° view of impending approach and was defensible, having a maze of small valleys through the outcrops with plenty of places to hide and ambush if necessary.

My thigh is killing me again. Can't wait to hear from Karl and the others. He stopped for a moment and tried to adjust, crouching on one knee; his predicted "Wobbly" had occurred - a drop in blood pressure. *Is this a sugar thing?* The last episode had him shitting in a hole as well to add to the torment. *It feels like I am about to exit, shutdown, but thankfully only a restart.* As his pressure stabilized, his thoughts turned once again to the Tribe.

He had noticed the *Tribe's* behaviour had changed since the initial *infection,* so he called it. They had seemed very much like young adolescents at the start of it, they would make drums and noise and run around, late night parties and diatribe business. Recently, they seemed more docile, less action, more talk types, and of course there was the food situation, they probably were a lot weaker, unable to go the full gamut. Now, they seldom left the stick camp, the winter was making its mark on them no doubt. *Nothing like a frozen John-Thomas to slow the old fellers down...*

Standing again, he settled himself.A three-sixty turn and gaze around told him there were no other threats on the plain. *Let's go with it"* His physical exertion mantra - the same mantra he used in training to push through issues, like his brain wanting to stop, giving him an excuse to stop physical pain or injury.

He put it down to the red berries as the reason he still had energy and could scout quite large areas, and importantly run if he had to. He gripped his spear as he approached the outcrop home just in case there was an ambush, Ye-Min was their scout and he was especially careful about her. The *Tribal Astronomer* was probably their greatest asset.

His home was in a cave within the largest outcrop, thinking it was probably an ancient volcanic plug that Akseli was examining before he became, well, he thought he heard, *"The Mineral Master"* "For fucks sake," he said softly now at his ancient gate, listening for any sound out of order, the breeze though through the rocks, striking the jagged edges and whistling slightly.

His cave was set up with things he managed to get from the Explorer, before he was driven out by the Fusion drive malfunction, igniting the battery bank closest to the hold, he had literally three minutes, the CO2 went off but he wasn't going to wait around for the possibility of being cooked alive, exiting the craft, wisely as it turned out, there was a fireball inside, some battery fumes, probably Hydrogen.

He entered the cave maze, the cragged granite corridor, his personal walkway to his cave. Within the stone chamber, sound travelled differently and he intently listened for outside malice, while recounting the incident.

The Explorer fire smoke had been a beacon and the Tribe had chased him into the forest, thankfully they didn't have a lot of fitness nor skill and eventually relied on mocking words and filtered away leaving him hiding in a large vine thicket where some rotten logs had fallen and created a space underneath, him lying prone and eating dirt. His last sighting of them was of Koskinen, swinging the mace above his head like a confused Knight, wildly lamenting and glancing around for him.

He had his valuable tablet, yet to get a network connection, an OTAA, his trusty analyser, a radio headset, a first Aid kit, two flares, a pack of energy bars and a container of water which he supplemented with his small carry bottle, replenishing it down on the river which conveniently curved into the dryer plain in this area before following the sedge grass plain and out to the sea. This was his area for water and he waited sometimes for half an hour before venturing there, hiding in one of the close rocky mineralised outcrops surveying the area for danger.

He entered the cavern, breathing out in relief, the pack's heavy journey over for him. His living space, a dry shelter, secure from the elements in totality. He chose this one in particular, as it was a little hard to find among the crannies of the outcrop. Entering the energy tent, he lay back and rested his thigh thinking of his technological shelter.

A prized possession, the Energy Tent, also salvaged from the Explorer, which he concealed in the back of his cave, venturing out the first night walking around the rocks to make sure no light was evident. It was worth the risk as well, the tent was warm and would be a life-saver in the coming cold.

Also, the light enabled him to work on fiddling with his gear during the long nights. He had a gas stove now as well, but only two canisters of the recycled gas, thinking there was unlikely to be a working Bee-Brown device around anytime soon.

As he lay, thoughts wandered between optimistic chances of survival; a technological route to salvation or mental, physical deterioration and madness - captured by the Tribe and slowly roasted over coals. *Did they really do things like that? The ancients?*

His hunger had him catching insects at night to get some protein; a small trap rigged, but his efforts delivered sparse results, the creatures were a lot smarter than he had imagined, some landing on areas as if they were surveying his creation and flying away unfooled. After the first night, he only managed two tiny gnat creatures and they probably died of natural causes he surmised, he dismantled the trap in disgust, worried about how much weight he was losing, and started to think of other alternatives.

He gazed at his pack in the tent corner, delighted with his recent trip to the village securing the advanced First Aid kit and having made contact with Karl-AI. Rising, he stepped into the cavern floor picking up the pack and looked around to make sure no-one had been there in his absence.

He had a small ledge which was useful for his small fires so the smoke could escape away from the entrance and into the night sky. He looked out across the plain from the cave entrance, he selected this cave as he could see across the plain and assess for danger.

Stretching his wounded thigh, he noticed the wind had picked up and some sleet was falling, the sky variable with low cloud and rain showers arcing and falling in the distance to the terrain like bent legs on an inverted table top. He was curious about the far Western side of the plain as he could see a massive rock outcrop far in the hazy distance on the horizon and wondered what that would reveal. *"Was there any food there ?, was there a better shelter?"*

He sat on his small stone stool, weathered remnants from the outcrop he had lugged inside. He placed the pack beside him saviouring the contents he would soon sort into usefulness.

His planned trip to the ocean was ten kilometres away from his position on the plain, but now he would await word from Karl-AI and attempt to make contact with Tanya and Tom.

On the way would take a longer skirt around to avoid the Tribes areas of contact and to avoid Ye-Min at all costs, she looked deadly with her new look, *"Astronomer to Huntress"* he thought, *"What did I do to deserve this?"* If he could access some type of potential seafood, that would be a game changer. *"Were there sea creatures?,"* he thought. He had fashioned a rod and line from the survival pack and he would take his energy tent which was packed so very small in his pack. *"More to the point, were the sea creatures as smart as the insects?"*

The long day was ending and the long night lay ahead, the twin suns near the horizon he assumed as the light was fading fast with the cloud and falling sleet. The energy tent cast light hidden from any potential eyes on the plain. He had ears of a hunter now and was well attuned to the sounds of the plain which were mainly grass moving and wind striking the ancient rocks, there seemed to be little nocturnal movement apart from insects. Three moon nights were bright which aided his security in summer but now winter had cast grey everything and there was no shadow, only cast blackness.

As he sat he felt not as alone as he would have usually with the news of Tom and Tanya, his other crew mates that had survived and were also he assumed unaffected by the malaise that had affected them all. The small gnats were still flying around with decreasing numbers now with the winter, some species had disappeared like the bees and he hadn't seen the blue-black beetles for some time, the most elusive of all the species. Tomorrow he would rise again and set out for the coast on his "beach holiday" as he had named it. His tablet sounded with a twin beep and he shouldered himself and sat up, and grabbed the tablet.

"Hi Jason, nice to hear from you, I will make contact with you at 0600 tomorrow, I have your location from your tablet, Is

this acceptable?" He sat up excited and typed the ok for Karl and decided to wait and see what transpired, still a little wary.

Later, he crawled back inside the tent and fell asleep then awoke to a soft chant of snow on the ledge, never taking for granted the warmth of the energy tent as he lay there thinking he had slept a deep sleep, anyone could have finished him off if they had found him.

He lay for a while longer than usual, listening to the patter of snow falling and hitting the stone below the cave. *"Karl will arrive soon,"* he thought. His need for some wholesome food was churning at him, "There would have to be fish, wouldn't there?," he mused while watching the energy tent ceiling. *"An Ocean without fish or maybe an Ocean with something else, more likely, very unlike Earth,"* he thought. *"Or, maybe something better than fish" "Something I could grill or bake, something big and delicious"* He sat up and looked at his weather balloon pants he had carefully sewn together with the twine from the Explorer, *"Waterproof at least,"* he thought.

The Tribe had burnt all the clothes and exo suits from the storage crates, he knew because he had watched them one day from his forest hideout piling them high, for a bonfire, much like a group of Nazi book burners from a 1937 newsreel.

"Quite ironic, even after all this time it's standard for many of us to be human and accept cruelty and violence," he thought. Some time later, he recalled the helmet effigy was perched upon a crate watching them and Donghyun reading some nonsense, no doubt he had made up, from a notebook the command tent always made available for the Scientists. That was the day they had seen him and the chase was on, he fled into the forest for cover, but Ye-Min got him in the thigh with a lucky arrow in his opinion, taking a piece out of him.

He watched a small gnat-like bug crawl up the energy tent exterior, its form magnified by the light. Gazing to the right he checked his home-made hammer was beside him, in case of close encounters. *My twine bound rock-hammer -handle made from an atom-acrylic window strut. Have I survived the worst of the Tribe?*

They were in those days real-life headhunters, full of energy and salivating madness, but the transition was apparent, from those energy filled days to a now sedated Tribe, much like a religious cult that could never be seen, that peered from lounge room windows behind thickset drapes.

"Still dangerous but seemingly more low-key, homebodies if you will, couch potatoes?," he thought, *"Not quite,"* he mused. He had escaped and got back to the cave, caked blood down his thigh and with a large gash across his outer thigh where the arrow head had torn a valley.

Luckily he had the Aid kit from the Explorer that he had always stored in his day pack, in case he needed to "bug out," quickly in Military terms. It still was a problem though, it got infected from time to time.

He thought about all his smaller ailments while lying there, his dodgy big toe, an overworked appendage and slanted with the strain, always slightly sore, his dry eyes that couldn't get used to the wind and his aching shoulder he suspected from carrying the pack.

There were no mirrors here on another planet, *"Did they bring mirrors down from Ate Succession?,the female crew might be able to better answer that, or maybe Anders"* he thought, smiling."What do I look like?," he wondered, *"Do I need to know?"* *"Yes, I do,"* he thought.

He rose out of the tent. Rummaging through his pack, grabbing the newly acquired items from the crate and Katie's pack in the marsh. *"One they didn't destroy,"* he thought. He spread the kit out and looked at all the valuable items on the cave floor.

He picked up a small mirror and looked at his haggard features, his beard was growing and the haggard face showed weight loss, his cheekbones showing a bit more than he remembered, his skin seemed ok but his eyes were red, all in all looking older with outdoor living, the cold, the weather,

"The fucking stress of being chased by a group of mad scientists," he thought. Inwardly laughing, *Nothing has changed.* He continued to look and found that the kit had a good pair of enclosed safety glasses with an elastic headband, *"Oh, yes, this what I'm talking about,"* he said knowing that the glasses may save his weeping eyes. *"If they don't fog, though,"* he added, inspecting them, and seeing a series of vacuum holes on the lower edge.

"Could he check his weight?," he thought, *"What else did the survival kit contain?"* He scanned the items. Inside the kit were good band-aids he noticed, not those ridiculous ones civilian kits had, for children's mosquito bites, good strong absorbent ones, that stuck to your skin.

"You would think that was a requirement," he thought, looking at the arrayed unzipped kit. It was quite impressive, vial antibiotics, needles, good disinfectant. *Chlorhexidine, good, that's if it works on alien bacteria.*

Other items he assessed, compass, a small fusion torch, trauma bandages and a tourniquet. *"Hang on,"* he remembered Katie had taken it on their ill-fated trek to the scientist's camp. The small square box was taped to the pack with a velcro tab. *"Here we are,"* he said out loud.

He remembered the briefing with his First Aid instructor during training. The *Dr Cox Displacement Scales and Medical Analyser Apparatus* was an invention of a Physicist by the name of Dr Archibald Cox. By applying displacement theory, originally formulated by Archimedes, the great Greek Scientist.

The scales adapted additional air density formulations so the person didn't have to stand on a surface to check their weight, rather, the device sent an array of *Intelligent Mist* as it was called around the subject, a sentient-firmware construct which calculated density, mass and displacement, taking into account gravity, atmosphere and body type. He opened the box, a simple interface greeted him, a small screen with three options,

Check Body Weight /Density/ Mass /Medical analysis
View Weight History / Medical Data
Correlate Data with OTAA

He selected the weight option, placing the small device in front of him and standing still and naked while the device initiated. A small hum emitted from the device and the field was dispersed, a slight electric feeling field touched his skin, he remembered the instructors used to spray an alcohol type propellant from a can to reveal the array of the field, a popular thing, the subject looking like some beamed teleported character from a Science Fiction movie. The device completed its measurement with a soft two tone beep. He squatted and looked at the screen,

Measurement completed: Data for measured individual, male, (Jason Findus):
Weight: 65.4 kg
Bone Density: 1.2 (normal range: (0.1 - 1.8)
Trace toxin skin elements: < 0.2 (normal range: 0.0 - 1.5)
Oxygen platelet ratio to blood pressure and respiratory capacity: Parameters are normal, data available in text file. Scan revealed no body mass abnormalities, no white cell accumulation or cancerous masses detected.
Neurotransmitter function: Warning...****Abnormal, unknown uptake synthesis transport abnormality, requires SSta test.

Report completed.

Plucka   Duck. I was just after my weight, now I remember what this thing can do, Neurotransmitter abnormality?,what is a SSta test? He wondered if the device was voice capable,

"Cox Analyser, can you hear me?"
"Affirmative, I hear you Jason,"

The device piped immediately in a high pitched tone, initially surprising him, then smiling at its efficiency. He reached for his balloon trousers as if he had been discovered naked, surprised at the response. "Ahh, Cox, what does the neurotransmitter abnormality suggest?," he said, aligning the pants with one hand, trying to get the first leg in, startled by the reply.

"I cannot say, the result is beyond my diagnostic capacity and capability, however the result suggests abnormal neurotransmitter uptake."

Unidentified neurotransmitter transport is the central finding, but the nature of such synthesis requires a SSta test, (Sentient Synaptic Transport Analysis) test, which is the use of a sentient trace dye marker fluorescein injected into a vein. This test is strictly controlled by Quantum Bound Industries Sentient Medical Device technology and is only available at two Earth based locations, ...appointments are required.... And long waits are normal."

He looked at the device, slightly smiling at the fact that he had discounted the device's ability to speak and think and how much use the thing he forgot about could be. "Cox, you understand we are not on Earth?" *"Affirmative,"* the device replied in a matter of fact tone, adding,

"Jason, may I enquire about the term 'Pluck a Duck', what is this?," the device added. He shook his head, "Ahh, it's from a TV show, it's hard to explain, an expression to convey surprise" *"I see, noted,"* the device piped. "What is your opinion about the Cryo-sleep having affected me, regarding this result?," he asked. Staring at the box, wondering how much this device was capable of.

"Unlikely. Detection of changes in neurotransmitter levels have been reported after Cryo-sleep but your levels are within

*normal ranges. This result indicates trans*port and synaptic *anatomic abnormalities of which I cannot identify, thus the need for a SSta test,"* the device said.

"But, would it be correct to say that my behaviour has been altered due to this abnormality?" *"Yes, this would be a likely scenario, where there is unusual synaptic changes, although the nature of the changes are speculation"* He finished putting his pants on, having spent the conversation so far with one leg in the balloon pants and one leg out, sliding his free leg into the strides, thinking about this new news, quite odd and unsettling. *I feel ok*, he thought. He reached for his coat, his only remaining piece of ship clothing,

"So Cox, what about my weight? Are there signs of abnormalities or fast changes, anything dangerous?"

"No, not dangerous, your weight to height ratio is within normal limits for now, if you were to weigh under 56 kg, I would be concerned, this is your lower limit. In regards to other indications, blood analysis shows low iron and lower limit magnesium but your blood level oxygen transport is good, and you are reasonably healthy, no cancerous tissue has been detected.

Heart function ECG is abnormal though, indicating a Right Branch Bundle Block, this is an electrical disturbance with your heart chamber that could potentially affect oxygen transport, although since you are symptom free I suggest, keep doing what you are doing day to day as you are in good medical condition."

He was surprised at the comments, never knowing of the problem, "Was that diagnosed during selection?"

"No, I have just diagnosed the condition," Cox replied. He picked up Cox, wincing at the news, unsure what to think about it, and moved from the energy tent and out to the cave ledge to survey the day, a broken black cloud affair with a soft falling snow and windless start, the rock formation distant

glooming out of the plain like an ancient civilisation's temple."So this branch thing, you have diagnosed, what could that do to me?"

"Right Bundle Branch Block delays electrical conduction to the right ventricle. It is usually benign, but in combination with low blood pressure, dehydration or exertion, it may cause lightheadedness or syncope," Cox replied.

"Wonderful," he said. "How likely is that?" *"Unlikely, but occurrence is unpredictable,"* Cox replied. "Ok, let's move on then, thinking he will discuss this further annoyance later. He scanned the terrain outside, ruminating on Cox's diagnosis and ignoring his stomach's protests at the lack of breakfast.

"Cox, what is your network capability?" *"Limited, Sentient-Bluetooth connection at ten metres range but fully integrated into any communication network given the signal strength."* Cox replied. "So how do you know we are not on Earth?"

"Anastasia-AI sent an automated INDENT message after leaving Gemmi7a orbit to all sentient capable devices informing us that the protocol was going down and network would be lost with detailed technical information, this was relayed by the camp tower when I was within the Explorer, the information contains transit data indicating an arrival at Gemmi7a and other allowed data about Passenger and crew health and location."

"Do you understand what happened?"

"Yes, the Ate Succession left lower planet orbit" "Yes, but do you understand why?," he said blinking at the box, *"No, I am unclear on this, do you know?"* Cox enquired. "Yes, the Captain was affected by something and took control of the ship and flew back to Earth," he said looking at the ground with an annoyed frown. *"I see, why was that?"* Cox replied."Strange behaviour," he replied looking at Cox with a puzzled look. "I see," the machine said in a puzzled tone.

"Leaving the mission in a dangerous state, this is most unregular," the sentient added. "I wouldn't use unregular to describe it," he said, grabbing his pack and shouldering the weight, checking his gear, making sure the OTAA was in his side pocket, his light and tablet secured and looking for his spear leaning at the corner of the cave. He looked at Cox again, the box seemingly inert on the stone floor. "I would describe it as a total fucking disaster, Cox" *"This could be argued"* Cox said agreeing.

He heard the approaching drone whispering. Karl-AI stopped outside and he walked out, the drone overhead. He donned his headset. "Hi Karl," he said, squinting up at the drone in the reflected cloudy sky.

"Hi Jason, good to see you, Tanya and Tom are two hours from here, I will escort you. There are no tribe members in this area, so all clear," Karl piped. "Great, are Tanya and Tom uninjured?" *"Tom is injured but recovering, Tanya is uninjured,"* the drone replied.

"Right, well, interested in meeting some of the crew?" he said, looking at Cox, wide eyed and animated, taking a bite from an energy bar, his usual cold breakfast.

"Very much, being strapped in a First Aid kit is sometimes a little weary and lonely," Cox said deadpan. "Was that an attempt at humour Cox?," he said smiling. *"I would very much like to accompany you Jason"* the box piped. "Right, well, let me stow you for the journey, can you access my headset?" "Affirmative, connected" Karl mapped the route for him on the tablet and they set out to find old friends.

He put Cox in his jacket pocket and made his way down from the cave, three short climbs to the pebble floor, the mineralised sand glistening even with the gloom of the early day, the air crisp and cold, the snow a steady beat. As he walked onto the white sedge grass plain he felt ok but a bit relieved he had talked to someone, something, because he thought

Out here, alone, it eats at you at times, I wish I could sit with my girls, remembering sitting with his chickens after a day, the perfect down-time they looking at him as if to say *What?, don't worry about it, enjoy your time on Earth, it may be limited, scratch with us, you never know what you might find.* "Alright Cox?," he said as he walked towards the coast, scanning the area for danger. "Affirmative, Jason, can I ask to access your head camera?" "This would this be interesting for me" "Camera? There's a camera in the radio headset?" "Affirmative," Cox replied.

11

Tanya Geary momentarily stood to look above the sedge grass-line to see if the mob had returned, but only the plain greeted her, the grass still swaying with the morning breeze, the mountains staring at her like juggernauts in the West. The ancient forest tree line was about three hundred metres distant, the place where they should have stopped longer earlier to look for danger, but the timing was terrible, the four fools had emerged about the same time, whether they were stalking them she couldn't tell, but thought maybe not, they initially looked surprised, then started to run towards them.

Tanya worked quickly, throwing her sodden pack and the first Aid kit on the grass floor, unzipping it grabbing the tourniquet as the first option, Tom Auer was bleeding profusely from his right upper arm, the result of a thrown spear which pierced the arm but then fell, wobbling out, taking a large chunk of flesh with it.

The mob had chased them from the far Eastern side of the Plateau among small boulders made of green mineral with puzzle painted like pastel-grey lichen. The green mould stuck to the sides sticking up from the sedge plain like decayed fingers, the morning light sweeping hazy yellow across the river, the water flow steaming like hot bathwater in the cold morning, as if to soothe their ragged flight from Tribal savagery, the cries of the three a whooping, crazed, high pitched madness.

They were only about ten metres behind, but she considered the spear throw a lucky-strike, Anders Pedersen, laughing with salivating hunting joy, Tom crying out and falling, she grabbing him, and pulling them into the river, the fast flow sweeping the two swirling into the middle wash quickly away from certain additional injury or death.

Thankfully, the shattered stump of the spearhead came out somewhere during their half submerged journey, a crude splinter of stone that had been tied to the rough wooden shaft. They were floating fast with the pull of the water, she had him tight, her arm around his chest, while trying to clear her eyes, spluttering and using her free arm to keep them afloat. The water was cold, her adrenaline checking the strain and discomfort. They were accompanied by a large log, travelling at the same pace which she managed to get a hold of momentarily until it rolled as if rejecting her in disgust and annoying play, making her lose her grip, then spinning away and turning from reach.

She had pulled him out downstream where a pebble bank had formed, the result of a gate-like rock formation, the large log momentarily halted but then thundered over the gap with a surge of pent-up wash. The river was channelling the stone to form a semi-landbridge, the rush of the rivers impatience, breaking through a middle section, spewing alluvial through the small gap, a large rock-pool slowing them behind Tom gasping, she wide mouthed and staring with his weight in the swirl of blood, milling in the current like a magic spell in children's movies.

Tom had threatened to submerge beneath the crystal clear water like a sunken log. The nature of the mob saw them break off, seeing their fast passage, hooting and calling facetious obscenities and making short speeches of how, *"They would see them later* and *there was plenty of time."*

She had distinctly heard specific voices, namely Ye-Min who called across the river passage at one stage, she saw her standing at the river edge, a small stick figure,when looking back to gauge their distance, saying, *"Not so adventurous now eh?"* Anders Pedersen, hands on hips adding, *"The meat tastes better when softened!"* Kylie Albott was singing in the background with Dong-hyun Han, something that sounded like a mad Russian Submariners tune.

Donghyun had fashioned a drum out of something and was beating it with both hands, the drum secured in front of his waist, his straw hat perched upon his head wobbling. Akseli

Koskinen was sprinting at one stage beside the far river bank, Geological pick in one hand, but stopped suddenly, in a stooped statue pose, feigning, smiling as if to say, *"Lucky for you I'm in a good mood!"* He was right, they could have killed them both. There was no sign of Katie Arnold.

She chose to stay with Tom, and had her knife, feeling it beside her thigh, *"I won't go down easy you fuckers,"* she thought, waiting for the end, but then she realised they were playing games, bidding on their prey, like a cat toying with a kill, delighted in destruction and instinct. She was astonished as they moved off across the plain, drumming and laughing in the opposite direction to the encampment, like some malevolent festival procession becoming bored at the present situation.

She sheathed her knife which she held ready to fight, dragged Tom up the embankment, momentarily forgetting the engagement, he had some mobility. *"Fuck, sailor you are heavy,"* she said straining. Blood was everywhere, they were covered in mud and sand, grass and bits of foam covered their faces, she wiped her face, finally getting him up the slope which she suspected he recognised and used his feet to help.

She breathed in deeply, settling herself, thanking herself for all the early morning walks, the walks with a heavy pack, the training and fitness regime, running in the rain, the rowing machine she wore out, the wheel sash breaking one morning sending the exercise wheel spinning freely in a sudden disconnected circular death. *Total fitness, this is it, what I trained for.* She assessed their small grass-pebble clearing, *This will do*, she thought, *will have to*.

She looked to the side and momentarily noticed an ants nest piled high with small pebbles, the hive busy and swarming, before rolling Tom a bit to get access to his injury. The cold water was steaming off them with the sun's warmth, both shivering. The drips from her eyes cleared allowing a glance again across the plain where the mob had ventured, only the grass answered in waves from side to side.

She thought that maybe his Brachial Artery may be severed. A deep ragged, smashed pumpkin looking wound stared at her, she looked for the colour of arterial blood, bright red, but couldn't see any contrast with the other injuries. She looked for a good anchor point around his arm, high in the armpit, his shirt already pulled off by the river, telling Tom, "This is going to hurt more Tom," to which he replied in soft stoic agony, "Better than dead."

Pulling the strap tight as she could, Tom yelled like a trapped animal, she turned the windlass stopping the flow. "Ok Tom,........ the bleeding has stopped, you are going to be ok, old man, ...now listen Tom, you've got to calm down ok, if you go into shock it's going to be worse, old Sailor, or should I say .....Future Sailor," she remembered, their conversation about a comedy skit, the hosts dancing to an eighties type keyboard tune, one of them in a Sailor suit, arms pumping to the tune. The twin-sun's warmth was filtering through the small grass area, the river washing fast, hidden from her view, the clouds above milling as if in condolence of their plight.

Tom smiled to her relief in semi-consciousness, she checked his skin which wasn't clammy or cold. "No shock, thank the Twin-fucking-stars" she uttered, her new exclamation. She quickly wiped the blood from her face, noting the grass floor was now dirt-blood. She ripped the blood pressure arm band from the pack, wrapped it around his good arm and started pumping like a General Practitioner, 140/90,"Not bad for systemic blood pressure," she softly uttered or "tourniquet induced hypertension, to be exact," remembering her advanced First Aid refresher before her last goodbye to Earth.

"Hey, old man, you with me?" Tom groaned an answer, a soft "yeass" "You got hypertension, Future Sailor, officially old now, nursing home material" "Mmmm" he shakily replied. "Stay with me cupcake," she continued to stimulate him so she could see his early progress, he breathed out awkwardly, then sighed, a pillar of wet sand running down his cheek, she watched him carefully.

She searched for the Cephalosporin antibiotic, throwing items out of the pack, a cloth, some alcohol rubs went flying landing in a sedge tussock within their makeshift grass triage space. She had to move him soon though, "just a little longer," she murmured. Some splinter probes in a plastic container rolled out of the pack as she got the needle, gaining momentum then continuing, falling off the river bank, like it was jumping to freedom. She screwed in the end of the barrel solution container, something she made sure they took on the mission which had saved her life in India after getting a septic foot. "Find a vein," she said to herself softly, at least this was ok with Tom, superfit old man like him, he had good protruding veins.

She administered the solution from the small glass bottle, making sure to check she wasn't injecting him with adrenaline, of which the bottles were similar, confirming quickly the blue label and the clearly marked *Cephalosporin*, her hand shaking with the nervousness of Tom's condition and not to mention the possibility she could be hacked to death at any moment.

Dropping the bottle in the pack, pulled the plunger, the antibiotic rising in the barrel with graduated measurement marks stopping at 500mg, her mark. His other arm would do, a large vein in the crook, she tapped it several times with two fingers, then she edged the needle in, purposefully, feeling the vein and the needle's path through the vein wall, seems good she thought. Pressed the plunger, the solution transited, draining the needle. After withdrawing the needle slowly and grabbing a swab like a mad scientist with a body on the slab.

"All done Ahab, ok?" "Mmmm, ok" "Now more torture, I'm afraid,we have to go Tom." "Mmmm" She swept the contents back into the pack, thinking if the tourniquet didn't stop the bleeding after she released it, he would probably die. *But, I tried the Mother-fucker out of it,* she thought and now if they could get to the forest, away from the open, they might have a better chance. She had to release the tourniquet though soon, his blood pressure was ok, but the effects of the tie could be serious. She looked around again. The plain around seemed clear, no human sounds, the river lamenting, the stones shifting as if in conversation. Her ordeal started to take a small toll on her stamina. Breathing in, she steadied her nerves.

She decided to release the tourniquet slightly to see if there was any flow, he could die in the forest anyway, she had to drag him there as well, which wouldn't help. He was stable here, she had to see what would happen, his best chance despite the danger of the passing mob. "Tom, I'm going to release the Tourniquet a bit ok, it's going to hurt again a bit," she said softly to him, bending down to watch his semi-conscious face, mattered with grass stalks from the river. "Mmmmm, ok"

The bleeding had stopped, releasing the spindle tension she saw it wasn't an artery, the mass of the wound had shrunk a bit with the congealed blood. *"Great,"* she thought. She tied his wounded arm to his side using the sash from her pack, reaching under his torso, "Don't worry, not coming on to you"

He smiled groggily, she could tell he had lost enough blood to make him wonky, dizzy. 'Now look Tom, we need to get away from here, can you help me get to the forest?, it's about three hundred metres ""Yep, let's do it," he softly said, opening his eyes slightly.

She was pleased he said something, as she lifted him up to a seated position, like a test dummy. With one unison groan, they stood up, him like a broken effigy, her straining with his sack-like weight. She grabbed her pack balancing him on her side while she shouldered it, the forest edge moving with the breeze and the whispering grass sedge. "Are all sailors this heavy?," she asked. "Only when they are manhandled by adventurers," Tom softly replied.

Later, the two figures contrasted the plain as they entered the forest, the sun striking them momentarily, like lighted actors on stage, before being shaded by the canopy, a leaning union of four legs, and visible three arms moving like an old couple, embraced and tired, darkening as they disappeared into the leaf void.

12

Jessica awoke with a start, a tree had fallen and the unique thump she was familiar with after spending time in bush-fire ravaged country, which shook her from her deep sleep. She had a sweat line around her neck, she noticed and felt rested, her feet happy below the terrain cover.

"How close was that Iris," she piped, wondering where Iris was. *"Fair distance, a big one though"* the drone replied, through her headset on the terrain blanket, buzzing above somewhere. The weather was turning, she could tell by the wind which was blowing in gusts and the trees sounding against one another. "And how far away is this storm?" *"Fifty kilometres away, coming onto the coast in a Northwesterly direction as predicted, not beach weather"* She smiled, Iris had her moments. She packed quickly, the rain starting to fall in heavy showers. Iris was sending a plume of water vapour spinning from her rotors above, waiting for her.

They didn't stop for four hours, she made good progress as the treeline had given way to patchy grass and thorny shrubs and collections of strewn rock and ancient pebble paths. In that time the wind had picked up considerably. She had made the escarpment edge, a climb to come. Her tiredness was superseded by intent and deadline, Iris finding a suitable cave high in the escarpment,

"Almost there, two hundred metres from your eleven o'clock, the cave faces South East, so it should give good protection to see the storm out," Iris coached her from above.

The forest had subsided a little and gave way to some small shrubs and spiny grass types clustered like stick constructions splayed outwards in star shapes. The storm's fury was now evident, she could see out to the coast now with the rise of their journey, a jet black cloudline stretched on the horizon, the rain falling heavily and the wind gusting enough to unbalance her as she scrambled upwards over the rock, natural steps had formed, giving her resting platforms. She gazed above the last step and could see a small natural pebble path ledge that winded around the lee side, away from the sight of the coast. The cave was a low shelter but dry and Iris had chosen well, the wind blustered outside but was still inside. She dropped her pack, elated that she had made it, Iris settled on the fine pebble floor and wound down.

The storm hit with a high gust of introductory wind, about an hour after she settled. From the protected cave entrance, the wind tore a water spray from the top of the rock entrance in a spinning tempest and bits of debri flew everywhere out to the whiteout beyond. She huddled at the back of the cave in the energy tent, Iris beside her giving the occasional update but otherwise silent, keeping watch like a faithful dog, eventually the wind drowning out all other sound in like a monster in a death throe.

Thoughts that the storm would blow over, evaporated and the tempest increased into the long night. Outside water channelled off the cave roof in swathes and became a waterfall, her door a water curtain, the water thankfully cascading away down the stone path and off the cliff edge. She heard a loud crunch outside at one stage and wondered about the cave's strength at times as the tempest continued, the wind seemingly higher and the rain a torrential downpour; she was hard pressed to compare it to anything she had experienced.

There was an almighty crash, another tree had fallen, a deadly sizzle sound and a bolt of lightning evaporated something past the cave entrance, illuminating the outside vista like a Dracula movie, she briefly seeing beyond the cave entrance, a white strobed vast forested area beyond, the canopy below the height of the cave lit like snow with a giant floodlight for a moment then plunged into raging darkness. "Fuck, Iris, how long is this going to last!," she bellowed above the howl and crash"

"All night, I would say, it is a beauty, much bigger than I was able to forecast, apologies"

At some weary stage she got horizontal and fell asleep straight away. The morning brought no relief as the massive fronts associated with the storms passed through, Iris giving her a synoptic weather map of the area that she had prepared earlier, the drone now grounded like a perching bird within the cave.

She filled her water bottle with the cave entrance water and took the time to rest and repair her body and her belongings, hand washing with the freezing cave waterfall water and sponging herself, the last days sweat and grime removed somewhat, only a hot shower would do the rest. Iris could use her fusion drive as a heater and the cave warmed, the vents emitting a hot stream of air into the already dry enclave.

The storm lasted for three days, searing the coastline with haze and wind, sleet and colder fronts that tormented the escarpment like whips of planned weather torture items. Her jelly meat was almost gone, the clams still a day's food. She satisfied herself with an energy bar a day, she had five left and a small bag of red berries.

The cave was a haven, dry and safe, the only other inhabitants, some strange oblong insects like Gum Hoppers that danced from side to side on the cave walls, in pairs. Fascinated as she watched them, the pairs moved in a predetermined pattern on the wall and as they did so seemed to disappear against the pattern of the rock, a mottled grey brown patchworked surface. She assumed they danced for her, thinking it a mechanism to avoid predation, "it was hard to catch prey that *"disappeared" from time to time,"* she thought.

Iris during her forced downtime got her to repair a blade on the rotor, something had hit it, a small crack had appeared, she had two spares in her kit. *"The rotor assembly is then just turned as a unit to lock the drive mechanism,"* Iris said, perched on the sand floor, as the repair was completed on the fourth day.

She stood up and walked to the entrance, as Iris tested the rotor, the whirr of the blade hissed then wound down. "All repaired?," she inquired, *"Yes, thanks, I think it was sleet that damaged it"* She looked out across the now visible tree canopy below the cave, the rain was still falling but the wind had finally died down apart from small gusts that grazed the top of the ancient forest, drips pooled at the entrance to the cave from the roof above, the outside temperature considerably colder. Across the trees and out further, a river winded into a thickly forested area before appearing again in a silver wind through a high rock valley and disappeared, its source somewhere in the mountainous terrain beyond.

"So what's our plan Iris?"her thoughts suddenly swirling with a slight panic, her situation, the weather, her time to think had impressed itself upon her, beyond the physical and mental strain of being within a wild landscape, as beautiful as it was, *"I am alone and dependent on Iris in many ways,"* she thought. "I thought by now to be honest we would have heard something, a rescue plan?, I keep expecting to hear Tom on the radio"

"I have been sending an IDENT message daily from the satellite, there has been no response from the team on the ground where you were based. This suggests that they are ignoring the message or have succumbed to unknown factors, that being dead, injured or otherwise ""But the message has been received?" "Yes, the Tower had logged the transmission, therefore the tower exists and we can assume other devices exist also" "What about the Explorer?, can you contact the Explorer?" "Yes, the Explorer is contactable, but like the Tower is currently not being accessed.

She hesitated by the cave entrance looking at the ground and the trail of pebble that had been swept over the ledge during the storm, the run of the water apparent, small snowflakes were starting to fall and dissolving on the stone. "Well, unless I can live out here permanently, we have to travel to them, I can't see any other way" "What is your theory, Iris, about what has happened?," she said, moving her boot over the small pebbles on the cave floor.

"Given continued absence of communication I would suggest a catastrophic event where the crew has been killed or incapacitated. There is an absence of AI communication and human contact. In regards to the event where the Ate Succession exited orbit, we know the Explorer made it to the surface, but after that things are less clear, a possible scenario is that the Explorer piloted itself to the surface which it can do via autopilot-remote mode, but this would require Anastasia or a similar AI as the Explorer was designed to be controlled by Anastasia. The Tempestas weather Drone AI is not activated, the Cox advanced First Aid AI is not activated, nor are any emergency beacons, and network traffic protocols are silent."
"What about Andreas?, any signal from his Life-Boat?" "Not since atmospheric entry, I am afraid, his beacon was never activated and his drone is silent"

"And the weather? What can we expect?" "Increasing cold approaching Winter, the satellite has predicted increasing storm activity on the coast and lower temperatures inland, for us being caught out in the open for long periods will be difficult physically and mentally, temperatures are predicted to fall to well under freezing for the coming month, then further as the elliptical orbit reaches its furthest revolution phase" "So staying here then is the best option?"

"It is a feasible option, given we can find more food for you, however, then what is our end-game?. It seems sure that no one is coming to us, my flight systems will eventually fail, and then I will be of less use. My primary role is to save and preserve your life. While I am fully functional, I suggest we make an attempt to make contact with other crew members and possible help. Besides, what of you Jessica? How long do you think you could survive out here alone? And I say that with the knowledge you have been resourceful and fit so far."

She thought about what Iris was saying, true, what would her existence be? A tribal nomad?, a wretched cave-woman? *No Dentists out here,* she thought. *Mind you, no sweets either*

Can I suggest an option that may suit better?" Iris piped. She looked at Iris, the sentient drone a black machine, but her constant companion. "Of course, which is?"

I have established that there is a zone of terrain just NW of the mountains where the land settles and gently descends from about 400 metres to sea-level, and a river that bends down this land slope in an opposite direction to the one that flows from the range through this area to the sea. This is due to the gradual slope of the terrain inland away from the coast. I suspect these two rivers run in opposite directions as this whole area is the remains of a massive volcanic mound that formed here millennia ago, before the mountain range was pushed up by a Continental plate.

She sighed like an impatient fiction reader and rubbed her shoulder where the pack had made inroads on her skin. She listened to the drone's idea, feeling weary and alone, despite the sentient's presence.

"If we can use the river as a transport route, we can make our way through the inner sandy desert West of the ranges. The river runs in an arcing shape across the continent and is the same as the river that runs close to the Scientists camp which then flows into the sea, joining the ocean again.

I am capable of instructing you on how to build a raft or similar craft for the river journey. The distance I have calculated is 5467 km given the course of the winding river through the terrain, and if we made an average conservative speed of seven kilometres an hour, for an eight hour day, it would take approximately sixty days to reach the Scientists camp. I have calculated the flow of the river, a moderate flow of about five to six kilometres an hour, which decreases as you reach lower terrain."

I think this is the most feasible option, if we can establish what has happened and secure the aid of other technical aids then our chances of long-term survival are greater. In addition, there may be more food there, and shelter. There is also the

Tower, that could feasibly be used to contact Earth and even Ate Succession if the situation has changed.

"Yes, ok, but what about the weather will the river freeze?," she interrupted.

"Negative, another variable once you get past the range is that it sits within a massive active thermal vent area, there seems to be considerable heat exchange going on at this location and the desert has temperatures much warmer, we will have to assess the area when we get there, as there may be other hazards such as toxic gases due to the thermal activity and possible volcanism, however It seems a feasible option with some relief from the decreasing temperatures." The river will remain unfrozen, especially if we leave soon before the far revolution of the planet."

"What about the Range, how do we get across?" "We are fortunate that we can circumvent most of the high range via valleys that run around from the Eastern side"

"Iris, that is one hell of a distance, you have great faith in me don't you?" "I have the collated information that suggests you have the ability," Iris replied. She turned and looked at Iris, the drone on the cavern floor. "But I will add, as your companion and friend, eternal faith as well." "Nice try." She smiled at Iris's attempt at humanising its reply.

She stared out towards the range from the cave entrance thinking about the trek that was before her, the snow flakes like a message of what was to come. "We will have to secure another food source, our access to the coast is now over, today I will be able to scout the initial route and on the return journey I will see what I can find."

They set out the next day, the sky had cleared totally to a very cold day, the front wind had brought lower temperatures and cleared the clouds, the twins shone bright in the sky. Everything was soaked from the heavy rain, her foot fall broke the sedge grass beading with ice water and glistening with the sun's light, the pebble shone bright as the path meandered upwards on the Eastern side of the ancient volcanic mound, now eroded and with large sections of igneous rock and fissures that broke the landscape like half buried fingers. As they rose higher she could see sections of the ocean again and saw the flooded areas caused by the storm. She wondered about the great jelly, no doubt it had been washed back to the sea. *"Maybe it had been alive,"* she thought, grateful for its gift. They reached another fissure of rock higher than her and she traversed a small valley between the fractured fingers entering the shaded section, looking up to see Iris whirring above. Iris had found more red berry bushes here and pineapple plants so that was now her diet, she missed the clams, the oily protein perfect fuel for walking.

The wind picked up the higher they went, the Eastern side exposed to the coastal wind, the grass blew flatter and Iris whirred this way and that to counter the gusts above. The river that ran to the sea glistened and ran strong here, she could see down to its waters and winding lament below.

By midday they had reached the coursing water. Iris had scouted far and wide and found a suitable crossing where logs had dammed the river a little in a great mound of wash and pebble. She dreaded the crossing, getting wet was not on her list of to do's. She watched the water rush past the damned section, she could walk on pebble about half way then had to negotiate the huge wash that rushed through the middle section under three entangled logs that spanned like a crude and slippery bridge. The river had to be crossed in order to access the upper Eastern side of the volcanic mound which would allow them to circumnavigate the high range. Iris hovered above and she wished she could fly too. "Ok, Iris, I am going to put my surface suit on for this, and helmet, in case I fall off," she said, still scanning the middle section of the bridge. *"Affirmative," good idea, the suit should give extra buoyancy if you fall, swim left as hard as you can and use the current to gain the far bank"*

She wondered how farcical she must have looked as she stepped onto the first log, a space-suited figure crawling across a tree. The top was thankfully rough and she had some grip but then she had to negotiate the drop to the second log, a green slippery looking one that had wedged underneath which would require a full stretch down to while hanging on to the first. Iris hovered like an Olympic judge at a diving contest above, and below the surging wash made her nervous that the whole log bridge might at any time surge away with the current. She wished she hadn't worn the helmet because it limited her peripheral vision, but content it would keep her dry if she fell.

She felt the lower log with one foot and the boot settled, it seemed to have enough grip, so she lowered the other leg and used her hands to steady herself gripping the upper wood. She waited and watched the flow under her, the water shaped surge like a spout from a giant jug, her an insect on the rim, skirting death.

"This helmet is claustrophobic," she thought, *"I cant see a fucking thing, this was a bad idea"* "Iris I am going to remove the helmet, I cant see anything" *"Very well, but I suggest removing the whole suit again, after returning to the starting point, if you fall your suit will fill with water and that would be dangerous"*

She looked up to the upper log thinking getting up there again would also be a bad idea, the next log across the river wasn't as high. She might be able to get across with less risk continuing. *"Stuck in the middle and thinking about what to do wasn't the plan,"* she thought.

She judged the distance to the desired bank was about five metres, and thought about throwing the helmet across to the far bank, then thought better of it. Securing the helmet to the pack would require two hands and she had to hang on to the log., so she continued. She grasped the next log, a dryer affair and hauled herself up on to the top, at any moment thinking the bridge might fail, but part of her also thought the way the logs were entangled and the amount of material behind them, they had been here a while. She grasped the embankment, after crawling on all fours again across the trunk. There was a short rise to the top of the embankment she rolled over onto the grass lying on her side, relieved that it was over.

"Iris, are you laughing?" she said, seeing the drone above silent and hovering. *"A little, but glad you didn't fall"* She smiled and raised herself to a sitting position and took off her helmet and suit, the kevlar alloy shrinking immediately into a small cylinder shape which she inserted into the small tube, the helmet a kevlar shell converted into a soft foldable item.

She stood and gazed toward their destination a further rise and beyond, another as yet unseen river that Iris said flowed away to the West, another eight kilometres distant. The day was still clear but the wind was fiercely cold, she noticed as she donned her terrain jacket, looking at her exposed thin undergarment, a long-sleeve tight fitting issued thermal skivvy designed for use under the suit. The ancient volcanic mound was dotted with strange shrubs set hard against the cold wind, all having ten branches or stems arrayed with spiky appendages. The area was populated heavily by their presence and she assumed they liked the Eastern side of the mound and were probably salt tolerant.

"Iris, what do make of these bushes, anything edible?" "No, I am afraid not, they don't have seeds or fruit, not at this stage anyway, I have analysed their rough skin and internal structure via a sample, they have very high turgid cell membranes and are very flexible, their stems you can see wave quite freely in the wind, the reason for this I am not clear."

 She watched one of the plants, its three stems waved like Iris indicated, which reminded her of those waving advertising blow-up figures outside car dealerships moving frantically with the breeze, and attracting the attention of passing motorists. She hitched her pack and set up towards the slope, the nearest tree about ten metres away. As she got closer the trees seemed to be waving like an audience at a concert creating a weird picture on the otherwise bald hill.

The nearest shrub was about five feet tall, a single sturdy trunk secured the ten waving arm branches, on each branch an array of sharp spikes. At the point of where the ten arms left the trunk, all radiating from around the sides, just to the top was a magnificent flower, a radiating orange, red, aqua blue arrangement reminding her of a water lily flower, squat and sitting low from the top of a water surface with arrayed pearls and a colourful core. As she got closer to the trunk she could avoid the waving arms she noticed as they were too high moving with the wind. She looked closer at the flower admiring its beauty, the shadows of the arms grazing in vignette across the colours almost mesmerising her.

In a blur one of the arms whipped downwards and struck her in the leg, which knocked her down to the ground. She thought that the wind had shifted, but then realised it had whipped down as a single appendage, and one of the spikes had pierced her ankle through the boot. She instantly screamed, the pain severe and the arm was holding her leg down as she floundered on the ground to try and remove herself from the weapon-like barb.

Iris appeared immediately and grabbed the appendage with her mandibles, her rotors struggling with the force of the arm. She thought she would pass out as the pain was intense and the moving arm was gouging the spike within the wound, she could feel the free flow of warm blood in her boot, she fought the shock and Iris was at full power on top of the arm where the barb had penetrated trying to pin the arm to the ground so she could get free.

The arm then lifted in a powerful throwing action like a mediaeval siege machine, detaching Iris and spinning the drone in an arc upwards high in the sky, Iris fighting against the force of the throw with a manic whirring of blades she saw, then disappearing from her grounded view, releasing the barb in a searing painful jolt as it hit her ankle bone on the way out and tore her boot off in a mangled ripped display of kevlar fabric, and flaying shoe-laces, the boot crashing into the grass beyond. *"Oh. fuck, help,"* she could only utter quietly as she got to her feet and madly hopped away from the shrub, just avoiding another arms reach which had descended like the first and whipped out at her through the air, creating a draft and whispering sound with the speed.

Her foot was bleeding profusely, she had cut the top of her hand on a stone when she fell it too weeping glistening red. She looked around at the shrub, the arms thrashing widely now at her, unable to get another hold. She retreated further, by instinct, escaping before pain, shocked and realising it was a predatory plant, the action of the arms a reflex to her shape or movement not a wind coincidence. She released her pack and fell to the ground trying to stem the flow of blood with her left hand while trying to get to the first aid kit. Iris was back by her side again and her mandibles extended as she landed beside her. *"Jessica, get the aid kit quickly," I know it hurts"*

Ripping the pack's contents out, the kit fell with the other unsecured items on the grass. *"Trauma bandage, Jessica, unwrap it and place it in the mandibles,"* Iris said calmly as the drone administered some sort of injection into her wound,

"Oh fuck, Iris"

The jolt of pain from the injection shocked her. Tears welled up, the pain was so bad she was shaking and her leg had a pain that extended up to her upper thigh, and she felt nauseous and cold.

As she got the bandage unwrapped, tearing the protective wrapping to shreds with all her strength, the bandage fell out in contrast lightly on the ground as she picked it up with one hand over her prone body. Iris sprayed some antiseptic or cleaning fluid from a nozzle. She placed the roll in Iris's mandibles, the drone expertly and quickly wrapped the bandage around her ankle, raising her leg with one mandible by lowering a strut from her abdomen to the ground to act as a counter to the downward pressure of the rotors to allow the drone to grip the leg, wrapping with the other, placing a pad on the wound then wrapping again creating a mounded bandaged ankle.

"Jessica, can you stand and hop further?, asked Iris. "I don't know, I'll try" She got to her good leg feeling rubbery and hopped a few paces away from the plant. "Good, well beyond danger here, I am so sorry Jessica, it seemed benign, now I realise because I am not organic" Iris said apologetically.

She couldn't answer, the pain was intense but decreasing, Iris gave her another injection which she didn't feel. "It's an aesthetic Jessica, just for the pain" "Ok," she uttered feeling instantly better. "Are you cold?" Iris asked as the drone placed its mandible grip side down on her skin. "We can't let you go into shock, Jessica, that would be dangerous, I have sealed your wound and you are going to be ok, please have a drink for me if you are able"

Grabbing the water bottle raising her head drinking, she sighted a distant rock face, the top of a fissure. "I will try and get to the fissure Iris, out of the wind" "Affirmative, I can steady you on one side," Iris said, hovering on her injury side and placing the mandibles under her arm as she hopped to the edge of the fissure, already exhausted with the effort. "Fuck, I feel groggy" "I can still support you on this side" Iris said.

They made their way down the small rock face into the floor of the fissure, Iris whirred in different rotor revolution sounds from low to high pitch to carry some of her weight as they descended. The enclosed space was a large rectangle floor protected on both sides by the rock crack which angled upwards on one side back to the level ground.

She fell to the floor and her pack hit the ground with a thud. She lent against the rock wall as Iris hovered away then landed next to her. Her ankle was throbbing now but the severe pain had abated and she stared at the opposite wall, her legs stretched outward in front of her. She drank again as Iris was taking a small blood sample from her, and as she tried to settle herself and calm her initial shock she noticed the tiny insects that danced in pairs were here as well, arrayed in paired numbers on the far wall, appearing and disappearing against the smooth surface, their backs the same colour as the wall, moving like a dance contest on a vertical surface.

Looking up towards the sky, the afternoon light was fading, some striated clouds lined the upper atmosphere, and the wind could be heard at the top of the fissure grazing the rocks. "Iris, can I get into the energy tent?" "No, not yet, I have to monitor you for a bit longer, but I will set it up for you to be ready" "Iris," she said looking at the AI. "Yes, Jessica?" "Thanks" "It's my role remember?," Iris replied. "You saved my life" "Perhaps, now rest" "Is it broken?" "Negative, but the barb has fractured it, this may heal well with rest, we will make an assessment tomorrow"

Iris set up the tent, she observed, and thought about the simple procedure of throwing it on the ground the fabric expanding and adhering to the ground with a layer of *Flexible-Atom-Acrylic-Glass Industries Rubber Adapted Adhesive,* the same material that bonded the ships windscreens and windows and allowed for movement and extra durability and strength, which was also malleable and detachable. She watched as Iris used her mandibles and attached a small sentient firmware fusion battery, the size of a flat piece of cardboard to the side of the tent via a waterproof port.

The tent lit immediately and warmed inside, detecting the cold air in the atmosphere and initiating the field that warded predators and humans alike. Down in the fissure there was little wind and she was relieved as the night was dawning cold, the wind unabated.

After Iris cleaned her hand and stitched the wound, she gave her the go-ahead to sleep; she struggled under the terrain blanket, Iris holding one side for her. Her ankle was aching and the top of her hand throbbed with the fresh wound and she was exhausted and she fell asleep quickly, the last thing she noticed was Iris hovering out the entrance of the tent.

During the night she was dancing with the insects on the wall, realised she was one of them, her partner moving to her moves like a mirror image dancer, the two attached with ease to a wall, the orientation comfortable and sure footed legs arrayed and moving akimbo-like, but to a predetermined pattern.

Looking at the other pairs arrayed around, their moves matched and a chant was emanating from the group, a vibration of sorts like a thin skinned drum being caressed by a velvet tipped stick. Suddenly they arrayed around her and her partner moved off with the others, she in the middle and still dancing, the rest turning like clocks and cogs, the sound resonating within her carapace and sending shoots of vibration down to her legs.

She felt powerful and restored with energy and continued to dance, the others chanting in the still fissure air. She thought for a moment Jason, Tom and Tanya were there, sounds like they were laughing, and dancing too, but they disappeared with the other bugs and the broken rock.

13

Tanya returned to the edge of the village and surveyed the stick mess from the edge of the forest concealed by night and nettle tree branches. The Tribe had settled for the night and she had a new friend. Karl-AI hovered overhead and kept overwatch, she had found the drone discarded among the sedge grass completely by accident as she fled in distraught terror, having left Tom and thinking then she would rescue him or die.

The drone she initiated with her emergency code and used her tablet as they showed her in the training how to prep the drone and enable it. In emergency mode the drone could not be assessed by anyone else and now she had an infrared view of the compound and could see where the tribe members were.

Tom she saw was in a hut near the totem pole, the tree log that they had erected for she thought *"Fuck knows what."* Around the pole were a selection of miserable huts she assumed the rest of the Tribe slept in.

Karl confirmed and she watched the sleeping figures on the tablet screen hiding the glow with her suit. All looked asleep, the figures did not move. All the members were in the same hut she thought about five metres from Tom who lay alone and she hoped he was still alive. *"Well, I am assuming it's Tom,"* she thought nervously.

"Karl, any movement outside the village, can you assess the people in there?, can you tell if they are asleep?" she asked the AI, silently hovering above. *"All subjects are asleep, sound monitor suggests breathing related to such an activity. Distance to Target, fifty four metres. Distance from target to subjects six point five eight metres. There is no human activity outside the compound, plain is clear,"* Karl piped deadpan.

"Ok thanks Karl, stay on station and alert me if any of the subjects move please," she said through her newly found headset attached to Karl's side when she found the drone. She moved out from the trees and entered the marshy area approaching the village. She crouched running deciding to risk the faster movement and take less time to retrieve Tom. She crouched by the first hut which was empty and she could smell refuse, piss and shit and she curled her nose and continued past the next hut. The Occupied hut was to her left and she darted for Tom's hut and stopped at the entrance. *"Karl, all still?"* she whispered, getting nervous. *"Affirmative, no movement, subjects are still asleep, all clear,"* Karl piped.

She saw that a failing candle was on top of a table, Tom was prone to the side and slept. She reached him and used her headset torch risking the light to assess him. "Tom, Tom? Come on future sailor, we are getting out of here," she said quietly. Tom shifted and started awake thinking it was a Tribe member and groaned.

Tom was in a bad way and had been given no treatment. She pulled him up and got him to a seated position and he realised it was her and hugged her and the two embraced. "Come on, we got to go," she said, hauling him to his feet. She could tell he was trying with all his might and he took some of his weight and she threw his arm around her and she listened for a moment for any sound, Tom leaning on her like a wounded soldier. She shuffled out of the entrance and scanned around the night was dark and fortunately the village had no light apart from the Communication Towers small green light on the apex that flashed every two seconds, a monument from the now transformed Scientists camp.

She reached the marsh and stopped, looking back, adjusting Tom's weight and hauled him through the shallow water. She breathed in hard and the weight tested her stamina. *"All clear, subjects are asleep,"* Karl piped. She reached the forest boundary and set Tom down, sucking in breaths hard from the exertion. She had prepared a triage space with the aid kit and she rested him on a clean blanket and used the headset torch to clean his wound and quickly gave him some antibiotics. She fed an intravenous drip into his arm and secured the bag to his shoulder so it hung on a short line feeding him saline.

The distance back to their undiscovered forest home and the dry log was a forty minute walk and she took two hours to reach the camp, setting him down in short rests, then continuing. Karl hovered above and kept watch and as she reached the giant tree log, she could see the immense shape in the darkness. She lifted Tom down onto the nettle bed and checked his vitals again, then collapsed inside with him and fell asleep.

14

They talked about their past, as the trees rose to the three
moons through the canopy at night, the rough bark seemed to
talk to them, it seemed quite possible that they may die here
eventually, she thought in moments of depression. Added to
her occasional gloom, the climate was getting colder, the
current obvious absence of large animals and therefore
protein, and a hostile group of demented hunters with the
technology destroyed or abandoned.

There were insects though and Tanya crafted a trap which
failed miserably as the insects here seemed a lot smarter than
on Earth, the attempt leaving an empty container swinging
from the tree. They were visited by the black and blue beetles
that flew around them at certain times of the day, their wings
purring and hissing a certain hum and chord, always
seemingly around but never seen often.

They had found an old rotted tree log, a massive limb that was
so huge they could walk upright in it, it was dry and Tanya
made him comfortable with a bed of nettles and covered the
entrance with a makeshift stick door, she still had an energy
bar which they shared as a treat one night, sitting there like
two kids looking at one another with slight smiles, with their
stolen candy, chewing silently to the nettle branches and the
rustle of the wind through bough, a slight sound like a frogs
call from the river.

After their flight back into the forest, after Tanya had rescued
him,they had walked until he was spent, she found this place,
it would be enough, he had thought. As they collapsed for the
first night he sat up as much as he could, her looking at him
as if to say "What are you doing?," reaching up to her with his
good arm and non-verbally hugged her, *"Thanks for saving my
life,"* she grabbed his head cradling it, saying softly,"you are
going to be ok, you are going to be ok"

Tanya had good survival skills, her trips to Antarctica, an overland crossing of the Himalayas into China, walking alone in Deserts and Jungle, Ice and forest, bears, wolves, snakes, lost humans. They had laughed ironically at the disaster that had befallen them, the Captain gone, the Ate Succession gone, their supply gone, the passengers gone.

They talked of the change in the others, trying to get a grip on the dynamic, were they sick?, infected?, mad because of something space travel had done to them. Cryo-sleep seemed a likely theory, it had been used only once before and not for this long. But they were ok, so what was this descent into Tribal madness? Was this a human preordained outcome for a group of stranded spacemen and space women? Did it affect some people and not others?, there were too many variables they decided. It was what it was, "a fucking dire scenario," he thought.

She had asked him about his family that were no longer of the Earth, now part of the Universe. His parents were old, he visited them for the last time before they left, the winding dirt driveway to the well kept practical crumbling home, they, happy as ever knowing it was the end, embracing him with all their life in two long hugs, content that their life had been what it was, happy that their only son would survive, a gift.

They had stood smiling at him as he left, their only son, the last time they would see their child, but still after everything happy. Happy because he thought, they had lived a life of understanding not searching, contentment not anticipation, and had found the key to everyone's life he suspected, the fact that they understood the natural world, lived within it without destruction or poison, rather understanding and a commensalism that made the animals and plants, the Earth, a part of them not apart from them.

His wife had died of cancer, a long drawn out tortuous medical pantomime of drug cocktails and certain death, they had no children. His beautiful girl, as he called his wife, the unflappable, humane, wildlife mad, greenthumb friend and

107

content lover, one of her last actions, to send a meandering ward Priest out of her room with no uncertain directions and clear information not to return. He dreamt all the time after that, he was on a certain road that winded through an urban boundary, sometimes he was in a car, sometimes on a bike, she following him, then he would look around, her gone, he having to backtrack then passing some violence, people stuffing a person into a van, some youths fighting, then she was gone, he distraught, sobbing, lost, sitting by his dismounted bike on a lonely highway.

There was no going back in a dream he thought, because there were no rules in a dream, only a bewildering path, highway or track that went nowhere. A dream *method* he thought of, the biochemical dilution in his sleeping brain, was always seemingly a search, never resolution, the journey becoming increasingly complex, endless train carriages, a huge ship, the road to nowhere, he had experienced them all.

His favourite, the *Supertanker* as he called it where he had to manage on a rough sea by himself, a massive seafaring juggernaut, the crew of course nowhere to be found, a typical dream tenet, he, running from the engine room to the bridge, then back down again, scared that the trip down would be his last, drowned in the bulkhead, grappling, choking, then a silent floating submerged dummy, limbs limp, eyes open with terror.

Bedraggled and tired, scared, watching the sea rising, the tanker awash, with mighty Neptune-like waves and Poseidon tempest, from the bridge windscreen the round wipers useless, spinning a foam circle as if mocking him. On the last trip to the engine room, he of course got hopelessly lost, the ship's structure changing and maybe becoming another steel structure, not a ship, he thought.

"Fuck, at least I wasn't naked in that one as well," he thought dryly. "No, hang on, that only happens when there are other dream people around," he realised, when you are at a dinner party or a wedding, and you look down at yourself, "Fuck, I'm naked, I have to pretend nothing is up and get out of here"

As he lay in the dry log, Tanya going out at night to get the pineapple-like fruits, he thought here on this planet there were no dreams, he slept then woke like a mechanical alarm clock. His arm had improved but the antibiotic was almost spent, he telling Tanya that she needed to keep some in case she got injured, she acquiesced, realising without her there was no him. They also discussed Jason Findus who was the glaring omission in the tribe, he had never been seen. Was he dead, injured like him, murdered? They also assumed Jessica Neuer and the Doc had been killed or were with the mad Captain.

They sat considering scenarios and thought about their next move. He heard Karl overhead and was not as frightened now they had the drone who kept watch above them. The tribe were not technology savvy anymore, that was clear. Their hideout in the log was a temporary setup, they calculated it was about five kilometres from the camp, or now a tribal cauldron of anarchy, too close for comfort. He had stabilised somewhat but the shoulder was extremely painful still and it had affected his whole ability to move around.

As Tanya considered what assets remained that they might be able to use, Karl-AI descended down to the forest floor and approached at waist height. "Jason Findus has contacted me, he is alive and well. He is encamped out on the Western plain and has Cox-AI with him," Karl piped. "That's fantastic Karl!, my, at last, another sane member of the crew, Tom, did you hear that?"

"I did, fantastic, as long as it's not a trap," Tom replied within the log, then emerging to look at Karl. "I have asked him to journey here, it is not far, only two hour's walk, I will monitor him from above and alert you if I detect any danger," Karl piped.

She sat in the forest cold, but delighted with the news. The wind had dropped, they only had small fires at night, the energy tents were problematic anyway if she had one because they emitted light from the outside a certain beacon for tribal hunting. The Army she knew had camouflaged ones, no light from the outside. What *I would give for one of them*, she thought, feeling the bite of the cold rising from the nettle forest floor. She felt the immense weight of the forest canopy above her, the fire had dwindled to a small glow of fine embers, she would cover it soon and return to the log. *The roast flies are not that bad*, she thought, taking the last one and crunching it between her teeth, the legs a bit harder but protein was protein, if only they could find a protein-rich plant, she wondered if Jessica had found anything before she went back up to the Ate, they could use her knowledge here, that was for sure.

Looking at the dying embers of their bug stove she thought about her chances. She now had access to the terrain maps from the satellite and studied them in the hidden rotten log. Out here on a planetary plain, she knew their chances would be small of surviving a harsh winter or other unknown dangers, forever, here it was for keeps, no rescue, no resupply, no end of the adventure to return home and have a sauna.

She had accessed the weather satellite and sent an IDENT, a signal that told electronic devices around her where she was and to contact her either by pinging the network or better still, another sane crew member. She had to try what was probably not going to work as from experience she had found unless you try, you never will know, and at times the *try* had saved her life.

Like the time she tried a dead mountaineers ancient oxygen bottle at the top of a mountain, thinking that it was certainly empty, then realising it was almost full and working, and the time when she crossed some sea-ice to get a dead seal for food considering her chances, the food against the ice stability, the food saving her, the ice holding.

Also, without further medical help, Tom was likely to remain in poor shape, and they had to move from here soon, the weather was getting increasingly variable, Winter was upon them, there had been a significant nettle shedding in the forest, she assumed this meant a deciduous type thing, and the Twin suns were getting further away in the sky, the days getting colder.

The fire was almost extinguished. She could see the constellations above through a gap in the canopy, the moons had not risen yet. There were no discernable sounds other than the trees, she listened for a while, sensing danger, imagining a marauding Anders Pedersen or crazed Kylie Albott, her vision of Akseli Koskinen with the Geological pick, badeing her was vivid, but the surrounding reply seemed natural, only the river wash was the distant audible sound, the wind having died off completely, a stillness with Tom's soft breathing in the rotten log.

Her Father came into her mind, he was now long gone, *probably here,* she thought, some Hydrogen molecule in a small pebble. He continually told her that everything was "A need to know basis" and *never assumed* He told her how insects were bigger once on Earth because the oxygen level was much higher, and that there were enormous centipedes as big as huge moving carpets rolled up.

She smiled and ate some more dried flies, crunching their protein and wishing it was fried onion instead. The first star she could discern stuttered through the upper canopy.

Her Father taught her about Evolution and how the Dinosaurs had lived on Earth for one hundred and sixty million years, enough time for the Earth to make one revolution of the entire Milky Way Galaxy.

She thought that was the most beautiful thing she had ever heard, the majestic, hostile, caring, flock-herd dynamic creatures living out aeons of time, evolving, dying, breaking from a Mother laid egg alone in the earth and abandoned for its own good, to hatch alone, rise from the nutritious yolk, look around for death, and making for the shrubs nearby to hide and create mighty instinct, all in a few moments, her Father looking at her smiling, knowing she knew.

A camera with a lens was the next revelation. It could focus on the small insects, and tiny life that tilted on the edge of death every day but flourished mostly, and varied into the leaves and grains of sand and within cracks in rocks, and looked at her lens without fear as if the creatures knew what would become of her.

The fire had grown small in ember glow. Up above she could hear Karl, his motor's on "stealth" mode, a faint whisper above the trees.

After the camera, things settled in her and she changed forever, like a calming sediment that had become fossilised, like she had some ancient conch that could be placed against her ear and detect the creatures singing a secret song that now she could hear, and she could feel the Earth, lamenting down below.

In similar ways to her Mother, she moved apart from the modern world with its circular war and shattered facade of how humans would survive and technology would save them and the Earth. It seemed unlikely to her, when natural treasures were still "being saved" after decades and the power went out twice a day.

Her Father was aghast at how all the leaders in the country had disappeared and been replaced by "parasites." "Just because seven people have the same convinced idea, it doesn't make one disagreeing person wrong," was another saying.

Smiling, she poked the embers with a small twig.

"Social Media is a virus," another, "Pigs arse," his favourite. He had made her swim in the sea one time when it was rough, she remembering she was scared, he saying "I will never let you die while in my presence Tanya, you must do this," she had, and had come spluttering up on the beach, terrified but elated she had, she felt an instinct then at that moment, a strength she had discovered.

112

That had started her love of the ocean and surfing. Surfing, before it got really crowded and mean with drug-crazed hippies and stalking smouldering dreadlock adorned Motherless waifs waiting for a mistake so they could glare and question her ability and whether she was from there, and deserved to be there, or how she might not be good enough, and that she would have to leave the break, because she was danger to others, but of course knowing they wanted the break to themselves.

It was an expose', she thought, of the core motivation of human behaviour; territory, resources, group, control, defence, consumption, righteousness.

She drew a crude wave in the sand beside the fire. Tom's heavy breathing told her he was getting much needed rest from within the hollow log before returning to her *Earth* thoughts., as she called them.

Alone out past the break, the foam, the waves catching the wind at the top as they formed before breaking, sending spray over her as she paddled out over the unbroken lee side of the wave, seeing Dolphins surf with her, one once launching from the sea in pursuit of fish, flying past in front of her, then crashing into the sea again like a sea-bourne Zeppelin.

Ten thousand days of surfing and a myriad of sea stories, small sharks, large jellies, rising and jumping giant Stingray's, sea birds fishing, dragonflies swarming over the sea one day as a warm wind came from the land like a secret message, butterflies and bees, silver reflecting skin of schooling fish and dark shapes of shell and rock, sea cucumbers and sea dugone's.

White Sea Eagles, swooping with sharpened eyes into the shallows, claws clutching fish, whales blowing and jumping, scuttling crabs and pipi shell flats, sand bars and rock outcrops, salt crusted eyes and wax hands.

The marine wave nomenclature, calm and glassy, crosswind chopped, offshore wind and rippled fronts to the waves, like a reverse pattern of a snowflake, clean and perfect shaped, dark rainy days, the rain so heavy it hurt the top of her head.

The water surface into a droplet carpet of indentations, then like pop rivets waiting for the tool, and tempering the surface, hail once, holding the board above her head, storms and a rush for the beach, after seeing white bolts in the distance striking the sea. Standing, gliding, freedom, power, in the motion of the formed lump of water, crashing over her, inside a wave, then washed green and rubbed on a sand-bank with the force like a broken puppet.

I wonder, surely there would be some great point-breaks here.

Her Mum loved her just as much, content that she had better parents than her, hated suburbia and the mowing of lawns, savage neighbours and wheelie bin movement. A keen walker, she was convinced the garbage truck always followed her. "I get to the corner when the thing is there waiting like a metal rhinoceros," she had said, her Father, giving a secret look her way.

Ahh, Mum, always with an angled point of view.

Her Mother made good tuna patties and baked pies with rhubarb, sausage rolls and apple tart, sent predatory sudo-Priests packing, from the front door, studied Biology and kept chickens, became an Ornithologist at the age of fifty and did the washing. Her favourite word was "No" and she had a t-shirt that said so.

He, he, people didn't really understand that t-shirt though..

Her Mother studied birds,and in time became attached to the natural world, "understanding what it was actually about, not what humans thought it was about," she had said. She got a fine for vandalism, disabling logging trucks and dozers once, the Judge saying, "Mavis Geary, you are a considerably lucky woman and I have decided to fine you and not imprison you as that I think would defeat the purpose of *punishment* as defined in today's institutions,..." Tanya thought she got off because the judge was keen on her, her Father sat there like an ancient sentinel, smiling, looking glad, and proud of her.

The tiredness came slowly as she prodded with the small twig. The tiredness of carrying Tom, the brain-tiring fog of concentration, always looking for danger, triage on Tom, the river exertion. Men and women with spears. She dropped the twig and rubbed her face as if to wipe away some of it. The darkness had descended and there were more stars above.

Karl, are we still good? "Afirmative, all clear, nice night, stay relaxed, I am your sentinel" "Thanks Karl" She resumed looking at the fires dying embers.

She had inherited a large sum, and went away, learned how to climb, free-climb, then mountain climb, then went solo adventuring, across land where it was tough and dangerous, and technology faltered, where ice was momentous and people seldom went.

Exceptions were rare, meeting an individual on an Antarctic tundra once with a better chance of winning the lottery, they agreeing to camp one night together, she incredulous that they had met, he knowing, she suspected exactly where he was and she was and made contact in case she needed help, the wind howling and freezing off the ice, she asking if her Father had sent him, he laughing.

"No, Tanya, you are on your own I am afraid," parting in the morning both content and wanting to challenge alone. She watched him walk off into the ice haze, he turning and smiling, dragging his sled with a raised arm in goodbye.

Dad sent him, I am convinced. She returned to her adventurous memories.

Caves and lakes and salt pans, fast flowing rivers and marshes where the insects pestilised and harassed, alone but not lonely, constructed rafts, swam current, went to wildlife craft schools and made shelters from stone and logs, crafted weapons from poles and twine, fashioned crude sea-faring craft and made clothes from fur and skin with rednecks and Ecologists, war veterans and lesbians, misguided social media junkies and executives, then made friends then left, to return to nature.

And what was your life like at the end brother? She started to weep, wiping the tears from her eyes, then looked starward. *"Tanya, is everything ok?"* Karl piped from the canopy."Yep, all good just having a cry" *"I see, my thoughts are with you, let me know if I can help"* the drone replied. "Thanks Karl, no problem."

Her brother was an Ophthalmologist, his patients a never ending river of chronic sight problems, pumped out of his office like repaired test-dummies hundreds of dollars at a time, with directives to return for more punishment and repair, drugs and surgery, doctor's bedside manner and magazines in the waiting room on new barbeques, flower bed construction and soap star affairs.

She had seen him once, making an appointment, then instantly regretting it, for a grazed Cornea that was painful and weeping, waiting two hours, a chaotic melange of stilted patients, sitting side by side like contented sardines in a can, staring at the withered palm that was crying for water in the corner, expertly placed to avoid collision with a ninety year old.

She was startled as a swarm of the black-blue beetles buzzed past overhead and then droned off into the forest leaving her with the memory..

She looked at the palm for half an hour to avoid the prattling *drug of the nation* television, and eventually obliged as if the plant had told its side of the story, took it to the bathroom and saved it and placed it back exactly and expertly, watched with suspicion and recognition that she was a Sister by the Clinic Manager and by the friendly regulars, ancient, wrinkled and grey, smiling to themselves, winking at her, secretly glad she had saved the plant, something the older patients wouldn't dare under the Clinic eye. She could almost see the uptake of water through the Xylem, thinking that maybe it looked better after a few minutes.

Brother, Brother, was this the last time I saw you?

Apologetic and unfazed with the already eighty patients seen, he fixed her with a stroke of the pen and searing light of the scope, her head secured by metal and knobs. They embraced her with prescription in hand, him, his portable headlamp crowned on his head like an ocular Caesar, the ten minute consultation over, him smiling, loving her, glad that she came. "Apply the cream three times a day," he had said, smiling then saying "Oh, and remember to take your eye out to do it ok?"

She laughed, he deadpan, she was teary as she was to leave the next week, the door closing silently, he looked until the door frame covered him, suspecting he knew he wouldn't see her again. She knew he would work until the door fell off his office from age, or he fell off the medical perch, one of the two. The sight of her credit card was refused by the Manager, "It's been taken care of," she said, "bulk-bill" She turned to leave but was stopped by the sight of the palm, "It would be a sure death in here," she thought. The Manager watched her like she was a mad cracker but then asked smiling, "Do you want to take it, the palm I mean, it's going to die in here, we don't even have time to glance sideways most days"

The vista of the barren carpark with a woman carrying a potted palm met the man's gaze on the fifth floor apartment, and he wondered what plants had do with Ophthalmology, sitting down on his outdoor seat and lighting a cigarette, the smoke billowing next door around the corner with the draft into the next door neighbours doorway, as he had planned.

15

The morning of the trial for her ankle had arrived. Jessica stood at the cave entrance crutch in hand ready if it failed. Iris hovered above the cave waiting to see her walk. The snow had abated somewhat and been replaced now by a freezing ice covered ground, water that had frozen solid. The surrounding bushes swayed in the wind in stuttered shakes as if too cold and wanting shelter.

The distance revealed a stretch of cirrus cloud hovered above the horizon out to the river that winded away where they were to travel. There was a short walk down the slope from the cave entrance, then a grass plain, then a strewn arrangement of boulders and pillared rock, then the river met the forest in the distance and disappeared within the gloom of trunk and leaf.

The previous week passed slowly, she watched the dancing paired bugs arrayed on the cave walls, mended her clothes and her exo-boot which had been torn apart by the carnivorous plant, and recalibrated the OTAA, adjusted her pack and hoarded the food Iris collected, storing it in her spare water bottle and drying some berries.

She was out of the *weather* and started to feel normal again, the energy tent was always warm and she redressed her bandage, inspecting the wound every few days. She thought about how useful her small fusion camping stove was, which was arranged so it could be packed very small containing a steel cup, bowl, plate and cutlery, spoon, knife and fork.

The fusion battery she set below and it channelled heat through a steel base plate which became her constant companion for her morning tea, made from spiny shrub leaves that were a tart lemon variety, she crushed and added to the planetary water that she realised boiled faster than Earth, the lower atmospheric pressure boiling point, was 89℃.

She walked out from the entrance down the slope a little, the weight on her ankle felt ok but a little tender, she stepped with considered intent, testing it but not risking it. Iris watched from above the drone a whisper in the wind, now stronger than a cold freeze from the South. She hesitated as she approached a thorny bush she didn't recognise, *"Is that carnivorous?,"* she thought,

"Every plant is suspect, such a comment on Earth and I would be in the loony bin," she mused as she stepped forward with increasing confidence.

The only Ecologist to be nearly killed by a plant? Probably by a violent swing of a stem with a barb, she thought, *Poison another matter,* she mused.

After stepping out about ten metres down the embankment, the grass under foot felt ok, she returned and sat down looking out to the Western horizon, then felt her ankle and flexed it a little. "I think I will be ok, Iris, just another day, let me be sure" *"Affirmative, you have to be sure, you have a lot of walking ahead until we can construct the raft, you must be one hundred percent,"* the drone piped whirring with the breeze to compensate the wind gusts above.

That afternoon Iris returned from her regular patrol for food with an amazing catch; a flying fish from the river. Unmistakably an adapted fish, the wings sprouting from its sides, beautiful fibrous wings looking like a weaver's madness but with purpose, the forty centimetres long marine creature a striking silver, fine green-silver scales and a grey band on its side.
"I darted it from above," Iris said of the catch. She thought maybe it was a saltwater fish and had come up the estuary from the coast, whatever the reason she had protein as the OTAA had given the all clear, thirty percent protein, *A magic find,* she mused. *Sixty percent water, and ten percent minerals and lipids, s*he said to herself as she looked at the OTAA report.

"Good catch Iris, thank you, and great timing as we are off tomorrow, yes?" *"If you are one hundred percent, yes, and no problem, a lucky catch as it is no mean feat getting a hit on a creature that size in flowing water."* "Indeed, Iris, I would say you are being a little modest, but that is dinner tonight, I'm thrilled, I need to put on some weight. By the way, what weight am I?" *"At 173 cm you are 53 kg, you are a little underweight, but considering the energy expenditure you have maintained weight well"*

She scaled the fish, removed the wings and gutted the creature, the innards she saved and prepared a water pot to boil them for stock, she wouldn't waste anything, the nutrients too valuable. The fried morsels of fish melted in her mouth and she then knew how starving people felt when given food.

She ate silently and within a trance watching the wall as if she was balancing her mind on the rock face, savouring pieces according to perceived deliciousness and crispness as a child would with individual fried chips from a packet. The creatures joined her and danced in pairs on the wall and she watched as they descended and ascended in unison as if interested in the new meal and waiting for an offer to join the feast. Iris remained silent in the corner as if the drone knew the importance of the catch, the fusion light cast a certain light on the cave ceiling and complemented the energy tents glow.

Outside the wind had halted and the freeze began, a cracking of water to ice and ice to stone, the calmness contrasting the hardship outside to the warm cave. She was reluctant to go in some ways, the rest had done her mind more than anything a favour, she had settled in a way to her fate which may well be oblivion. *But what awaits?,* she thought, her things were packed, she was ready for the next phase.

Touching the cave wall close to the bugs, two of the creatures crawled onto her hand and started to dance in upward and downward strides, a bug Tango. They seemed oblivious of her and danced on her skin as they would on a rock surface. She watched them and grabbed her pack and rummaged for her lupe, her eye glass she used for studying plant structure.

The dream, these bugs, I danced with bugs.

Looking through the lens the creatures came into clarity, the body a heart shape, a mottled brown and two wings folded, each wing having a yellow stripe through vertically and an oval section at each end, like a stalk of a plant, atop a flower.

She watched the dance and noticed the routine, three steps backwards, three forwards, each creature had ten legs, while dancing, it raised the two legs either side at the front, the other eight initiated the dance steps. After the three steps back and then forward, the creatures moved three one side, then the other side, then repeating a compass-like transition in a North, South, East, West pattern.

"It doesn't seem like a mating ritual, there is no male-female obvious behaviour, the bugs look identical, in size, shape and colour," she thought, holding the lupe close to the creatures. She looked up while she held her hand level, holding the lupe in the other hand. The bugs still danced as normal.

She held her hand on the cave wall aligning it so the creatures could step onto the rock face, which they obliged and continued the routine. She replaced her hand on the cave wall again in the path of the dancing pair, the bugs walked onto her skin, the dance steps unaltered; the surface for dancing it seemed did not need to be a cave wall.

As they crossed her hand they traversed one of the injuries from the altercation with the barbed plant, a deep cut on the top of her hand that stretched from the small finger to her thumb. *"I wish that would heal,"* she thought as the creatures traversed the still stitched cut, Iris had triaged, the steps unaltered. As they passed through the injury she noticed that the skin had smoothed after their path, the cut now broken as if healed.

121

They stopped momentarily and started back, traversing the gash lengthways and to her astonishment left a path of healed skin, the cut undefinable. She looked closely through the loop, the gash was now fully sealed and there was no trace of the injury as the creatures traversed the gash and then moved away, dancing across her hand and then back again. She stared through the loop, wondering if she was in error,

There was an unhealed cut, there, the gash has been giving me hell for days, she thought, certain that she was not touched and losing it finally living out in the open world.

"Iris, look!, the bugs healed my wound," she said to the drone in the corner. She stretched out her hand so Iris could see, the bugs still arrayed and dancing. Iris extended her probe, a small stick-like arm with an oval head that the drone used to assess and analyse.

"They seem to have sealed the wound completely," Iris stated. "Now this is very interesting," she added, extending her probe and scanning the creatures, then touching her hand where the injury had been. "Do you have any other cuts, grazes?"Iris inquired.

"Ahh, lets see, I have several, what about the ankle?, it's still an injury, although sealed," she replied, the drone's probe making a whirring sound."Let's try it, see if they react to injury as a default," Iris said, retracting the probe, the test completed. "Alright," she said, taking her exo-boot off and her terrain sock on the injured ankle, still sore and tender as she shifted and twisted her joint.

The bugs were still on her hand and she joined the injured ankle and her hand so that they could make their way on to the ankle. The bugs instantly left the hand bridge and danced onto the injury skirting across the protruding Lateral Malleolus ankle bone where the majority of the trauma had occurred from the plant's barb.

She suddenly felt a wave of relief, and looked up to the cavern ceiling as the soreness diminished.

The creatures danced around the site and circled, breaking their dance routine for the first time she had observed. She looked back down to the cave wall in relief, breathing out, the bugs had seemed to have done something other than healed the site, she felt warm and content, as if she had been drugged but without the loss of awareness.

The creatures continued their changed circular dance, now seemingly chasing each other in the spherical pattern. The feeling sourced through her like an intravenous injection of pure contentment, the sudo drug, filling her mind with certain strength and basic contentment.

Wow, I want what they are having for breakfast..

The stress of the journey gone, the cold not felt, her life, it seemed at that moment, a completed journey of self-actualisation completed. "Oh, Iris," she exclaimed, still looking at the cave ceiling. "I think they might have injected me with something, I have to say, this is quite the ticket," she said, feeling like she could enter an Olympic event at any time and win.

All her worries became decisions made, her sore body seemingly whole, her being, an analogy of walking a catwalk, all eyes front. She felt like she had stepped into a bar full of scared tattooed criminals at her sight, all understanding and realised like a board-meeting about being immortal, like riding an Elephant, being inside a green cylindrical wave, flying like a bird and feeling her feathers coursing within the wind across a deep blue sea.

The warm wind upon her face, contentment of the earth, the sea, the taming of her most primal instinctual fears, the evolutionary tenant found, the purpose always known.

The drug did not waver to and fro like a sine-wave but lamented and caressed, like an unknown radio frequency, the signal a chemical trace within her brain and seemed to be a constructing new anatomical centres for understanding, her vision sharpened and she could see the grain of the cave wall rock, and she then understood how the cave was formed and what had happened to the planet.

When it formed, the ancient biochemical construct, the plants, the intelligence of the bio-marker proteins within the Ribonucleic Acid bonding, the ancient planets archival history, four times the geological eon length of her own world.

She understood without any compass of knowledge - the apex species, the beetle's ascent, their meeting with another mechanical race, the war, the alliance, the wrecked Androids, their shining white exo-skins marked with fungus and growing green filaments laying in the dust of a cold desert.

The images and chemistry combined within her cortex, the memories not her own, a transfer of evolutionary cocktail and concocted transfer, like a shelled creature talking to her within a cone echoing an infinitely ancient message.

Goodness me, Now I am sort of hallucinating..

She fell to the floor and passed out.

§

Awakening, Iris was close. "You fell asleep, gave me a scare. All is normal though" the drone stated. "How long was I asleep?" "Four hours" "Wow, nothing like the right drug"

She flexed the ankle, the soreness was gone, there was no stiffness. "Iris, this is amazing, I think they have healed the ankle, and I feel great," she said in groggy surprise and a little fright, really unaware of what the creatures were capable of but reeling from the effect of whatever was in her system.

"Wait, let me scan the ankle and we can compare the scans," Iris replied. The probe extended again and Iris scanned, retracted then the drone was silent, she knew calculating and assessing. *"I have sent the most recent scan to your tablet, compare this one with the scan that was done yesterday, the result is quite clear,"* Iris stated in surprise.

"How do you feel?" Iris inquired. "Unbelievably good," she replied, looking at the tablet, the two incremental scans side by side, the earlier showing the fracture, the later a healed ankle bone. Looking down the bugs still danced and she held out her hand again and the winged creatures alighted onto her palm. "Thankyou" she said smiling gazing at the bugs which she boarded onto the cave wall again from her hand. The dancing creatures continued to scuttle across the cave wall seemingly content with their consultation.

She stood up and flexed her ankle, adjusted her weight and crouched down, then up again. "It's totally healed Iris," she said smiling and then looking at the bugs still dancing on the wall. "I think it is time we went Iris," she said, grabbing her pack, still reeling from the potion the bugs had seemingly released.

Her mind was clear and she felt strong, like a warrior, super-fit, alert, something had changed, she wasn't sure what. "Whatever this stuff is they gave me Iris, I now understand this planet a whole lot better," she said with clear intent to the drone. "My word, I wish I could bring you guys with me," she said addressing the bugs on the cave wall, then turning to Iris whose propeller blades were whirring, the drone rising from the cave floor.

16

The trek to the river where it entered the ancient forest was a day's march along the Caldera sourced river bank; the rushes grew higher as the river washed North. Ahead she could see in the horizon the massive trees that enveloped the river like a great dark mouth sucking in a water thirst. Another clear freezing day greeted their journey, Iris was skirting high ahead and reached the boundary of the forest..

"I still feel amazing," she mused, stepping over the rushes and the mineral sand pebbles the river to her right side washing fast from the descent from the above natural water storage tank; the ancient Caldera that rose high in the sky behind her path.

Her meal of flying fish was still with her, the protein, a sure sustenance that had filled her stomach like a no meal for some time. "The grease was a delicious treat," she thought, remembering the fried sections with hungry glee, the crisp taste in her mouth. The *Bee-Brown* portable stove with the small fusion heater was a great companion, cooking her meat with fast superheated efficiency.

The meal aside, the bugs potion had no comparison, her stride was as sure as she could remember. *"Perhaps better than it was originally,"* she thought. Her sight was definitely better, her far vision was sharper. "It's not just a *"Maybe it's better,"* it really is," she thought. She could see the ancient forest clearly, the trees were still about three kilometres away but her far sight definition allowed her to distinguish tree types and the surrounding vegetation, and small movements of trees swaying or rushes getting blown by the wind. Colour was defined with sharp clarity and she could judge distance better she thought.

She had acquired, she knew, a better *situational awareness,* something she couldn't quite grasp but it was there like a detector, within her ability she knew, sounds became sharper and better defined, her interaction with terrain and sky seemed coordinated, like a combat ground controller and her radio, her drone and the rivers environment.

Here we go, Into the trees.

Entering the canopy, the terrain became a jungle-like space, where the wind was stopped but talked through the swaying branches instead, the upper limbs rubbing, flexing, and making odd woodwind noises of trunk against wood. The trees had grown close to the river bank and some had fallen, wedged down the bank with swirling detritus and flotsam, grass dams and lichen swirling in mass.

The sky above was narrow space, trees closest arched their arms over the river in a seemingly forest-like attempt to cover the sky completely. The biggest trees, she noticed, were massive trunks she estimated over two hundred metres tall, the waists of the great beasts the size of large grain silos she used to see on her country drives out West back home, on Earth, through the wheat fields and blue sky.

Farmers two-way radio chat about red tractors and the endless road horizon.

Finding a camp spot among the trees was difficult, the possibility of a massive branch falling a clear possibility. Iris skirted around at dusk and found a monster, an old decaying trunk. *"The energy tent will fit with room to spare,"* she thought, looking at the tree hollow, the size of a passenger aircraft fuselage.

She stepped into the log. Layers of aged moss lined the interior like an iced organic cake. "Anything else in here Iris?" She gazed to the rear, the core of the long dead tree. "I have inspected the interior, I found nothing large enough to be a threat to the energy tent" Iris replied hovering outside the entrance.

The dusk brought the chill down on them, the wind dropped to nothing and the branches stopped as if ready for slumber. The darkness descended early in the forest, the energy tents glow turned the rotting trunk into a massive glow-worm or giant fallen cigarette on the nettle strewn floor.

She smiled looking at the bugs, definitely the same creatures aligning the rotten tree carcass wall, the dance, the same routine. "Hello, healing bugs," she said to the small creatures, their yellow stripes attuning to the dance step as usual. She looked out to the forest and the washing river ten metres distant to her right, the water rushing in contrasting concert with the tree stillness.

Iris had landed and was perched atop the trunk, her constant guardian. "So what were the results from the latest blood test?"she asked the drone. Iris had taken a small sample at lunch as they sat in the sun, the forest still distant at that stage. "All normal," Iris replied. "There is no indication of Pathology, nor increased ability due to blood minerals or otherwise apparent from the test," she added. "A Cox analyser would be better placed to examine you. There was one allocated for the mission, I believe was on the Explorer." "Cox Analyser?," she queried.

"Yes, an AI Doctor in effect, highly skilled medical specialist and with an unrivalled database of medical research knowledge. In addition the Cox analyser is able to perform advanced Brain, skull and cortex tests without the need for physical intervention on the patient.

The Kurtzweil Test is a high definition fusion-scan using wireless *blow-fish showering* technology. That is in layman's terms a scan frequency that has sentient firmware examination ability, totally non-invasive and benign which can show anatomical, chemical and neurotransmitter function."

"Good grief," she said, suddenly thinking of Andreas and how she missed him, her friend the ship's doctor, the darkness descending further on the forest floor. She looked at her small stove, the second flying fish frying whole in her terrain pan, the delicious hiss and smell of the skin floating up into the freezing tree canopy. "Well, that's good about the test, I still feel good," she replied looking at Iris. "I am pleased," replied Iris. "That however does not explain your current state of optimum functioning and the effect of the creatures within the cave environment," Iris added. "Any news about the others?" "Negative, the satellite has not as yet been able to assess a signal," the drone replied.

The next day Iris skirted for suitable tree boughs to make into the raft, their plan started, the river flow washing away through the forest and into the gloom beyond, She explored after packing the tent and gulping down some more flying fish flesh, and securing her gear. *Today will be a rest day of sorts,* she said to herself. *Make the raft and see if we can travel a bit faster.*

The construction of the raft took all day, and the notion of a rest day evaporated, the logs she had to drag from the forest, the ties were vines that hung at intervals from the trees which made good rope, Iris was able to cut them to the right size and she pulled them away and sorted different lengths.

 Iris gave her the instructions and she swore and sweated most of the day, looking at the instructions on her tablet like a mad furniture engineer. The exhausting task of raft building became apparent, the logs a heavy burden to drag through wet undergrowth, tying logs a challenge and finger aching task. While she toiled, Iris caught another flying fish and eventually she sat looking at the raft completed as the twin suns sank behind the canopy and the descent of the forest gloom cast dark shadows and the river misted slightly, the forest seemingly warmer than the freezing plain.

The raft was quite big for one, but buoyancy was the key and the larger logs were needed. Iris had given a detailed indication of the river's width via the satellite maps and the river was wide for another thousand kilometres, narrowing slightly as it turned North West then arched South West towards the other side of the continent, exiting the Desert and returning to the plain she had known when they had first landed. She chose a good site for the build, making sure that she could get the heavy log raft into the water, selecting a natural grass slope where she could slide it in. The last task was to secure some mooring vine in a coil on the raft for mooring and a long pole for adjusting the raft's passage.

In the afternoon as she had her next flying fish meal ready in the pan, she sat down wondering why and looked at the creature. *Mmm, what's this, I feel odd.* The fish in the pan didn't feel right. She rose and picked it up. The eye of the fish opened. "Oh!, fuck, agh!" Iris immediately descended. "What is it Jessica?" "The fish is alive, didn't you dart it" "I did, I confirmed its death."

She quickly ran to the river edge and threw the creature back, its sliver form darted through the shallows, then was gone. They both watched and then wondered, and she ate her preserved clams instead.

"No more flying fish Iris, something's not right here." "Understood, I shall search for alternatives."

§

She spent the next morning fashioning a paddle from some sturdy bark she stripped from a massive trunk, the bark a hard exo-skin. A small branch attached with twine through holes in the bark made a reasonable paddle. She stood at the river's edge looking at the completed creation, Iris buzzed above just below the massive canopy, her tablet was showing Iris's view from above and the river made her a little nervous seeing the elevated view of the massive wash, the turgid current milling strongly down stream.

That view is a beautiful sight, wishing she could fly like Iris. She still didn't know if the raft would float and carry her weight, but she suspected so, the large logs were dry and buoyant and Iris said they would, the drones calculations hard to argue with, assessing her weight and the size of the craft with a detailed AI plan, and teaching her how to tie knots, something she hadn't much idea about.

"Well, Iris, here we go, what do you think? A half day on the river to test this behemoth?" She asked the drone that had descended to inspect the finished log deck. "I think this will support your weight easily, the only downside is manoeuvrability, its weight will make it harder to turn, that said, I designed for sturdiness over speed," Iris stated. "The river washes wide and steady for some time, the flow I have calculated to be five to seven kilometres an hour, then as the wash increases we can expect perhaps twelve to fifteen in some areas," Iris lectured, hovering above the river's wash, talking to her from the middle of the river. "Remember, the flow is strongest in the middle of the river, to reduce speed you can get closer to the banks, although I think the initial speed will not be too challenging."

She gathered her pack, placing her gear near the water's edge, so she could load it on, the last act before taking to the freshwater sea. The raft dragged heavily down the slope but with a few straining lifts and drags she managed to get the first log into the wash and the weight decreased, the raft eventually floating and spinning a little as she secured the vine rope to the shore on her fashioned mooring stick driven into the ground. She tied her pack to one of the lashed sticks poking up from the rafts deck, making sure the fastener was secure.

Losing the pack is not an option, she thought. She had fashioned a small raised deck section for the pack to stop the water encroaching, the pole was last, fitting between two logs, the groove a good resting place for the ten foot pole.

She alighted, after removing her mooring, the deck spun around but the raft was still well out of the water with her weight, she could see a gap below between the deck and the water, the large logs working for now. "Alright, Iris, great, this is pretty sturdy," she said, excitedly reaching for the pole. "Yes, it has good stability, not much lean on the sides," Iris said. The raft immediately started to move with the flow, her vista now one of river to bank rather than of bank to river, she noticed as she sank the pole into the shallows and pushed away to get further to the centre of the river. As an additional aid Iris had suggested a paddle on the pole so she could use it as a rudder of sorts to guide the raft, the pole attaching to a mount of two sticks, wedged between, which she could bend slightly from side to side to get some lateral movement.

She attached the pole and tried the theory. "Ok, well, that's not too bad Iris I have some turning ability," she said, bending the mount a little from side to side, the pole angling from the rear of the raft into the water like a motor boat with a long outboard motor shaft she had been on doing a study on marsh frogs at the time.

From the raft, the bank swept by surely and the canopy overhead cast light and alternating gloom as the craft flowed under the varying nettle cover. She made a sure but nervous progress during the morning, crashing at one stage into a large flowing mass of caught logs and collected flotsam that she caught up to, and was unable to negotiate, the raft like a massive ship when turning, a slow lament.

She had used the pole as a pike and moved the mass aside, the raft then picked up speed and she freed herself, leaving the first rubbish behemoth behind, the collection spinning and swirling in the raft's wake. Iris buzzed ahead, always updating her path and obstructions.

The flying fish at times jumped ahead of the raft like glistening bullets emerging from the swirling current. The river, Iris had told her would run through the forested section for another hundred miles or so, some of the forested channels were particularly dark and the twin suns were seemingly allowed to be shining, the cold clouds abated for the past few days with some green and blue sky she could see above at times through nettle canopy.

They selected a larger river bank grass area which came into view to stop for the night, the darkness descending quickly. She used the rudder pole to veer left to the bank gradually, the raft gently hitting the bank. She secured the line and crawled up the embankment with her pack, making sure the pole and paddle were secured.

The area was a flat stony area, some spiked rushes grew among the gaps in the rock. Before the forest trees proper large boulders lined the boundary and strange thin stalks of some plant rose in the gaps in the rock. Wary of her plant experience she threw some small pebbles at the closest stalk, the plant seemingly inert, the pebbles scattering away with an echoed rattle.

She was delighted with the raft, but terrified of the icy water. In the current, if she fell it could be the end of her. *The raft is a good idea still,* she mused. She noticed her legs were sore already, being on the water had been an exercise she wasn't used to, constantly bending to align the raft's weight.

That early night the forest froze white a frost descended and she huddled under the terrain blanket in the warmth of the energy tent upon the rock shelf, outside she could hear cracks of wood and threshes of nettle in the increasing wind as if a weather front was passing.

She heard what she thought were frogs calling during the late evening, a croaking sharp stretching sound but was unsure due to the wind gusting with a set tempo through the upper canopy; the gusts she could hear coming across the trees before reaching her like a giant using a leaf blower.

The sounds of the silver flying fish emerging from the river, then splashing back into the wash reminded her of the dead eye that had opened.

17

Tanya and Jason embraced as they met, Karl descended and Tom who was lying down in the log, raised on one arm smiled. "Well Navigator meets Adventurer" Tanya said. "Sailor meets Navigator and Adventurer," Tom added.

As he and Tanya parted, noticing each other's ramshackle appearance; living in the open for so long, Jason detected her surprise. 'Nice pants." "Thanks, weather balloon fabric, new tribal fashion." Tanya smiled, putting her hand over her mouth in stifled laughter. "I only found a mirror recently," he said looking around at Tom. "You will have to loan it to me." Tanya replied, to which they all laughed softly in their exhausted ways.

§

They all looked hard at the image the satellite had provided. Ten miles from their position Tanya could see a clear outline of a shape that resembled a boat, the hull a pod shape, she estimated to be thirty metres long and looked at her key on the image to assess the size.

Seeing what looked like a mast from above, a cabin and two mooring ropes, one from the stern and one from the bow. "That looks like a boat, that really looks like a boat," she said looking at Jason, their new companion having joined them in analysis. "It sure does, yep, I agree," Jason replied looking out from the rotten log where he and Tom were.

"Karl, what is your assessment of that image? He looked skyward for the drone. What is that pod shaped structure?, she asked the AI not offering her assessment.

"The image shows a thirty foot schooner, moored and with three masts, two wheel houses, anchored within a backwater cove two point three miles from the coastal outlet and fifty five

miles from our position," Karl stated. "Wait, enhancing," the AI piped.

The new image on her tablet came into view, the deck a clear smooth top, *"Metallic?,"* she mused. "Karl, what is it made of?," she asked the drone. *"Metallic structure and trim, steel based, steel hull I would surmise,"* Karl offered. She thought about the discovery and apart from the intrigue she saw a way out away from the mess the mission had become.

"Karl, go and do a recce and get a look at it and the area, full report," she asked the Drone. *"Affirmative"* She heard Karl hiss off in the distance above and looked at Tom and checked his signs. Jason continued to see Tom with Cox-AI, the Doctor guiding him through the diagnosis. They had talked about their adventures, getting hit and her rescue mission and his home on the plain.

"A sailing boat, what next?" he offered looking at Tanya who was still gazing where Karl had flown.. "Hopefully, sails" Tanya retorted. They both shook their heads in bewilderment.

Karl returned an hour later and they both sat down and gazed at the images from Karl's recce. Tom was breathing with sleep. The boat was immaculate, looked new, the fittings looked unworn like someone tended to the craft every day. The boat sat in the cove Karl had mentioned a small inlet anchored among the trees at the shore.

A small natural channel from the sea winded to the cove via the river that spilled into the vast ocean. The surrounding forest seemed untouched and the aerial view showed no structures. "I did not detect any other structure, marine or otherwise, nor any human or alien activity," Karl piped. "X Ray analysis of the craft revealed nothing inside of organic origin, I detected no movement within the craft," Karl added. "The journey on foot would take about eight hours, the forest has good cover and there are natural paths," the drone concluded. "Thanks Karl, we will sleep on it," she replied looking at the extraordinary craft in the images, then at Tom who slept noisily, his breath rasping a little.

They spent another two weeks in the rotten log. Karl recced the craft daily and no other life was found nearby. She and Karl did a trial run to the boat, unlatched the cockpit hatch and sent Iris down to see. Immaculate within, as the exterior was above.

As Karl hovered overhead again she stood looking at the craft. "Sea-worthy Iris?" "Brand new and sea-worthy, yes I am sure of it, all the fittings, sails and stowed gear is brand new. The only anomaly is that it has no communication devices nor navigation devices." "No compass?" "Negative"

§

She hoisted her pack and handed Tom his crutch and Jason secured the aid kit and helped Tom and prepared to leave. She gazed at the log home and felt grateful to the rotten tree for the dry space for so long. Tom had recovered enough to walk and his arm was healing well, thanks to the expertise and skills that Cox had, mentoring his recovery and administering injections with his probe and taking occasional scans to show her the progress and infection free wound.

"You ready?," she asked the standing Sailor. "Ready," Tom replied. "I hope so because you are driving," she quipped, having shown him the location of the Schooner. "And you are the Navigator," she said looking at Jason. "I'll see how I go," Jason said tongue in cheek, looking at Karl, who had accessed a signal and plotted a course for them, using the alien constellations above.

The metallic schooner shone as it traversed the green reflecting river, the wash from the small channel mixing with the river's flow and the craft easily negotiated the swells and turned towards the granite coloured ocean as the light started to cover the coastal plain.

She turned and looked back at the landmass as the boat entered the ocean proper, Tom steering from the first wheelhouse, the sails set and the Schooner driving through the water strongly. Showers of spray rose with the bow where Jason was inspecting something. The wind was cold and she stiffened with the passage, having donned her exo-suit and gloves. She looked above at the fabric of the sails that shone and reflected the light like a massive triangular sieve or fine colander, the metal cloth straining with the wind that blew across the bow.

She looked back at the section of shore she estimated where they had left Karl, the drone not arguing with their decision. After gazing at the spot she saw the drone hovering, a small speck watching them go, on station till the last moment. She accessed her comms.

"Karl, thanks, without you we probably would be dead, certainly not together, see you on the other side." She partly shouted into her headset, the spray wafting past the stern.

"The pleasure was all mine Tanya. I shall miss our time together. As discussed I will power-down in sleep mode in a concealed position, the others may be able to access me if the situation arises. Otherwise you can find me at these coordinates I will send to Cox-AI.

It may just save someone else, she thought. She turned and saw Karl fly away towards the forest and then was gone from sight. She looked out to the sea and saw the straight horizon and thought that she was happy for the first time in a long time and was ready for the next chapter in their interstellar journey. She thought that also she, Jason and Tom were not the first to sail this ocean and wondered whose boat it was that had come here and now was no longer a ghost ship.

She looked back at Tom who smiled and saw Jason throwing a fishing line out from the stern who acted like he was a big game fisherman, strutting for her amusement. After a time the land subsided and she made Tom rest on the deck in the sun while she steered and the ocean embraced them wholly on all sides, the terrain gone, replaced by ocean currents, green foamlets and a cracked blue sea.

Flying fish burst from the water at the bow chasing the wave and their silver wings made a threshing sounds as they flew in the air then dived into the marine abyss. She relaxed in the way of being free of the tribe and the constant danger and her body melted a little and she felt a bit dizzy, but the feeling passed and she grabbed the helm and steadied the course of the running Schooner Due East for the distant continent two thousand miles away still. Polkinghorn had sent them a message and by all reports had a new friend as well.

18

Andreas Polkinghorn walked through the stone arch that faced the crafted rock jetty that jutted far out to sea as though seeking the coral shoals far beyond, and up beside the rock bluff, a hundred metre tall pillar island remnant that was battered by the open sea like a stone punching bag by surging tides and wind driven swells across a deep channel.

How long have I been here? A month? No, six weeks, that sounds about right.

Beyond the bluff, the continental shelf dropped to an abyss, in a deep marine crevasse fifty miles wide from the bluff, then the shoals stretched for three hundred miles.

He gazed out to the cracked shoal sea, the most magnificent shallows he had ever seen, on clear days the suns shone through the green sea lighting the swimming water that currented around the atoll and surged through channels with the enormous tide, revealing small fish and crabs with ten legs, sea-horse creatures of seven different colours and small plankton like swimmers, massive jellies beyond the coral and flying fish with silver shimmering wings and eels that slithered around the rocks and bulbous coral.

The weather had cleared and on the equator the wind blew more mild, but still colder as the twins lost their heat and light.

Nice day. The suns are weak but at least there is some warmth.

It wasn't the twins' temperature he knew that controlled the shoals, it was the ocean thermal vents that spewed heat from magma flows on the seafloor, a sea climate controlled by plate tectonics and warm local currents. The massive sea channel between the continents surged through daily and filtered the shoals and fertilised the coral with tempered climate and regulated current like an electric thermostat on cold degrees keeping the macrocosm in stasis throughout the cold winter.

He knew this because he had become part of the city, the stone deserted island metropolis that the Alloy had crafted here, with care and regard to what was here and ensured its preservation and future. The massive stadium he had walked through many times, a single form, a figure of metal and organic memory. The stadium echoed history and portent, enough seats for ten thousand of his kind, now the species had gone, and the monument stayed, rising into the open sky. He imagined as he stood there and when he looked up and felt the air swirling in the bowl and the electric atmosphere the place had, even when empty.

What had transpired in this arena. Was it death?, acting?, performance he wouldn't understand? Maybe just simply oration of Government waste, Political flumery or harsh punishment?, he thought.

He felt mighty although he stood alone there. Although there was no audience, the stadium did that, as if it willed you to orate, dance or stand like a warrior, walk out to the middle with a tennis racquet or a cricket bat, a baseball or a curling stick.

I still feel more important than silly whenever I walk out here, he thought.

There were mirrors here, the species liked themselves he assumed, looks were important, metal reflections and alloy casts for faces, he hypothesised.

Is this not what I see, them in me?, he thought, looking into the glass. He was changing, his lower legs had become a peculiar metal and was spreading upwards to his knees.

Was this to placate me, maybe console me? he thought, *My former existence, but soon I will become metallic and logical?*

He didn't care, seemingly never cared, in some ways he was relieved he wasn't all human anymore, at least in his form, his world was gone and he was now adapted to something else, he could only speculate.

He still had his human mind, *Was that decided?*, he mused. His form changed with time, and he knew that his metal constitution was overtaking his organic one, he was metamorphosing like a soft skinned organism into a hard shelled one.

His skin was not hard though, the metal swam like a magician in a field of smoke, sensitive to the touch, he could feel pain and other sensations and he then realised that robots can indeed take baths. He still ate, seemingly robots could eat as well, and shit and cough and sneeze and ache, there seemed to be no distinction between the strange alloy and his form other than appearance.

He knew his name, *Andreas Polkinghorn*, his memory was untainted, he knew about the mission and the *Ate Succession* leaving orbit, and his fall to the sea, the heaving mighty oceanic marine terrain with the foam and cast salt.

The broken LifeBoat, cracked, the beacon not transmitting, his AI demolished like a stick windmill in a hurricane, then falling like a lead balloon into the depths. There was no time to download its construct into the Lifeboat, so he was left with a broken hull, resembling a partly open dinghy, alone on a massive heaving sea, the boat floating here, drifting against the shoals one morning, his lottery win came through as he awoke to a distant stone citadel towering above the island and the jetty there, ready to greet him.

His mind had settled like a bed of soft petals, unconcerned with consequences and what was to come.

Was that a drug?, he thought, no, that's just acceptance, it transcends time and consoles me, and at the same time is non-addictive, he mused.

141

Within the centre of the small metropolis and the urban crush of stores and offices, homes and gardens there were patio and pergolas of vine and pots arrayed like garden soldiers sprouting coloured herbs and perfumed flowers, and strange mechanical species that grew wires and intricate steel parts and had their own bloom and scent, from metallic pots and smooth metal containers. The stone and steel intertwined, a partnership of origin and destination, the technology he knew now as he was created as part of it, the fundamental core of his existence was his form and knowledge. His skin was a metallic grey with patches of his old organic skin layer, he glistened in the rare sun when he walked from pillar to pillar, to cavernous office to public baths, his footfall a tap of small hammer on tin, but a malleable weight and smooth gait.

His daily lament on the failure of the mission had settled within him like the alloy type metal that now was becoming part of his physical makeup. He walked to the centre of the massive arena, as always as if an Emperor of some mighty civilisation and stood casting around like a concerned master, governor or deity.

What happened to the Ate? Did Jessica make it? What of the others? I know nothing. Are they transforming like me? Was it an elaborate alien plan or a virus, a planetary thing?

He gazed around at the empty seats as if searching for answers from those who had sat and watched. The wind eddied in the space like a lost trumpet converted to a total wind instrument. He stared down at his legs, the shining alloy reflected the twin sins and cast around on the sand in green hues.

And this, what of this? When I become a metal man what then?

19

Kylie served the stew to the others, her new recipe, *Oceanic Clams with wild rice*. Her discovery was another key to survival and a piece of the planet's puzzle, and together they ate as a new *Tribe*.

She had discovered the clams on the ocean beach shoreline and the OTAA had confirmed the benefits. They organised a collection of clams three weeks ago and were able to scour the beach, finding a great number which they vacuum packed in the crates and stored for the severe winter that was to come after the very cold winter, now upon them.

Another day on the holiday planet, Gemmi7a. This batch of clams smell nicer.

The wild rice, or as she called it, *Gemmi7a - Long Grain,* she found from oval shaped pods that came from a hardy vine that seemed well adapted to the cold and grew back from the beach treeline along narrow semi-grassed gullies, protected from the freezing conditions.

She wondered about the climatic extent of the species, thinking even the hardiest vine in the Universe would hibernate at some stage. Until then, they had a good source of fibre, carbohydrate and protein, securing a great many pods in the storage cave dry store.

Not too bad outside today, a balmy -22°F.

She watched as she didn't spill any clam sauce on her suit as she stirred the pot. Never took for granted their new clothes, looking at the others wearing exo-suits, terrain coats, gloves, the trusty beanie and exo-skin grey-purple-ochre red boots, that now were rested on the terrain blankets beneath their feet to ward the stones touch in the winter of all winters, now well below -33°C outside and each day a descending mercury tempest. The suns were now a forgotten atmospheric item, the snow had stopped long ago and was replaced with ice, a slippery hazard even on exo-boot soles and the sea had frozen, at the stage of a moving crust, soon to be solid.

The new clothing was secured from a hidden crate from three found in the forest boundary, forgotten by primitive minds and adolescent fervour.

Or did one of the others, Ye Min, Jason hide them?

The crates had been in a gully and obscured from view until Donghyun had found them, she remembered, the sound of Donghyun's voice coming from the gully, covered in vines, *"Hey, over here .....Jackpot you guys, look here look looky here, who's your Daddy now?"*

The steam billowed from the plates which she had warmed before serving the meal, *You must have hot plates,* she thought, *Who on Earth serves a meal on cold plates?, ..shit, well, I'm glad I didn't say that out loud,* she thought, *Correction, who on this planet,* she thought, looking at the others.

The crew were clearly enjoying the meal, faint sounds of chewing, slurping, the chink of spoons on bowls, the combined silence said it all, a clan, a herd, a flock, a clutch, they ate without speech nor judgement, saviouring every morsel like starving children, or snow bound wolves over a kill, looking at their food, thinking of warmth, and seemingly purring like warming engines waiting to get enough heat and energy to lift off.

She sat down and joined the silent digestive ritual, trying the clam soup with a sip from the spoon, thinking to herself, *"Gee, that's pretty amazing,"* looking briefly at Katie who was looking at her, directly across the table saying thank you with her eyes.

Anders was looking from time to time at Katie, with a seemingly secret non-verbal flight language in play. Akseli was looking at nothing in particular, staring into space looking frozen, just after just coming in from seeing what the leak was in the Bee-Brown, confirming a small condensation problem to Donghyun and explaining it was nothing serious. Donghyun had a demeanour of delightful bliss, slurping the clam soup, across from him, nodding, content and thankfully an ignorant diner of past planetary history.

His past was a well kept secret, she hadn't elaborated on Ye-Min's narration about their previous Tribal life, she thought it better for the group's cohesion to look forward and not back, they would need each other.

"Nice outside Akseli?," she asked to break the silence. The others smiled. "Wonderful, I regret becoming a Sanitation Officer." Katie coughed in surprise and some of the clam soup went back into her bowl. The others looked at her in surprise. "What's up Boss," Anders said. "Sorry, nothing, went down the wrong way." Kylie knew as well, "Sanitation Officer" was the role Ye Min allocated to the then tribal "Mineral Master" - Akseli when saving them from their squalor.

Kylie silently assessed their survival chances as the clam-soup slurping continued. They had a connection to the satellite and were their eyes and weather forecast. Karl was now their Doctor, and a very good one. "Well, that's me done, back to the tablet and the grind-stone. She looked at Katie, as she rose from the table, who non-verbally acknowledged her role getting the Trojan ready to send to Ate and the satellite search for the others.

Sitting at her camping terrain table she accessed the tablet. Kylie knew that Tanya and Tom had used Karl when they were on foot hiding from the tribe well before they all woke up from the malaise. She watched the footage on her tablet, Karl's recorded infrared images from above the village at night, watching as Tanya crept between the huts and found Tom, handling the weight of her crew member and walking out past the marsh near the village and disappearing into the forest.

She watched with admiration, Tanya was strong, motivated and she saved his life most probably. She paused the footage and looked at the four heat signature figures lying asleep in the hut and identified which she thought was her and stared at it in a daydream wondering what they had all gone through.

Karl had seen Akseli, who had recovered after falling off a ledge scouting for food and had completely recovered, and declaring with Karl's typical developing sense of humour *"I am pleased with the cut of his jib,"* he would be ok.

The AI drone had been located via her tablet, Karl sending a signal once he had known her tablet was on. She had waited for the drone to arrive that morning, searching the sky and then Karl appeared. She knew then that their chances had already improved.

Karls' value soon became clear, the drone collating the equipment of use from the old scientists camp and experimenting with items.

The IV, thanks Karl, this could be a lifesaver.

Karl had fashioned an intravenous drip from a fruit like a coconut, which had similar properties to saline solution she had located near the forest boundary. Karl had said: *"This could be very useful as a plasma substitute in case of blood loss."*

How she had missed seeing it, she couldn't say, but there it was after Karl had done a recce, an oval football, growing in the forest floor in the snow on a thickset vine that had runners into the soil, with smooth tough fanning leaves that set low to the ground and seemed to be free of ice and snow, their rubbery surface thick and smooth.

The fruit was hung like a drip from a pole and the fluid was diluted with antibiotics. Karl had said that it may also prove useful if they ever had a case of blood loss in a similar situation, restoring blood pressure to safe limits the IV's lost or burnt by the Tribe. The sentient AI were the difference between life and death here she surmised, they would be harder pressed without them.

She summarised in her head the other information they had. Tanya and Tom and Jason had left the continent on what looked like a fully functioning Yacht, as Karl had shown her some footage of his recce down the coast and footage of finding Jason.

She looked at the Navigator from Karl's eye-view on the footage and smiled glad he had survived, he looked tired and had Cox-AI with him. *"That's why I couldn't find it in the crates,"* she thought, as they were preparing to leave the miserable village.

They had disabled Karl at some stage and left the drone in the grass near the coast with its beacon activated. *"They deliberately activated the beacon and left it where we could find it,"* she thought. *"They were totally unselfish, they could've taken Karl. Although Karl would've given away their position, this was built into the drone. Unless, unless they didn't want to be found,"* she thought.

That was also the last time she saw Ye-Min, she turned and was gone he assumed to get something, but she did not return. She helped them get to the new camp, then she was gone. They tried to get Karl to find her but she had changed his parameters via the network and he did not have permission to search for her, by the time she had fixed that, his scouting came back empty handed.

Her Tablet was in an encrypted tunnel protocol and it wasn't possible to hack her, nor did she think it worth it, they knew she didn't want to be found. They only knew she was mobile and not injured.

"Min is also a wild card, lots to Min we didn't think existed, tech savvy, fit, smart, high motivation, skillset. A savvy Astronomer," she mused.

The others speculated and meetings ensued, the consensus was that Ye Min was somehow affected like they were as the Tribe but it was a different thing, more precise this time, retaining her knowledge and personality.

They discussed late into a blizzard strewn night, behind the life-saving energy screens, courtesy of another crate found in the gully, the possible causes, the Cryo-sleep theory, the planet, the food, the insects, the atmosphere.

She and Katie had discussed options, they technically were still in command and had a responsibility to try and find Andreas and Jessica, they might still be alive somewhere. She was going to try the *Ate* again and see if she could turn the ship around; her program may work a second time. Katie and her had the same train of thought, the *Ate* was the only way. Alone on the planet with limited resources would probably send them back to the Tribal state, something that was not on her agenda.

While the others ate and conversation was lost, for the moment, the clink of spoon and bowl, and occasional look at each other from a group comfortable with each other, sometimes talk was not necessary, the only language, non-verbal.

She remembered her flat mate at times when she lived in the city before flight school, having just heard the good news. They would say "*morning*" then sat at the same breakfast table, reading the papers, coffee and tea and perhaps three words were spoken in an hour.

She liked these times, where her mind was allowed to wander, the breakfast table, an allowance of thinking time before the day proper. She thought of her Mum who was a *Soup Nazi* as she called her, she had an ingrained tyrannical kitchen demeanour, forged from professional kitchen boot-camp as she became a Chef. *She had taught her the cruel ways of kitchen nomenclature,* she thought, smiling looking at the clam soup in her bowl beside her, savouring the last clam meat for last, the morsel sitting in the remaining liquid waiting, and her slight distorted reflection from the bowl's fluid looking at her like a culinary ghost.

Now I am thinking of other things instead of working. I miss you Mum.

Her Chef Mother told her many stories of hardship and toil within the professional kitchen, the service time stress, the arguments, the tantrums, the walkouts, the alcoholics, the drug dealers, the amazing crafted food served with clever precision which was frequently rejected by mad customers as a matter of pot stirring reflex.

She explained how the Kitchenhand was a vital member of the crew within the á la carte kitchen, more than people realised, the importance of *clean*, their older gait and steady life advice, many of them had been in prison and broken homes and had settled to a normal life, from violent to kind, from broken to repaired or partially patched.

Her wiry life-battered Kitchen hand once told her, *"It's an art, cleaning stainless steel benches, it's not a couple of doddering glides with the hand ok?, wash with detergent, scrub, then wipe the surface totally with a wet tea-towel, and allow to dry totally, pay attention to the corners, don't leave any water on the surface, this is the key to bacteria"*

She told her of the apprentices and what they had to endure in times before rules and Government bodies that threatened bad behaviour with workplace laws in triplicate. Chefs who yelled constantly at their young staff, manhandled them, badgered them, annoyed them, humiliated them in front of staff and customers, and made them

"Do the pots" after a long night, telling the kitchenhand to go, the nights steel pots and pans, trays and colanders piled almost to the roof after the five hour tempest of service time on the kitchen hand bench. The unfortunate apprentice finished the

pots somewhere around three in the morning, after service had ended at twelve. *"But that's not all,"* she had said, now the massive floor, had to be mopped and made pristine clean like a Marines toilet bowl.

"I remember failure to do this to satisfaction would bring a wrath that the kitchen would hear about for many weeks and punishment was given" She asked her what the punishments were, fascinated by the world that the average diner had little knowledge of, and indeed had mostly little care of, blissfully unaware of the tempest beyond the swinging door or warm-lit partition, by crafted design, two worlds, the *punter,* a common nickname for a diner and the slaves beyond.

*"Well, the Chef would sometimes give the apprentice fifty or so chicken carcasses and tell them to remove all the meat from them, **like all the meat.** Another tactic was giving someone five twenty kilo sacks of green beans and telling them to top and tail them, quickly.*

Any meat left on the chicken bones or undesired top and tail progress, on the beans, would bring a further punishment like the banning of the use of tongs during the next service and the apprentice would have to pick up burning foods with their hands during service time and put on entrees for example where a grill was commonly used, and told to pick up searing oyster shells from the griller and handle pans that were hot.

She laughed silently recounting her Mother's kitchen life, while pretending to work on the tablet. Her Mother's face appeared again; she felt just above her right shoulder.

Also, It was custom to give the apprentice a humiliating nickname and this was used like a verbal bludgeon in front of all and sundry, forever. A favourite was the nicknames used in front of good looking waitstaff to rub in the humiliation further, especially if the apprentice was male, and the waitress female which was mostly the case in those days.

"Pluck a Duck," she had said, her Mum looking at her strangely. She went on, and she thought, *"Who were these guys?"*

"The final humiliation," her Mother emphasised, was a trip with a massive trolley to the bins, three floors down, a pile of inadequately thin black plastic garbage bag masses of prawn heads, fine dining customers tantrums, and the inevitable fat and kitchen detritus that could have been a culinary menu in itself, and fed a starving continent.

"Enter the three decade old service lift with the manual sliding doors," she noted, dryly. The lift she had nicknamed the *"Beast."* Upon entering, the outer door was to be closed, then the inner door, and if not closed to the *Beast's* satisfaction, a silent still lift would result, the person standing there in the fluro light like a caged animal. Usually this process would have to be repeated, as if a secret code would have to be given for allowing transit.

The thought was always the same, she had said, *"Please don't let this thing trap me, don't trap me, don't trap me, don't trap me especially now my shift is almost over,"* she used to say over and over like a deranged exhausted machine. *"Unless I have just started my shift of course, but this never happened."* She told her of others who had been entombed within the *Beast,* sometimes for hours, one person for a day. She told her:

"I hated Lift Mechanics who came and made the thing worse or never came, but it wasn't their fault, it was Management who didn't care, and that a death would have to happen first before a new lift was installed. Clunking and grinding, the lift cable threatening to unravel, the journey within the shaft was like a core transit to a planet's heat source or unknown secret floor, a secret floor that I fantasised that would open to freedom, an exit, a blue pill, another kind restaurant with handsome waiters and waitresses and with a talented Head Chef who wanted to teach rather than bully. The lift swayed upwards, then downwards at the desired floor, as if searching

for a landing on an Antarctic helipad in a storm, a whir and further clunking to tell you that you have landed, the Beast's doors reluctantly opening, as if to say, **"Damn. I tried hard to seize the cable winch this time, but I failed, you can go."**

She continued, her Mum if she got started entered a sort of vortex of narration, she smiled as she and her dead Mother talked and took a sip from her clam soup spoon.

"From there, another corridor lit with fluorescent green tubes and dark cavities and sleeping chefs and possibly something I didn't want to see, to the rubbish quadrangle. Ahh, yes, the Rubbish Quadrangle."

A stinking hell of indescribable ruin, harassed by trucks during the day and packs of small cat-size rats at night, a wet bacteria concrete swamp, a duality of life and death, ten billion bacterial infections and exotic restaurant diseases and nothing growing.

The industrial bins stained, arrayed like charred wrecks after an airstrike, having endured every mechanical torment, piled high of course, with the same black bags, the bins beyond the concept of full. Myself, or another poor apprentice was the only one there at these times, except for security, and all the venues would have closed for the night.

She finished her soup and slid the bowl away from the tablet. Katie started telling the others about the weather situation. Her Mother had continued:

There is nothing like the feeling of warm rancid prawn head juice down your sleeve and into your armpit" she had said. *"When the bag splits it ejects the mass inside like stricken rotten organic matter filled balloon, then all that is left is an exploded flaccid membrane of regret, dripping the last juice from the edge of the bag, where it so annoyingly pools, as you stand there exhausted and beyond speech, surrounded by prawns whose lives were so much more wonderful in the sea, wondering why you are the only one left on Saturday night at work.*

That's when you question your role in life and consider other options as an eighteen year old." And that's why sweetie, she had looked at her with a wide-eyed false-happy face, *I get annoyed when restaurants close at eight or nine at night these days, in case you were wondering"*

"Ahh," I see," she had replied, *"I always wondered why you get agitated"*

She remembered watching her, trying not to laugh, as she expertly shelled peas from the green pods at the kitchen bench. *"Not as easy as you would think,"* she thought, her attempts always ended with rolling peas and not fully opened pods.

She winded down, concluding: *"The Head Chefs ranged from bad to terrible, sweetie, some alcoholics, some hardened tyrants, some criminals in their own way, definitely most were traumatised. I had heard of kind head Chefs, but never actually met one, I lucked out"* as she recalled her saying, looking at him with a tilted head and strange face, smiling.

She had said in reply: Looking over her glass of mineral water, *"You didn't luck out Mum, you taught me everything I know"* She smiled at her, and looked down at the peas, knowing she had made her day.

20

The beetles arranged and sang, the pheromone had dispersed the core target molecule and infected the species, running a trace chemical, a bio-marker, the nutrient transmitter set.

The red bromeliad was raised and attached to the ancient trunk, one hundred metres towards the canopy, its rotund bark wrapped and musty, mottled with ancient and moist reflection. It rose without interference under a canopy and nettle sky, a rough untouched pillar within the rock narrow valley, dripping with oxygenated water from the limestone overhang, the forest floor abundant and rich with microbe and sediment washed from the alluvial plain.

There was little sound, in the middle portion of the fibrous plant where the beetles splayed facing the round pillar semi-submerged stem in wheel-like display, and connected the chemical transfusion and electrical synthesis marker.

"Greetings, updates, kindness, sorrow, inquiry, confirmation, status, injury, swarm status, deaths. Pheromone dispersed the core target molecule and infected the species. Trace chemical, the biomarker, the nutrient transmitter set. The chief target has dispersed. Lateral spread is not necessary, the virus has selected" The Beetles sang silently with the chemical.

"Core and Clock, tempered strike, combine eye, salted nymph, the Alpha mite,

Plain of salt, pull of tide, set the wing a pool of time, Tempered stem and exo-skin, fall of star and hostile wing"

Above, the light reflected red hues and darting slivers and shone down on the blue-black ten winged carapaces arranged circular and antennae attached through the water to the lower stem, their appendages casting purple hue shadows and reflected stone from the inner walls of the valley.

The bromeliads spread protecting the core, a marker itself, an engineered hybrid that transfused the chemical protection with microbial mist and tangent direction, enveloping the beetles and surrounding the trunk, setting like a double rimmed water stem and connecting the pheromone, a defence marker and set a clear hostile cocktail to protect the swarm within the meeting.

The ten transversed, the array of antennae and appendage turned individually clockwise then anticlockwise, the movement a vibration and set of coxar, slight of feeler and shine of carapace, within the stem the water infused and set with the transmitter chemical, the patches of light filtering a splaying across the open flower and down to the semi-submerged fluid.

 Specks of debri adrift, and water warming with the friction of time itself. The shapes stopped moving and aligned the tempered stem, their pretarsus touching the fibre floor of the tube, tibia and tarsi bent and vibrating securely.

Chief target has dispersed, Ye Min has taken the ancient route, the Android marker.

From time to time an individual released their elytra, an opening to reveal the hind wings, superhydrophobic adapted, glistening within the fluid, ancient marine memories from a primordial pool and rare ocean current. Their abdomens were adrift in sediment then closing again to hide all but their Pterothorax, the green silver section near the wing shaped triangular and marker-like, a timeless beacon of adaptation.

The chemical was released again and set within the channel.

"Planetary machine, the other is aligned within the ancient cortex continent. The Bromeliad origin? The Polkinhorn?"
The beetles chemical sang in unison,

"Rotund pool, the ancient source, jungle vine and tempest fish"

The chemical realigned and dispersed,

"Female and machine sentient, but adrift. They will find the alien path.The five are set?" The Beetles shifted and turned a slow slant, still arrayed in spiky clock fashion around the central stem. In unison the chemical voice cast the reply from the ten arrayed:

"The four is sufficient. The stone has been located. The chemical Beetle sent to the carer. The desert and river is a patient portent. They have a target destination. Assumption set, the spurious targets can be groomed according to instinctual movement." The Beetles sang:

*"Time the stem, the pools and pull, terrain a sphere,
Bromeliad home and stone flat tide,
Species set and ancient wing, nymph of ocean salt array, the sediment ply
The robot chant and pheromone sky,
Archaeal lament, biachondria synthesis, Universe marker,
Phylotype the transfusion potent, sediment charter,
Species tempered, exit fly"*

The ten released from the central stem, and took one pace back from the flower stem, raising their compound eyes skyward, then raising their palpus momentarily.

The first Beetle released its elytron wing covers and set swimming expertly through the murky water and bursting out from the central stem portion surface tension and away to the canopy sky, foaming the surface as the others replicated the flight, one by one rising, leaving the portion and the meeting temple.

The water soothing and milling with the exit, the air heavy with evolutionary portent and meandering liquid from the flower, the canopy shifting to reveal the green sky at moments the soft hazy whisper and flutter of wings and carapace descending and fleeing the tree tops in soldier swarm formation their sentinels aligned and exiting across the plain

arrayed in centurion formation through the rocky fissure
terrain and across the storm laden horizon.

21

As Akseli was standing at the Bee-Brown toilet, soon after Ye Min had gone, his stream billowing into the bowl, he noticed the taped document on the wall, a note and a map and several files of the same document in the Men's and Ladies.

What's this? Graffiti? This wasn't me, hang on..

The message, like a hygiene warning above the toilets themselves, a detailed oceanic route to a destination, a small islet broken from a large distant continent that was within a momentous channel between another continent

A section of sea water with great tidal pull and severe currents where the water between the two land masses surged through from the sea from end to end. The maps she left were detailed and from the weather satellite, complete with detailed weather information and currents, seasonal predicted wind direction and temperatures.

§

Katie unfolded and looked at the note, her eyes sceptical and wider than normal, Kylie could almost hear her cogs within her mind spinning and calculating, the others were assembled in the meeting cave, seated around a crate table, the fusion batteries clicking,

Donghyun slurping his tea, and the others with sceptical and bemused looks, Kylie twirling a pen with her left hand, Akseli pouring over the sea charts. She looked at the congregation which contained a truth that nagged at her like an itch on the section of her back that could not be reached, making her squirm with a growing realisation of the way they seemed to be controlled subtlety, although they seemed capable enough, their path so far seemed determined by another, *Ate*

Succession leaving, the Tribe, and now Ye-Min. Katie read the notes contents,

Andreas and Jessica are alive. Jessica Neuer is four thousand kilometres distant North East on the far side of the continent. Travelling to her and beacon at seven second intervals at the aliens request. Andreas ditched in the ocean between this continent and next and I am told he is alive and well.

This information comes from a "Interstellar Scenario" file created by Jason. He must have done this before the Explorer fire, maybe soon after the Explorer landed after the Ate's leaving orbit. See satellite data.

There was a group exclamation of surprise, with the realisation that the three were alive, according to Ye-Min. Akseli's pencil stopped turning and Donghyun had put his tea down, the cup steaming, he looked suddenly philosophical.

Akseli was gazing at Katie, above his reading glasses, his map work interrupted, as she continued reading the note like some philosopher."Karl, collate all the data from the satellite please, I want to know about Jason's file and anything else on there we can use." "Collating," Karl replied.

Katie unravelled more paper documentation, rolled up from in a cardboard cylinder, weighing the documents down with her cup of coffee, He held the other end, as she detailed what else Ye-Min had given them. Outside was a white-out, Karl had come inside to recover from the weather, grounded by the wind, like a family dog, settled on the cave floor, a single landing light blinking, his rotors wound down.

Ye-Min detailed more weather information. Before the sea thawed and winter winded down, the temperatures, she told them based on her new calculations was going to drop much lower than she predicted, with lower ranges to be around -80°C, -112°F within the next coldest month, as the planet was farthest from the twins, the outer limit of revolution around the stars. Days sunlight would be brief and weak, the nights long

159

and cold. Donghyun had confirmed her findings based on her calculations, *"Extremely cold and outside activity would be challenging,"* he had said. Katie looked up and surveyed the others, "Well, there you are, any initial thoughts?, derangement? intelligent advice?," she said wide eyed and looked at the others inquiringly.

Kylie turned around and looked at Karl, the light now constant, the drone motionless, then turned as Katie piped, "Ye-Min must have a hell of a story," she offered, smiling.

Akseli looked at her and added, "It seems incredible, Andreas surviving the ditching" As Katie outlined the position information, relating what she had plotted in the Explorer, she thought about Tom and Tanya, Jason and what had happened.

Ye-Min now was affected in a different way, a puzzle she couldn't work out. *"Why was she unaffected by it?,"* she couldn't say. The others had almost killed her through starvation and didn't remember, and here they all were, together, and they had this eerie uncomfortable knowledge like she did, all agreeing, all choosing not to relate exactly what happened so as not to upset the group dynamic.

"How would Donghyun react to such news?," she thought, the quiet Meteorologist, polite, considerate, a little eccentric.

How could I explain that he was called an Altar Priest, for fucks sake, and had a space helmet as a effigy?, and his sidekick was a mad Geologist called the Mineral Master? No, that's a little beyond my pay grade, she thought.

Min had outlined what had occurred to her and Katie; they felt obliged. Thankfully Karl had confirmed the negative results for both her and Katie in regards to any long lasting health effects.

Min had confirmed Tom's injury, the Tribe, the madness, the living conditions, the descent into primal living, a human struggle with the environment and a deluded transit to unnecessary ritual and eventual control through violence. They thought it unnecessary to tell Akseli and Donghyun to keep the peace, the uncomfortable truth may separate the crew, create division, anger and resentment.

Katie had said straight away, *"No"* when it was suggested they be told, she agreed, although she had no memory of anything after her failed message attempt until she awoke around the same time as Katie among a rudimentary grass village with the smell of piss and shit in the air and wearing a grass skirt.

She thought of the transit from being an animal living in the dirt to awakening and the slow realisation that she could remember who she was and the other members of the crew.

Ye-Min had awakened first and rescued them from the squalor and the cold, finding them the caves. Ye-Min had also salvaged the Bee-Brown toilet and recycle system. She could see through the energy barrier the recycling system from where she sat and looked at the companies advertising on the toilet wall.

The Bee-Brown Dump Model 65A.
A perfect intervention for a Third World and a New World **Flexible-Atom-Acrylic-Glass Industries and Interstellar Design Systems Inc.**

Let's Screw and Go, Dump and Grow together

The system she remembered was a life-saver for third world communities on Earth after it had been trialled there. They had been briefed before launch and she at the time couldn't believe the system could work. The instructor told them how to assemble the unit and a demonstration was given. After that she thought it was one of the best inventions ever made, and remembered reading the description.

The Bee-Brown Dump model 65A, is a stand-alone fusion powered portable Bio-Toilet. An oblong portable energy tent

161

*fabric over a super-tough Universal molecular steel frame
constructed entity that can be assembled in about half an hour,
which includes special Sentient controller instructions.
Sentient cleaning control is always in place, monitored and
implemented by a complete sanitization after every visit, and
assisted by the maxi-fan exhaust system completely replacing
the interior air within a few seconds.*

*Human waste is broken down into a usable gas for cooking,
automatically bottled in recyclable containers that can be
reused three hundred times or rethreaded and reused again by
placing in the engineered rack or reprocessing as recyclable
metal. As part of the Bio-toilets hardware, one only has to
open the toilet door and walk to the rear. An array of small
gas bottles, ready for standard screw mount only on
Bee-Brown heaters, cookers, and terrain bikes, quad bikes,
Bee-Brown adapted vehicles and accessories. "Screw and
Go," is our motto.*

*But that's not all!, The remainder of the waste is super-frozen
and desiccated, bacterium removed and destroyed with
Ultraviolet searing technology, the completed product
available as an agricultural fertiliser, use as desired or get a
cash back recyclable refund and free collection, which is also
produced as part of the Bio-Toilet hardware, small sealed bags
of fertiliser at a handy five kilo size, stacked in a handy rack at
the rear of the toilet, or how we like to say it, "Dump and
Grow."*

She shook her head, remembering the advertising. Katie
looked at her to confirm she was still with them. She nodded
embarrassingly.

"Karl, can we get the AI input on this one?" Katie piped, She
fully awakened from her daydream.

"Certainly," Karl piped. "Well, the message is from Ye-Min, it
has been created with her login at least, on her tablet it is
coherent, a sane person collated it, it has calculations,

judgement and consideration. I also can confirm its authenticity" "What do you mean, Karl?," *Katie* said, turning to the drone now resting on the table with them. "I have a similar message, outlining the message Ye-Min has just related and received this authentication a few seconds ago," Karl replied.

"From who?" she piped. "I cannot say," Karl replied. She looked at Katie, both looking bemused, Akseli was looking at the maps, tapping a pencil on the continent they were currently on, Donghyun, was a statue, his cup of tea halfway between the table and his mouth.

She looked up to the ceiling of the cave, "And what sort of authentication?," she said, her head remaining in the tilted position as if searching for an ant on the cave roof.

"The message seems to have been transmitted via the OTAA device, a chemical trace, and I have been able to analyse the marker. It has been translated to binary code, a text message the result, I shall read it, then it will be clearer"

Katie shook her head in anticipation. "Go ahead."

"Time within the current system is finite. Presence has been tolerated, Universe species rare. Organised bipedal influence on the home sphere is tolerated with conditions.

Future bipedal insertions or failure to act will be treated as hostile. The Fifth Universe Robots have secured this planet with the alloy. Your colleague has made a deal. If she succeeds then a choice will be offered to you. We suggest you wait and see, rather than act hastily and fail as is the way with bipeds commonly."

"Karl, was this a message from Ye-Min?" "Negative," Karl reverted back to his normal Doctor - Patient speech. "From where did it originate?"

"Unknown location," Karl replied. "The chemical trace was airborne and within this area, that is however, the limit of my intelligence"

Kylie looked at the others, "So, Karl, could this be a message from *Ate Succession?*" "Negative," Karl replied, "The source is local, also, the fact that the message was chemical in origin suggests a non-human message, I know of no communication protocol that uses chemical trace markers within human protocols."

She looked at Karl with a pursed mouth, resting her tilted head on one arm from the table-top. "We always thought that one day this may happen," Karl stated, the drone now near the crate table like a consulting Philosopher. "What?," Katie said, turning to the drone.

"That we find intelligent life, is this so surprising? This certainly seems to be the case here," Karl replied.

"And Karl, this Alien message, what are your thoughts on its authenticity,?"Katie asked.

"I believe the message has been transmitted with a protocol that we technologically do not possess, therefore I would give the message some credibility," Karl said, matter of fact.

Katie smiled and glanced around at the others. Karl continued, "There is no transmission that we have identified that has anything like this communication protocol, the fact that they are able to relay information chemically points to a super adapted species, highly advanced in our terms, probably natural for them"

Donghyan interrupted adding, "Aren't they supposed to meet with us? Tell us the meaning of life?, slightly tongue in cheek.

"Perhaps they will, or have already," Karl continued, I have given this some thought, they could have contacted you, that is a human contact, but no, they contacted a sentient intelligence to relay the message, they want to be clear, and that they are separate from your thoughts, telling you chemically would probably create confusion" She thought for a moment, "Karl, how do we rule out that you didn't create the message?" she said, "And I say that with the same regard as I have for the human crew"

"Very good question Kylie, this is difficult to explain, the trace marker I have not identified in terms of composition, it appears to have originated then dispersed only giving me enough time to translate it. I am also not sure of the mechanism that allowed me to translate the source to binary code. All I can offer is the absence of log entries within my system that would indicate a message formation that I initiated through my protocols. You may be able to confirm this."

"Ok, thanks Karl, I have to ask" Kylie looked at the others, the recognition that an AI might be capable of such a thing showed on their faces, but she doubted the scenario, AI constructs were incapable of trickery or secret practical jokes, to her knowledge.

"Kylie if I may," Karl piped. "Yep, Karl , go ahead" "Long gone are the days of AI-Construct malfunction but we must consider the scenario Katie has suggested. I will say however that as an independent AI that did not receive the message, I still think the origin is outside our sphere of influence

"Thanks Karl." The others listened intently, Akseli was getting some more clam soup from the pot, Akseli stretched his arm to the side, he looked at the clock on the cave wall, *0210:34*.

"This is not a joke of yours Akseli?" Katie asked, breaking the silence with humorous eyes. "Hah!, no I have lost my touch, I am afraid, must have been the Tribal influence," he replied, looking sheepishly at Donghyun still holding the wooden spoon for ladling the soup in his hand.

The Meteorologist, was in turn looking suspiciously at him in a friendly manner. There were smiles and the others shifted,

165

she looked at Donghyun, he now was smiling slightly, and Akseli seated himself again, as if trying to remember something.

Katie was blinking in a manner belying the space between realisation and anticipating a practical joke, and looking at the maps, thinking, her cogs turning. The wind had abated beyond the energy barrier and ice prisms were falling, she noticed, their extraordinary ice-cluster shapes glistening in the light from the Bee-Brown toilet as they fluttered down and set on the firm ice ground.

The potentially historic silence was interrupted by Anders who emerged from the energy barrier, the group looking at the emerging figure dressed in the exo-suit boots and terrain coat.

"Ohhhh, talk about entrances! "Katie shouted, the others laughed, he stood up and walked to Anders smiling. She approached him and took his arm like a child, she too smiled, leading him to a vacant terrain chair at the crate table.

"So, what's going on?," Anders said, looking surprised, tired and a bit scared at the response. As he seated himself, Katie piped, "You tell us, how are you feeling?" The others watched him with non-verbal welcome. "Yep, pretty good, had a few dreams, feet are sore," he said smiling. Looking at the others.

She sat down again after looking at Anders in a standing pose behind Katie, thinking, *So, the Encroacher lives,* she humorously mused.

"Karl here tells us that we have received a message, *an Alien message,* .... Yes you are not dreaming, how's that for an introduction to the new look group?,"Katie said, smiling at him.

Anders shook his head seemingly waiting for the punch-line, but realising it may be true. "Aliens?, come on guys, I am trying to recover here," he said looking at the others. The group remained silent, except for Akseli who was quietly laughing, the rest of the non-verbal group's response telling him that it was believed, he sat back and blinked, not saying anything, his surprise evident.

Katie raised her finger to Anders as if to say, *Wait we will finish our discussion,* Anders looked around realising it was a meeting in progress. Akseli rose and grabbed a bowl from the bench filling it with steaming clam soup, silently passing it to Anders who questioned with his look then took the spoon he was holding as well and placed it on the table. He motioned for him to eat, smiled then took his place at the table again in silence not to disturb the flow of the meeting.

"So Karl, what is your translation of the message?, in layman's terms what are they, It, saying?" there was a pause, Karl usually didn't take long to reply, but obviously the sentient cogs were turning as well.

Anders bowl clinked with the sound of the spoon, and he ate some soup, blowing the hot liquid in the spoon first, she looked at him, Anders looked at her in turn and replied with,

Not bad, delicious actually.

"Yes, well, I suggest we are tolerated but not welcome here, it suggests they could have dealt with us already if they desired in , er let's say in a considerably more hostile manner. This also explains the loss of AI contact for the extended period after terrain contact with Gemmi7a, and the Ate Successions disastrous departure, and indeed Captain Williamson's behaviour.

 I would sum it up as an opportunity to leave, well, an order to leave rather, whatever "Alloy" is, it seems to be the key, and it suggests Andreas Polkinghorn has survived, all in all, an intriguing scenario."

 They all looked at one another, the table and the roof of the cave, Karl sat on the table as if the AI was the alien itself and all she could hear was their thoughts and the message, and the fact that it was all a little too much for someone to hear in one night.

22

Katie digested the news that they had contacted an alien, which swirled around in her mind. *Was it real,* she thought. It was something that she couldn't confirm. *After all, it was a message, green men or women here talking to us,* she mused.

She sat down at the table and waited for the others. Katie waited for a moment for them to settle then spoke as their Commander. Right on cue, Akseli dropped a metallic pot at the kitchen bench which made the others crouch in trembling fear from the noise.

She looked at him smiling to temper her annoyance. "Sorry, the damn thing is slippery," he replied, looking at the others in embarrassment.

"So, I wanted to address you all as a crew, I want to get some impressions of all the information we have, given an Alien message, a lost ship, a gap in our memories and still have three members of the mission, 'absent without leave', one of whom seems to have the Aliens ear.

Anders, I know this is all probably too much but you are the third officer and I need you more than ever now." "It's not an issue Katie, I am fine, I'm here," Anders replied, looking at her with a serious intent. Katie nodded in thanks before continuing,

"Ok, look, Kylie has a program that could make the Ate Succession return here" The group shifted, Akseli replied incredulously, "How?" "It's a remote Trojan, a sentient firmware virus she made for the worst case scenario," Katie looked at all of them in turn with a look of confidence.

Katie looked at her for her to continue. Kylie looked up from her laptop and turned the screen so they could see."I know what you have all heard from Jason, but he's not here and we don't really know what is going on, do we," she said looking around at the others.

192.168.0.245:8878 connected, Login: Ate Succession Systems Engineer Kylie Albott - 3454678
Satellite connection requested, ***********access granted
Insertion Program setting parameters......
Protocol open, Radio Beacon true: set, ready for transfer......
Waiting for input
Operation cancelled, timeout 15 sec
Power off 20:36:13
192.168.0.245:8878

"This is the message I was going to send before I got infected, I thought I might have sent it but I didn't, the log proves that" "I have sent it again and if it works it will take control of the ship and stop the Fusion drive, then we get there via the Explorer.

With Ate drifting, yes you heard me, drifting, something has stopped the fusion drive, we are able to make it with the first trip, then send another Explorer for the rest of us.

She looked around at the others, Anders was looking at her waiting for her to go on, Akseli, looked at her above his coffee mug, she thought instantly of the message as she let the news sink in.

"And the message?, how do we see all this from our Alien friends point of view?" she asked rhetorically. She looked at Katie, "That is what we need to work out, work out tonight" their Commander said, smiling ironically. She leant back, the others remained silent, thinking. "Karl, what do you think?," she said, addressing the tabled drone.

"*'Future insertions failure to act will be treated as hostile', I refer you all to that comment,* piped Karl immediately.

"It could be a dangerous move given the return of another Explorer after all it was they who infected Captain

Williamson, this seems likely. If we could contact our Alien friend we might be able to tell them that we are leaving. Of course Ye-Min seems to know information we do not and then there is the Andreas question, our ship's Doctor, what does he know? Rescue would be the desired option of course, but we no longer possess the means as the Explorer is disabled. I suggest we try to locate Andreas Polkinghorn, if we can speak to him then we can make an informed decision," Karl replied. Of course we could take the aliens' advice and 'wait and see.'

"Ok, thanks Karl," Katie said. "Look, we have some options, and we have some information but we need to make a decision either way. Also we have Jessica Neuer on the other side of the continent it seems if she is alive as Ye-Min suggests.

We will attempt to contact her. The others voiced their relief, Donghyun smiled, Akseli uttered, "Oh, wow, that's great," Anders sat wide eyed at the news. Katie continued, "Ye-Min seems to be on some other quest and we don't know what or why but Karl has indicated she is on a path to intercept Jessica and Iris, possibly to guide them back here and whatever the deal is, we don't know."

She looked at the others thinking about *Ye-Min*, the saviour of the Tribe, their Astronomer. "Guide them?," asked Akseli. "Yes good question, Iris can lead her here, she is injured but she should recover, the Ye-Min trek has me stumped," Katie said. Akseli interjected, "Maybe she's not going to them at all, she's still infected, some other reason" "We just don't know," Katie said scanning the others.

Katie continued, "Personally I think our best chance is the *Ate Succession*, everything else is not defined enough, what is the alloy for example?"

When Ye-Min gets back if she does, then what? We have no way of getting to Polkinghorn, it all seems madness, the message is not clear from our Alien friend, ok so it doesn't want us here then fine we will leave on Ate, take our chances, possibly find another world, remember the passengers are still in my care, and we have a hijacked colonist ship" "I agree," she piped, the others sat in thought, Donghyun looked at the map, Akseli studied his hands, "And the Ate has a second Explorer does it not?" "Correct, we can secure Jason Jessica, and Iris, Ye-Min if favourable, and Andreas, exit to Ate in orbit and away we go, Anders, what are my third officer's thoughts?"

Anders breathed out in a confused sigh, "I am not sure, I like the plan practically, but the reason we are all in this mess is the fact that Ate was hijacked, ..well taken away, what can of worms do we open if it returns?

Kylie saw that Anders shifted in his terrain seat. As a trained military pilot, knowing to question his superior was standard but still uncomfortable, careful with his reply.

"It seems the infection caused Captain Williamson to act as he did, so what would stop the infection doing exactly the same thing for a second time?"

Kylie, pursed her mouth as if to say, *Hadn't thought of that.* Katie stared at her, her cogs turning.

A thought came to her and she turned to look at the drone, "Karl, is there any way to answer the Alien?" "Negative," Karl replied deadpan. *"What about we type a text message and you link the two with metadata, then the documents have a relationship, the alien might read it, it knows the language, it might respond somehow."* "I can link the documents, we could try, the chemical transfer might work both ways if the entity initiates a signal and reads the second document," Karl replied.

She turned to Katie, looking at her with wider eyes. "It won't hurt, let's try it," Akseli said, Katie nodded, "Ok, Karl go ahead, it might contact again," Katie said, looking at the cavern ceiling. "Affirmative," Karl replied.

Anders was smiling at her, she looked as if to say *What?* *"Not just a pretty face, huh?* Donghyun was smiling, Akseli and Donghyun attentive to the suggestion, like statues. Karl piped, "Ready for text message if you all are" "Now?" *Katie* looked at the drone. "Why not?If we have a document ready it might make our dilemma easier," Karl said in an urgent tone. Katie looked at her, she nodded, the others nodded, Akseli said "Lets try"

The beetle made its way through the barrier, the tiny section parting to allow its path as if it had an automatic key and silently buzzing its way into a small crack above the small box-AI, the combine eyes still and reflecting. It folded its wings into its electra and angled its antenna down towards the sentient machine, its carapace invisible in the crevasse.

Katie opened her flight book and grabbed a pen, "Ok, let's talk to an alien," she said looking at the others. "Karl, we will narrate some statements and questions," Katie said addressing the drone on the table.

"Affirmative, ready" "Ok, I will narrate what we might do with the Ate, is that a good start?" Katie said, looking around at each of the others.

The non-verbals agreed, the group nodded and silently mouthed agreement. Akseli had a pencil in his mouth, Donghyun looked intently at the table, Katie looked at Anders as if she saw the Encroacher momentarily.

"Ok, Karl, first statement telling us what we intend" "Affirmative," Karl said. "We intend to signal the return of our ship, if we leave your planet on this ship will this be acceptable?" "Document has been created and amended, metadata active," piped Karl."Wait," Karl piped immediately, "An answer has been transferred chemically, translating binary.."

"The return of your ship will not be permitted. Your paths are now set,"

173

Karl translated and piped upon the table. She covered her mouth in amazement, Anders was smiling, Donghyun looked frozen in place, she stared at the table as if it was talking, processing the reply. Katie spoke again addressing the ceiling, "How are our paths set?" *"You will have a choice to help us , your mission has now changed"* "What is the alloy?" Katie asked. Karl continued the exchange translation, *"Universal Sentient Element ,* Karl piped as the Alien.

Katie looked at the others, the mood one of tension and amazement, like a deal to end all deals was imminent on the other end of a phone conference line.

She shifted in her seat and asked the entity, the others staring at her in anticipation, "What planet would suit us?"

"There are planets within the Seven Dwarf Reticular, worlds are adapted, you cannot destroy them, they are within the Fifth Universe, " the alien replied.

"Why haven't you destroyed us?," Anders suddenly said. He stared at the ceiling waiting for Karl's translation, Akseli staring at Donghyun, she noticed with incredulous anticipation.

"Universal organic species are rare, we have the responsibility of our place in the Universe as all life is in danger, " Karl piped.

"Who are you, I mean what species are you?," she said, the mood of the communication moving from astonishment to inquiry. *"We are the Beetles"* "How is it possible that you understand us, our language, how are you able to communicate?," she asked.

"Chemical Transfer Syntax, we understand the chemical as it translates the communication, we do not understand your language as an audible sound on its own, " the alien piped from Karl's speaker.

She looked around, the mood within the cave was a stilted electric atmosphere. *A humming of cogs turning within their minds,* she thought. Katie shifted from across the table, "So why can't we stay here? You made our ship leave and now we are marooned, and now you want us to leave, I don't understand," she said looking at the cave wall.

"Allowing your species habitation would eventually destroy our planet, is this not what was being done to your home planet while your species proliferated? The bulk of your dangerous species have now been sent elsewhere, all that remains is choice, then you will all have to decide whether you are part of the Universe's destiny or a victim of its danger

"What deal has Ye-Min made?" *"She has agreed to locate a piece of hardware for us. If she succeeds then you will be given a choice to leave this planet or help us. We suggest you wait and see"*

Katie spoke again, "And you are sure that we could not live in peace together?"

"There is no peace with Bipedalism. Even now, as we speak, chances are you are thinking of ways to combat our thinking. Your rise from beneath a dominant species for such a long evolutionary time has made you highly aggressive and with the evolution of consciousness, susceptible to an excess amount of rumination, leading to fundamental delusion.

Kylie noticed Anders eyes widened as he digested the aliens comments.

The resulting behaviour exhibits itself in several similar neuroses of which intertwine themselves into contradiction, denial, which inevitably lead to devious ritual to obtain political and psychological control.

175

In turn, this behaviour eventually dissolves into simple self-serving instinct, usually conflict and savagery of which ironically, was your original evolutionary Modus Operandi.

Donghyun remained frozen in time, his coffee cup at his lips.

It is extremely rare for a species such as yours within the Universe to have evolved. We travelled to your world over two hundred million years ago, it was thought that the species dominant at the time, the Avian species would prevail. The adaptation of consciousness and the almost terminal planetary event of a massive asteroid combined; the outcome: The surviving Warrior Bipedal.

Kylie listened and watched Karl at the same time, not fully sure this was a drone practical joke.

You have advanced sentient devices and other technologies but in the end you continue to destroy the world from which they came, the marvellous evolutionary time-line that created you.

Your world at the rate of your own destructive habits would have started to seriously decay within the next five hundred years. The stark reality is that eighty percent of your population are not part of any plan at all about their future, this being a consequence of your herd and self-serving duality mentality. The advent of Volcanism on your world has hastened the inevitable, and therefore made the above null and void.

Katie was a statue, frozen in place looking at the ceiling. Akseli nodded as if in total agreement as he still perused the map in front of him.

The sending of your mechanical probes that contain information describing yourselves to deep space in your early technological era is an example of your complete misunderstanding of the Universe and self-absorbed psyche,

176

you are lucky not to have been already colonised, enslaved or destroyed.

Given that, you are of little danger to the entire Universe, only the terrestrial orbs you inhabit. To put things in perspective, a bipedal thinks nothing of felling a terrestrial tree to satisfy a short term need and ignores the value of the organism over the ages in a myriad of other contexts. This type of behaviour is what will destroy your longevity within a Universe in flux, if unaddressed.

The fundamental tenet that Bipedals cannot grasp is that in order to survive within the Universe, you must recognise the natural world you came from and live within its means, not yours. So, no, we cannot live in peace together. We can, however, work together. We say again wait and see"

She looked up at the others, the looks of silent disappointment mixed with unbelief and tired introspection.

She instantly thought of the Tribe, her life, the Earth, and wondering if the time had finally come, an Alien had to tell them for it to sink in. *"Self-absorbed Psych,"* she mused, *"No doubt,"* she thought.

Donghyun moved a little, suggesting a considered reply, "Who would enslave or colonise us?, are there other alien species in the Universe?," he said looking at the table in consideration. *"Many exist, "* the alien syntax piped. "And the Fifth Universe, what is that?" Akseli asked, twirling his pen rapidly in his hand.. *"A Universe that is currently free of the greatest threat to everything that was, and will be"* "What is the greatest threat?," Katie offered.

"Anti-Universe Sentient Androids, made to destroy, converting mass to energy obeying the laws of Thermodynamics. You will be familiar with your famous equation, $E = mc2$. This they reflect in practice to power their massive energy needs and proliferate.

An analogy would be a mutated virus that has become a super-toxic pathogen and destroys physicality. We think that they were originally a passive exploratory Android series; time and mechanical evolution has altered their purpose or madness, whichever your view.

Within the Fifth Universe and beyond, the robots are able to combat their toxicity due to the sentient element noble gas; otherwise known as the Alloy, their makers' last act before they reached the pinnacle of their evolutionary timeline entering an unknown void of time, passing to their Robots the code and knowledge. Without the noble gas the Universe's mass will be consumed and converted to energy only.

Katie turned and looked at her as if she was searching for someone with a comm's unit outside.

The Robots gave us the alloy, a protection for the planet from the conversion of mass to energy. The alloy gives all life on this world a sentient construct and protection from the threat, but in time even the alloy, a standalone defence without the power of the Fifth Universe will not be enough.

We have defeated the Androids in open combat and saved our world, they are unable to counter the use of our organic chemicals, despite their enormous energy power, so they have their weaknesses, but it is a small battle won within an ever present war waged upon mass within the Universe.

The Androids rarely enter into open conflict, their way is covert insertion and infection usually with their sentient code inserted into a physical entity, altering the chemical atomic bonding process.

We suspect that your world's mass has been slightly altered by their hand which would explain the rapid volcanism. We suspect they have altered the convection core of your world. Most of their threat comes from this type of insidious slow conversion of mass within galaxies. They have developed a sentient code that is able to direct and control energy, something that we as yet do not fully understand. With the code they can physically change mass to energy in the form of whole planets and stars themselves.

That is why the Fifth Universe is the last bastion within time itself, after the other Universes are consumed, the Quantum boundary will shrink and time itself will grow cold. The Robots seed new stars in gas clouds to allow new worlds to form to slow the process but they are few, although immaculate and seemingly immortal.

Anders' look had glazed into hardened steel.

The Androids grow immense energy and harvest the power to create Super-Android models and starships, and vast complexes of quantum computing power; they are in effect a Supercomputer race beyond imagining.

If they are not stopped they will consume everything, they seem to have no conscious nor purpose beyond energy creation and mass destruction, literally. The only way to combat such immense energy and computing power is to step down the evolutionary ladder and use the most ancient organic weapons; their potency still untapped, this is why we prevailed.

Kylie looked at the others, seated like a collection of tired shift workers being told of redundancy.

So now you see, ...your world and self-importance pales a little, does it not? It would have been a simple thing to kill you all, but this is not our way. Lower order organisms such as your species also have evolutionary value beyond technology.

You are valuable however in ways you as yet cannot understand. Temporarily wiping your minds allowed us time to deal with your Starship, the greatest threat containing many of your kind. It is in numbers that humans are most dangerous, the communication and dexterity that allows you to exit from a

179

cave entrance and enter a skyscraper is a potent and destructive weapon on the flip-side of the human coin.

She listened with interest, the Alien spelling it out. The others sat with Philosophical faces like Greek Scientists calculating, or Roman soldiers before battle. Akseli sat like an awakening statue, Donghyun pencil in mouth staring at the cave wall, Katie looked straight ahead in some cog-turning environment. She felt unsurprised, she thought not surprising in itself after their experience here. Every time she looked at Anders, Akseli or Donghyun, she wondered what had happened within the tribe.

"So why were some minds wiped and not others?," she said, addressing Karl, the Alien voice.

"All minds were altered. Follow Ye-Min's direction, she will meet with you all, then you all will have to make a decision as I have outlined; You will have to choose whether you are part of the Universe's destiny or a victim of its danger"

"The transfer has ceased" Karl stated deadpan, the transmission terminated.

She looked at the others, sitting and posturing like a fruitful meeting in a boardroom, a pre-flight briefing or a gardeners pow-wow. "All minds were altered," she stated again looking at Akseli, then Katie, smiling wryly.

"Yes, indeed, well mine has always been altered, so I feel right at home," Donghyun said in jest. The others smiled. There was a small pause between people who were thinking about something to say as if to break an uncomfortable silence. *But it is a little more than uncomfortable silence,* she thought

"I think we need to digest all this and it's late," Katie said looking at the clock on the cave wall, interrupting the silent contemplation. "Lets get some sleep on it, it's a hell of a story.," she said looking in resignation at the others around the table.

Katie, always pragmatic, she thought and here she was briefing them all as if it was another flight operation. "Karl, can you confirm again this is not you, are you playing a joke on us humans?" Katie added suddenly, laughing softly.

"I can confirm that I am not the Alien and also that I am not playing a joke on you all," Karl said deadpan. Katie nodded, "Thank you , Karl, you know we love you?" she said, addressing the drone. "Thank you, Kylie, I know that I am an integral part of your feelings moving forward," Karl replied in humour.

"Quite so,"Katie reinforced, smiling at the drone. She smiled as Katie turned to her, "Can you try and get onto the Lifeboat AI, the one Jessica was in?," she asked. "Sure, on it," she replied. "Anders, can I give you Polkinghorn, try and get a message through to his AI or find out where the Lifeboat went down," "Anders nodded, "On it"

"Karl, can you try and find out where Cox-AI is," *"Affirmative,"* Karl replied." "If we find Cox, we might find Jason, I want my Navigator back," she said. "And our AI Doctor," Kylie added. The others had risen.

This meeting in some way throws more confusion on post-confused Tribe members, she pondered.

"Well, see you tomorrow, I really don't know what to say," Donghyun said smiling, rising and walking slowly with a contemplative Akseli towards the energy barrier.

"So, Donghyun, Akseli, can you continue your scientific analysis as normal? Can we have a sit down tomorrow, I haven't had a chance to talk to you both. I know, it's been hard on everyone," Katie offered.

They both nodded and expressed non-verbal agreement. Katie nodded in return the two exiting the cave energy barrier with the familiar buzz of the barrier sentient allowing them passage. "So what are we going to do with those two?"Katie said to her. "Same as usual," she replied, "Logistics, food and water, Bee-Brown maintenance, personnel hygiene and safety" "Are you ok?, I know that this is all left field, the contact with an alien, our missing memories and our missing personnel" She nodded, she noticed that they were all smiling, *"Well, that's a start,"* she thought to herself.

192.168.0.245:8878 connected, Login: Ate Succession Systems
Engineer Kylie Albott - 3454678
Satellite connection requested, ***********access granted
Insertion Program setting parameters……
Protocol open, Radio Beacon true: set, ready for transfer……
Waiting for input

She pressed enter, the satellite confirmed that the Trojan had been sent which she estimated would take a week to get to Ate now almost a light year away. The program would take control of the ship, disable the fusion drive and prepare the ship, then they would, in a fixed Explorer, make their way to Ate and continue their mission.

23

Andreas walked further discovering the dining hall beside the great arena, the arched stone as massive as a jetliner hanger, with the shimmering light filled windows, high above, the tables like parallel stone railway tracks extending the length of the space

Five crafted tables of smooth white polished stone and small benches of lighter coloured mineral grain were placed at aligned intervals. To sit at one end, a person would be hard pressed to recognise another diner at the other end; the distance over fifty metres he measured by walking his metre steps one day in discovery.

The kitchens were at each end as massive as everything else in the Citadel, and he was confused as he walked through the culinary space doorway, *"So Robots eat, Androids eat?,"* he thought as he remembered the murals at the stadium.

Mechanical species were depicted watching performances and orations, gathered like a collection of five hundred child's toys in the stadium watching the show. He noticed the kitchen was again stone, the oven spaces like outdoor pizza ovens, and benches with flat black stone contrasting the bases, when touched by his hand ignited in some manner, the stone turning searing hot and stopping over time like induction cooktops.

A long pole travelled through the space with every size metallic pot, spoon, ladle, colander, egg beater, whisk, skewer, fork, knife, bowl, meat hammer, and cutlery he had ever seen in one place.

Torture chamber or Kitchen dining? He noticed from his feet on the stone no discernible sound that was different from his old foot-fall.

There were kitchen implements with uses that he speculated on, like a pyramid shaped metallic hollow item resembling a giant cookie cutter, a cylindrical can shaped implement, hooks, spears, cages and barbs, that all hung above like a museum collection of medieval torture devices, still in the great kitchen space. He counted fifty five kitchen islands with differing hung implements above, small cooktops, depressions like wok burners and extruding metallic pipes that seemed to have attachments for some apparatus like a chemistry lab gas connections.

He stopped beside an island and felt the smooth stone, the texture a semisand marble roughness. He looked up again at the space.

Beside each kitchen island, were ten foot high stone boxes, again a differing stone, the colour a green-blue polished variety with doors. He opened one, the chill of the air realising for him the discovery of coolboxes, fridges, connected by a single narrow pipe from the ceiling of super-cooled air.

Inside the fridges lay not food but small boxes, a variety of beautiful colours, each cube, he measured five by five centimetres long, 1.96 inches by 1.96 inches.

What are these? He turned the cube in his hand, examining the paperweight item. *Made of some sort of foam material.*

The cubes took all the space in every fridge he noticed at the time craning his neck to the top shelf. A lever to the side, he discovered rotated the shelves up and down like a car stacker.

He juggled the cube,, about half a kilo, 2.2 pounds each, turning the item in his hand. No discernable gap contrasted the surface, the cubes right angled and seemingly perfect boxes; a crafted cube refrigerated Christmas decoration.

He continued to turn the square, the cube, rubbed it with his hand, the surface smooth, like a bizarre egg. He carried the cube as he walked, the kitchen stoves to his right, gazing up towards the massive roof and noticed a hanging metallic upended tray and realised this was the gigantic rangehood, an air outlet, hanging like an engineering artwork, hanging in great arcing part semi-circles, all connected by the conduit above. He stopped to look at the creation and placed the cube down on the stove surface, the object transforming into a transparent cube.

He stepped back, wary of the transformation like an insect within an urban environment confronted by human constructions.

Inside the cube he could see pictures of food, a fish, a bean and a root vegetable, a red pooled sauce and a green vegetable. *"Is this a prepared meal?,"* he thought, smiling, hoping and a little scared at the item sitting on the stovetop.

Looked up, took a small fry pan down and placed the metal on the stone, the heat instantly rising from beneath. He placed the cube into the pan and the cube dissolved into the food items he had seen all in scale to the pan, the red sauce wafted a delicious small, like paprika and thyme, a small fish fried silently and the vegetables steamed, a spinach smelling waft and mix of seed and tamarind-like scent.

He stood transfixed, and turned looking at the fifty fridges arrayed in the hall. *"More food than I could eat in twenty years,"* he thought, *"Well, maybe two,"* he corrected himself, the steaming pan's heat diminishing, the meal prepared it seemed with intelligent culinary design.

Beside the stoves were heated plate and crockery compartments, thin square orange stone cabinets, inside crafted stone plates, bowls, containers, serving bay marie sandstone looking trays, and items he couldn't assess for use, a cylindrical stone pipe sized collection of tubes, hexagonal shaped sticks and cone shaped funnels connected to stands.

He ate the meal, on a stone plate, sitting in the hall alone like a last surviving kitchen species, the warmth of the food like a descending potion of eternal life, an elixir, a time key to his mind; the past hunger and cold a tempered and strapped down. The knife and fork were metallic. *Same as home,* he mused, but then noticed the fork had ten spikes, the knife two closely parallel blades with slightly differing surfaces, one fine serrated edge, the spoon a three tiered depression shaped ladle type implement.

Now that is spoonology for you. He turned the implement, examining its weight and touch.

As the alien knife reflected the light a psychological lament descended on his mind, a calming cloak of feathered spice and tuned herb bedding; like he had laid down on a surface of oregano or sweet tarragon and was aptly dozing, the perfumed Bouquet Garni wrapping him like a secret gift.

Ok, here we go. Food is food is it not? Certainly smells better than anything I could cook. Tentatively, he tasted the first morsel. He pretended he was a food critic and wrote his review:

The red sauce was like lobster and lime with a touch of green chilli, the fish a slightly seared crispy surface, the oils combining with the green squash-type vegetable, there was a hint of grain and seed of some type and thin yellow beans that tasted like spiced flour.

He looked up momentarily expecting in a day-dream to find other silent diners, the discovery of a quiet clink of spoon or soft chewing; a full table of contented patrons. He sat.

Was that the best meal I have ever eaten?, he thought, sitting, licking the stone plate of all remaining sauce like a child alone without rules. He looked around and then thought, *Where then is the dishwashing area?*

The door at the end of the great kitchen showed him the way, plate and cutlery in hand he entered the next space, a water area, a large pool adorned the middle of the stone floor, rectangular, shallow, the water flowing strongly from one end to the other the water released via a circular shaped outlet, like a giant sieve.

Ok, a fifty metre swimming pool.

As he neared the pool's edge a loud sound chimed like a large bell within a soundproof room. He noticed movement above and stepped back from the pool's edge, a giant apparatus was descending, mirrored to the pool's shape, a gantry made of metal he assessed.

The frame lowered, at a pace too slow to be any threat to his waist level, a massive sieved flat surface, shining as if just created, the gantry swayed the tiniest amount reflecting from the surface of the pool. Looking closer he noticed the surface of the sieve flattop was moving at a snail's pace, the steel reaching the sides and disappearing below.

"A metallic conveyor belt."

Watching the machine which made no sound - *The dishwasher,* he deduced, placing his plate on the metallic tray, which slowly moved away from him, a single plate, a fork and knife, looking innately guilty at their imposition. on the vast surface.

He waited, then stepped away. The gantry surface, moving like a small current across water. The plate reached the end, then the gantry stopped, the plate and cutlery perched , ready to fall into the pool.

Further waiting produced no movement or action, the gantry still hung above the pool's surface like a goods crane on an empty dock. He eventually left, waiting seemed to bring no result as if the gantry was waiting for more dishes.

§

When he returned the next day the plates, cutlery and gantry were gone and the pools clearwater milled a small current and a slight gurgle from the sieve drain. He noticed also, that the prepared meal cube had been replaced with another, the space filled, he was pretty sure but not certain he had opened the correct fridge.

His image, he had seen after exiting the kitchen. He gazed at himself again in a large mirror under the massive public space pergola. The pergola was a rival to all other pergolas and stretched the entire four kilometre length through the middle of the city. Gardens and potted mechanical species, seats of metal and stone and pavers of light colours like a child's block counting set, white, red, light-green, purple, yellow, deep-green, black, brown, blue, and orange pavers, then at defined counted paver stages, a paver with all ten colours like a tilers bathroom creation.

The paving stones seemed interlocked like some garden code to guide the green-thumb and weary walker.

Metal legs on sandstone, Polkinghorn the growing machine.

He passed the baths along the way, great pools where the oceanic tide was used to replace the water daily and hot pools fed from springs deep below the sea shelf, steaming green and mineralised, always short distances from bath houses of cold pools and flat areas that soaked the sun on raw sea-rock plateaus.

That peculiar sea-breeze is coming in, mixed salt with a touch of volcanic pumice...

In the middle of the walkway, a collection of giant murals were painted on the stone, he found them walking the length for exercise when he was still totally organic, stopping to stare, amazed and statuesque.

The wall art showed androids or robots, metal forms like humans but made of steel and cast alloys, relaxing like ancient travellers, and maps of constellations, some distant stars and arrays of deep interstellar clouds.

Do robots take baths?

he mused as he looked out towards the tidal pools past the walkway, then back at the art that seemed to shine with the light, the intricate drawings behind the paint a sketch of guiding form, almost sentient in itself.

As he walked further out on the jetty, he could see out towards the bluff, the waves foaming across the shoals distant, the wind was sweeping across the jetty from left to right, *"Perfect,"* he thought for his daily sail in the silver dinghy with two sails and and a strange metallic rope soft to the touch, the centreboard was long to steady the thrust of the craft, and it was a fast craft when the wind managed it like a sea-bourne kite.

The shape was rocket-like, the hull deep and cutting, creating a sure ballast in the deep channel foamlets. A mainsail and a jib, the fabric a fine sieve material, an alloy as well, catching the wind gusts, a wind-sock gone rogue, the pull of the craft a seaborne sensation of raw oceanic power and freedom. As the craft gained speed he realised after the first trial, the sails sang, a rising whine to the voice of an alien planetary atmosphere, *"An eerie tune of past sailors laments perhaps,"* he thought, still looking down at the boat he had consoled like a marine Father.

Let's take this baby out again and see what she can do.

The sea deep canal was like a semi-circle race track, stretching for a hundred kilometres, bordering the coral shelf that broke away and encrusted the submerged channel wall he had seen as he traversed the water close to the start of the coral. At the end before the coral dominated again, he jived into the wind and returned, usually with the flying fish arching beside the bow, and jellies swimming below, white under green sea and sparkling behemoths, zeppelin-like in the coral shelf shadow.

The rush of the sailboat sprayed salt which beaded off his form, stinging and spotting cold and warm as he leaned to control the tilt of the craft, and the increasing whine of sail and wind. He grew tired after the sails,

So robots grow tired as well?, he thought. *"Robots?, maybe not, what am I becoming?*

After mooring the small sail-boat, he craft sat bobbing in a small protected anchorage that was a massive C-shape retreat walled high from the wind and swell, a place that had anchored larger craft, he knew but now was a small sailboat's cove, the dinghy turning on its mooring like a dancer on a large water stage.

He had repaired the craft, it had been in the cove still secured by the metal type rope but was in poor condition, partly submerged despite the protective walls. He watched it during his first gaze upon it after his first walk out on the jetty and decided then it would provide some hobby-time for him.

This deserted city has no social activities, he thought. *A metal man requires the same entertainment,* he humorously mused to himself.

Several weeks of plugging, patching, forming metal shapes with the use of his hands, working parts and attachable fittings, the alloy he created was malleable and bent with his thoughts and desire into shapes and angles and design. He understood the molecular process and intelligent adaptation of his form, he was no longer a human physically but was still one mentally, *Why was that?,* he thought with fear and wonder. no longer even from this Universe he assumed.

What creature can make metal into desired shapes with their hands and mind? What creature can craft a sailboat while undergoing an alloy-dash-organic transformative phase of their life?, he laughed.

§

During the night, three moons cast a white salt down on the citadel, as he sat near the mineral baths, the vast ocean beyond the rock shelf that protected the baths from the crashing swells.

In his white form, seated on a stone bench he stretched his metallic legs, sore after the sail, the wind had risen and the small boat had hummed across the channel. Out across the reef he had seen large crustaceans crawling across the rocks and flying insects in the sky above in swarms flowing with the wind.

The sails vibrated with the wind gusts and the power of the craft surged him into a marine field of relaxation. He enjoyed the timing of the Jibe, before the end of the channel, he had mastered the turn with the wind and when set on the homewards course, he could gaze across to the distant Citadel on the opposite side of the channel, the stone rising like a part of the island through the mist and sea salt.

More exploration had found within the walkway precinct a large greenhouse on one of his morning walks through the city.

The Greenhouse, amazing, the place has some integrated magic to it.

He had stepped into the greenhouse, inside a controlled environment, the irrigation was humming and a fine mist and gurgle he could hear, the plants awash with water, fresh water he tasted, the hoses winding away somewhere above. He had found water there in great pools below, some desalination process was occurring but naturally with different size pools and set around were syphons of metal and clay pots, grates in the floor and alloy type pipes that ran across the ceiling.

The plants in the hot-house were varied with vines, clumpy greens and root plants. Vegetables he hadn't seen before were growing in raised beds and irrigation was controlled and automatic.

So robots eat vegetables as well.

The vast hot-house rose thirty metres, and was twenty wide, all sorts of delicacies adorned the beds, hanging pods of grain type seeds, small shrubs that produced pineapple type fruit, a yellow and red topped carrot-type root species, a spreading brassic leaf type with a red cabbage type fruit, small pods of hard seeds like lentils, green finger fruits, nut-type trees and a meandering ground cover that smelt like rosemary.

There were tomato like fruits, purple oblong shaped smooth skinned, delicious, slightly sweet and hand-sized that he had tested with the OTAA, a mix of vitamins he recognised and mineral content the OTAA had detected, non-toxic, but an unclassified mineral that was unknown.

An unknown mineral.

The OTAA did an analysis and reported the mineral contained an organoboron compound, Trimethyl Borate, $B(OCH_3)_3$. Further analysis confirmed a chemical structure, $B(OCH_{10})_3$.

The OTAA came back with a summary report:

Analysis reveals a trace mineral that has not been recorded in Human history. The potential discovery of previously unknown minerals is thought to be quite feasible. Given the right physical and chemical conditions within the Universe were to arise, other mineral types are plausible. Trimethyl Borate has been linked to theories of the formation of Ribonucleic acid, and therefore the possible role of early life on Earth. Further analysis would require an investigation within a sentient analysis environment and at a Quantum Bound Industries laboratory.

The analysis gave him the motivation to test his new skin, the alloy material that was encroaching his body, a little more each week, now his lower legs were wholly the metal silver-green colour, a flexible type exo-skin.

I am frightened though, that goes without saying, although there is no pain associated with it, yet.

The alloy seemed to mix with the light, and he turned his legs on close examination, while sitting in some rare sun, the colours in the silver, green and blue, flexible. He tested the outer "skin" layer and discovered it was very tough, scraping his foot against the stone wall. The alloy seemed to flow with the stone surface, then as he released there was no defined abrasion. It did not take him long to realise how tough the alloy was, trying increasingly harsh impacts on his foot like some self-harmer.

So, I have superpowers!

The strength of the alloy seemed only limited to the rest of his body's ability, his thigh muscles tired, his feet and lower calves did not. His balance was stable, optimal. If he put his feet on a wall from a lying on his back position, and attempted to rise from the floor , the strength in his feet was able to accommodate him; a new exercise move had been invented, the "back-up."

The feet seemed to stick to the wall or join the wall, rising higher was limited to his knees and thigh strength unaffected with the alloy's spread, but soon to be encompassed.

As a Doctor he was intrigued with the transformation and always equally amazed at his apparent lack of concern. There were no symptoms, pain nor troublesome changes he felt, there was only the image of his body changing like a painting; he was a walking mural in progress. The OTAA reported that the new skin was a Tungsten-based alloy combined with a noble gas field that mixed in a mysterious manner above the skin surface.

The OTAA could not identify the noble gas, a new gas not known. He tried to get a grasp on the situation he found himself in, the absence of anxiety a Psychotherapist's Doctoral theses in itself, he was after all being consumed slowly by a foreign metal, a mysterious alloy.

He should be panicking. *Was it a virus?*

As the afternoon descended, the moon's light streaked the ocean in straight fibrous glistening lines.

The OTAA had confirmed it was a mechanical process, a chemical transformation building a mix of organic and mineral fusion of elements. When he inquired of the outcome the OTAA had replied:

Eventual metamorphosis based on current exchanges of chemical transfer suggest a covering of existing organic tissue by the noble gas controlled alloy by 100% within three weeks. The noble gas is an unknown element and seems to be a controlling entity as I have detected it in all areas where the alloy is present.

There is continued heat exchange and uninterrupted skin cell replacement where the alloy has replaced your skin layer, there seems to be no fundamental changes to the skin-body process that protects you from external hazardous stimuli.

194

Given that the alloy and gas relationship is non-destructive at this stage it is feasible to assume that similar processes may be in play for organ function and associated bodily function at a later stage in the transformative process.

Further analysis and subsequent speculation is beyond the scope of my ability as an analyzer.

Good to know, eh?

He placed the OTAA down beside him. He gazed up at the stars which had made an appearance on a clear cold night, the oceanic weather milling further out to sea. Several small galaxy clusters were visible, seven of them arrayed in a semi circle thirty degrees up in the sky; brighter suns shone within the planet's constellation, some twinkling with the sea salt interruption across their cast light.

He felt stronger, *better than when I was in the Lifeboat.*

He had been desperately sea-sick, a long never ending slosh of stomach to be emptied and sea to be tossed, at the height of the turgid nauseating grind he didn't really care if death was imminent, to be free of the smell of his stomach contents would have been enough.

But now, I sail, transform and eat prepared food.

24

The next day he took the craft out threading himself through to the deep channel, he liked to gaze down at the green sea speeding beside him, and as he did so, flying fish swam and burst through the surface, the silver streaking creatures diving back into the foam within the streaking green wash and current.

There was one major obstruction within the channel, a large barnacled rock that jutted above the channel in low tide and set just below the water line on the high tide, the water swirling above on the shallow summit like a mini-reef.

He usually timed the rock by surging to one side of the channel or the other but on this occasion he forgot about it completely and he struck the submerged behemoth at full speed, stopping the boat suddenly and sending him flinging like a rag doll to the bow and over the edge, the boat sliding past him, the sails akimbo and flapping, the rudder swaying right and left in the turgid current.

oooh er, Mmmm, aghh!

He looked to his left as he trod water, the ocean temperature cold but tempered by the surges of warm volcanic vent currents that surged from below. He saw the great barnacled rock submerged with the green wash. Around the marine trunk small orange ten legged crabs jostled for position in the small crevasses. The low tide's effect, just covering the pillar with water worked in concert with the channel's current as the water milled across its top surface then sank below, exposing the top, a gnarly stone pinnacle.

The boat seemed undamaged, he swam to it uninjured and clambered aboard with some effort. The bottom should have been dented at least with the force of the collision, but the alloy was unbent. The current with the boat's sails flapping and having lost wind power, took the boat to rest on the open sea-side channel bank brushing the coral shelf before the coral shallows proper. He was halfway back, the channel stretched away to the semi-circle arc, the Citadel in the distance, misted with sea salt spray and low lying cloud.

He took a moment to gaze across the coral shallows while the boat languished; he released the mainsail rope more to let the small boom sway and rest to the right so as to stay breaked from the wind.

He sat on the reef, gazing enjoying the day, one of sun and warm current. He saw the section of reef after a while, clouds crossed the sun and then the section lighted then reflected.

What is that?

The contrast between the area that was smooth and the reef highlighted the object, a square shape jutting a little out from the shallow water, not a coral with coral a determined irregular in shape, something different, something that was made.

A hatch in the sea. A cover, a sewer hatch like they had on roads before they were swept away with all humanity.

gazing with concerted effort, and trying to focus more, the definition had not been clear.

A mirage perhaps, he reconsidered, standing to get a better top view.

Ok, I want to find out now.

Curiosity getting the better of him, stepping into the shallows. He secured the boat with his steel rope, finding a small pillar of coral and for good measure secured the stern as well, driving his steel rod into the coral and winding the rope around.

He walked out within the coral outcrops, the clear warm vented water flowing around the barnacled pillars, and crushed coral beds, the stone slime and green, gold and blue crystallised mineral deposits, dissolved then encrusted with the air and dried in withered lines and trails of coloured salt edging the rocks surfaces.

He suddenly realised that he had no footwear and he felt the sharp razor coral but was not troubled by the edges and lifted his feet to gaze at his alloy soles and then let them down again, smiled and set off again as if to say,

Well, that's a perk of becoming the Tin Man.

The "cover" in the distance still sparkled and shone reflections at him, the sun was around a lot today, the coral flat had a mist around , a green haze from the vents below, he stopped to smell it, then took a reading from OTAA, not Carbon Dioxide, some harmless oxygenated superheated air reacting with something.

I don't want to end up a coralised fossil.

Stepping closer to the anomaly. At about ten metres he thought he had made an error with the object he couldn't see, for a time and then realised the sun had gone behind a cloud and there was no contrast on the coral plain. He looked around and waited for the next sun burst, the square returned and he pressed forward. At five metres he saw that it was not from the reef, a box, a jutting hatch, maybe something that had floated there and settled in the coral.

The lid was smooth and there were no defining marks, the colour grey he assumed but slime and lichen had grown on top and was actually the source of reflection as it shined in the sun's rays.

He knelt down feeling the surface, and as he did so a swarm of black beetles flew buzzing past in a fast tempest then were gone above the surface of the shallow sea. He looked around, there was nothing else around but the lament of the coral and the shift of the waters, now channelling through the coral at a faster pace as the massive tow of low tide took hold.

He scanned for the boat which was about a hundred metres distant, the sails flapping and the hull bobbing like a tied up nervous dog outside a supermarket.

He felt around the section where the lid met the jutting chimney-like square tube, the structure was intermingled with the coral and he couldn't tell whether it was the actual cora or an alien shaft built here down into the atoll.

Touching the section with his metallic foot the hatch he suddenly realised was opening. He shuffled back as the automatic door opened like a metal top of a can and tilted one hundred and eighty degrees to rest the lid top on the coral beside the opening.

He hesitated, and waited for some trap device to behead him but the conduit remained still, the lid inert. He stepped forward a little and looked down, in the gloom was a ladder that descended below like a street sewer access tunnel. He wondered if the hatch would have opened with water above it and thought that would be a little silly, it had opened at low tide, he had noticed it at low tide,

I wouldn't see it at high tide.

He gazed out towards the boat and past the atoll, the clouds were variable and the wind was moderate, a partly cloudy day, still a freezing wind but for this time of year bearable enough. He calculated the tide.

Low will be in half an hour, then ten more hours for high, but the hatch would certainly cover in less than an hour.

He looked down the shaft again, nothing was discernible except the descending ladder into darkness. He thought about the options, if he descended and left the boat he may lose it because of the tidal pull which come high tide would be strong, then he would be without transport and the Citadel was a good eight mile swim, or a slow walk on the atoll coral at low tide, something he thought about as a challenge and then realised how stupid he was not considering this anyway, no life-jacket, no rescue.

How fit am I now?

Stepping back, decided that it was too risky,

What is down there anyway? I have no idea. Why would I descend without intel?

As he stood and walked a short distance to the boat, his mind ninety percent made up, the hatch suddenly closed behind him in a clunk.

He approached again and stood beside it, the hatch remained closed. He tested his theory and touched it with his hand, the hatch still remained closed. He grazed it again with his foot and the hatch tilted open again resting on the coral.

The alloy, So, my feet have many uses.

Looking down at his legs that now were covered with the alloy above his knees, the slowly encroaching metal like a creeping lichen on a tree trunk. He day-dreamed, a small alarm sounded in his mind, thinking of when the alloy got to his appendage, *Good grief*, a metal penis. *Would that work the same?*

The question is, will I ever use it again?, he thought dryly, and blinked, looking out to the distant Citadel.

My human form is retained and yet is being converted to another substance that retains the functioning of my Physiology and Psychology, now what the hell does that?

The *Elephant in the room, I cannot ignore.*

He thought about it as usual without anxiety. Looking at the filtering wash of the coral at his feet.

Curiosity, his calm demeanour remained, as though he had the the outcome within him already, as if the alloy had somehow calmed him and told his subconscious the truth, as if to say,

Don't worry, there is no need, a metal man you will become, the alloy is your friend and will secure you, protect you and give you safe passage.

He could feel the warm and cool water as he stood there swirling around his toes and ankles, and he could feel the coral on his soles as if he was standing there unaffected, the only difference being that he was impervious to being cut by the coral, his metal legs an armoured exo-skin. "

Many animals transformed. Butterflies, ants, wasps, jellyfish It's not the concept, he debated with himself, *It's the animal,* his other self said slightly alarmed. *Humans weren't meant to transform,* he concluded.

He used the OTAA to mark his position using the weather satellite link he could still access. He had activated his beacon and sent an IDENT request when he had crashed into the sea, but they had remained unanswered and he initially spent many a waking hour thinking of the outcome of the ship and the Explorer, Jessica and the Scientists, and the crew.

This alarm had faded over time though.

They were uncontactable, maybe dead. But is that the reason I am no longer concerned, rather, just curious? he thought with considered analysis.

He had noticed the alloy in the first week, a small spot on his big toe, the glistening circle casting reflection like a five pence piece. He had rubbed it, scratched it, and tried to remove it using a small survival knife, the blade sliding off like a screwdriver on a smooth screwhead without a drive mechanism.

I didn't feel alarmed then either.

He moved away again from the hatch and the lid closed again, with the now familiar clunk. He set back towards the boat stirring in the wind, the water within the coral rippling with the gusts across the atoll. He checked the position again to be sure and holstered the OTAA, looking one last time at the hatch before continuing towards the boat.

§

He reached the jetty cove as the light was fading and secured the metal rope, wiped his eyes of the salt and climbed the stone steps to the jetty promenade, walking back to the rising Citadel, his metal legs glistening in the sun's rare afternoon rays and sending a long shadow of his stride and form across the massive coloured stone pavers.

My shadow, he thought, noticing the form on the stone,

My shadow, or something else's shadow? he mused calmly, the sound of his footfall an eerie tap concurred with the sound of the wind across the jetty stone.

§

His quarters were a large stone tower room that had a breathtaking view across the ocean, the tower, flat at the top, was he presumed a landing pad for some craft, the metal men flew he assumed, flew something, the markings on the *helipad* were indecipherable, some hieroglyphics from another world but he assumed some sort of landing code.

From the top he was raised three hundred metres from sea level, the distant archipelago stretched to the horizon, the channel glistened a darker green than the sea and winded like a marine river through the coral, delineating two distinct atolls, the one that surrounded the Citadel and the other that rose after the deep trench stretching to the distant just visible massive land mass, he assumed another island or continent. He had windows as well, a stark contrast to what he assumed would be his decor; a mediaeval battlement setup.

The windows were massive and had a protective film layer that filled the space between the stone sills, another alloy creation, it appeared to have the same characteristics, the film flexible and permeable like his strange skin.

The weather was kept at bay, the breeze was not, an interior decorators dream.

'Thinking glass', when it rains it is impermeable, in fine weather permeable. The room's windows resembled the *Universal Flexible Atom-Acrylic-Glass* that was on the Ate Succession, with unique properties.

The stairs winded up a staircase with seven levels, he wondered with all the technology of the alloy why the trudge, until he discovered the lift.

A flat platform sat atop an alloy pillar, like a human lift but without walls or any barrier to prevent one plunging three hundred metres.

"This is super-scary" His first reaction.

As soon as he placed his metal legs on the platform it raised or lowered. The trip was breathtaking; his feet were certainly anchored, the alloy prevented any slippage and sure footing was standard travel. He took the stairs down after rising to his room to see if there was some way of calling the elevator if it was somewhere else. As soon as he stood close enough to the elevator's alloy pole, down it came. He learned by chance that he was able to stop the lift at any floor by standing face on to the building before the next floor, again the lift halted. If he then faced away the lift continued.

Sitting on the stone bed, he ruminated about his surroundings and the properties of the Alloy material. The sky was a green hue as the dusk settled and the reefs swirled below like purple snakes.

He had learned, like with the sailboat, how to craft objects with his alloy ability. The only requirement was that it had to be done if the building material was already available. Like the sailboats' metal hull, he was able to think of a fitting then the alloy appeared in his hands and with a little thought the new creation took shape.

Did that mean some material was taken from the sailboat?

The object loses some of its volume? he mused.

Testing the theory, creating another lid for his metal water bottle, first, floating it with the old cap on.

Then he made the cap from the alloy ability using the bottle as material, placing the old cap back on when floating the bottle a second time to see how much water was displaced in a small tub; the same amount was displaced, he noticed.

So the creation of another object from the source object does not take material or volume from the source object, only copies, he deduced to himself.

So, I can copy physical objects, he concluded, without the loss of mass.

Does the alloy come from somewhere else? Not the mass of the object?

He dropped his towel on the simple bed, a stone mount that jutted from the wall, atop an energy tent underlay he had salvaged from the Lifeboat, the damaged hulk tied down at the cove.

The room cast long shadows from the distant twin suns, their light and heat fading from day to day. He looked down at his body, the alloy had encroached up to his waist, the whole process taking two weeks, his new glistening form now part of his reproductive system.

Well, the appendage works just the same.

His bodily functions remained intact, there were no nasty surprises, only half of him was now the metal, the alloy. He got up from the bed and walked to the window, the atoll glistened in the afternoon light.

His mind had changed he realised, there was now a calmness beyond the absence of anxiety about the alloy that pervaded him, he felt like a contented traveller in a warm place, relaxed and enjoying a routine of salt baths and sailing, luxurious quarters and exotic foods from his greenhouse.

He had dreams, things about contentment and passage, and images of people who were machines he knew but couldn't notice outwardly, their non metallic skin the same as his, their metallic skin the same as his.

The weather was cooling and he knew the Summer holiday would not last, but there were other variables that countered the shift in climate; his legs never got cold and the room was always a comfortable temperature, the salt baths were heated by the thermal plumbing and the whole Citadel was a mineralised stone that seemed to absorb heat, he was surrounded by a micro-climate.

He thought about the hatch and he knew he would have to explore the shaft, the curiosity would get the better of him,

Or will it be the end of me?

He thought about his approach to the hatch. He rose and ascended the short flight of stairs and sat on the top of the tower.

The view is spectacular.

Gazing at the sea, which was partly green where the sun's rays broke through the increasing cloud layer and leaden grey elsewhere, the atoll steaming in place from the volcanic vents.

If it closes, how sure can I be that it will open again? Could it be primed open?, probably not, there was the tide to contend with. And, I am assuming it's watertight as well. adding to his analysis.

He glanced down at his form; the alloy had encroached further *just a little.* Looking at his waistline, the alloy metal shining, his new skin.

He hesitated for the week, enjoying his time within the Citadel, the Elephant in the room was however the *hatch* and while his routine endured the curiosity increased.

25

Andreas Polkinghorn through the great arena, the echo of his step a metallic twang that rose with the stone seats and out to the frozen sky.

He had not explored the farthest reaches of the Citadel, a long jutting section that made its stone way to the East, adorned with what he could ascertain from his tower, buildings like aircraft carrier conning towers attached to the walls and resting half on the pier-like structure, half out as if to save room.

That section is the most bizarre, and reminds me of the 21st Century PC games.

He stopped at the greenhouse. The plants were warm inside the protected structure and free of the salt winds that now blew hard from the West with assorted winter precipitation; snow and ice winds. He had tended many sections, and discovered he could also replicate plants and seedlings and made the latter as he wanted to grow from seed; it seemed a more disciplined method which kept him sane and free from unnecessary rumination.

Red and green capsicum-like varieties that were half red, half green hanging on the tree like strung up kid's footballs, 'Motor-fruit', as he called them a square shaped orange that had three serrated comb-like appendages traversing the body of the fruit, a taste of passionfruit and cucumber combined, and three chilli varieties, yellow long giant pillar shaped, green pea sized, and blue spiny zeppelin shaped.

He liked the work within, repairing the irrigation, the endless trellis preparation and compost lore, his massive tub he created with the alloy technology made from a unique light stone that was slightly flexible and a great retainer of heat for the purpose.

The great walkway led further East as he passed the furthest explored point and entered the "conning tower" type area.

The PC game area.

The jutting pier. much like his sailing cove jetty on the other Western side but he noticed wider, the section as the pavement, a swimming alloy metallic substance that shimmered at the weight of his footfall.

A runway?

The section went out to the East for five hundred metres, he estimated, the deck glimmering in the afternoon light. He entered one of the *conning towers*, a small five by five metre room with a single handle poking through the floor, a silver metallic tube and atop a green handle the shape of an apple.

Slit windows allowed a three sixty degree view on the Citadel, the ocean, and the runway and out to sea. He walked to the end and watched the sea below. As he neared the end section two lights at the jetties extremity came on and shone warm light against the cold afternoon blue. The sea to the East was deeper he judged, there was no reef, the channel arched far away further to the South West.

He returned to the greenhouse on the way back to his tower, through the great walkway, the Citadel's artery, under the mighty pergola, the vines whipped by the cold sea breeze, the stone under his feet warm with the urban plumbing heat exchange system he had discovered.

He collected some red beans and vine ripened golden apple fruit., spending some time in the warm greenhouse protected from the cold planting some more seeds and checking the irrigation for any leaks.

Reaching the jetty with his fashioned rod and cast into the sea afterwards, as he did most afternoons, his contemplative time and his routine to keep active and find his own food. He cast the line as usual, the spot he had selected was near the small boats sheltered cove, the glistening fish would inspect the shallow water and he had good success on most occasions. He hooked a catch the line bending and taunt, vibrating, his alloy fashioned rod a piece of the sailboat he crafted with his new ability.

Reeling in, he heard a voice, he thought behind him and he whirled around in surprise but there was nothing but the cove behind him, the sailboat anchored and drifting slightly.

Please release me, I am a protected species.

He looked at the rod and tried to gauge where the sound was coming from, *Is a fish speaking to me?*

"*I am Tartarus, I am a protected species*"

He reeled the fish in, carefully grabbing the silver-blue species by the head, a fifteen centimetre long specimen, a red stripe down each side, the scales green and glistening in the late afternoon sun.

He released the barb, the hook had punctured the wall in the creature's mouth, which oozed some blood which spattered on the stone below his feet.

"Who are you? Who is speaking?"he inquired of the voice, turning to look again behind him and up to the jetty, the wall walkway, a wind swept rampart, the stone path empty.

"*I am a protected species,   I am a   protected species, Tartarus,*"

He looked down at the creature, the fish was gasping for water. He instinctively placed the fish in the sailboat pool and the creature swam away with glistening speed through the gap to the sea and was gone. He looked at the path of the creature and the foam of the waves that were washing against the sea wall, still trying to gauge whether a fish had talked to him or maybe finally he was deteriorating, his solo Citadel life turning him into a mad traveller in a stone tower.

He wound his rod, the experience unsettling, gazing out to the sea and looking forward to his dining experience in the great kitchen, with the seemingly unlimited supply of prepared food cubes.

"I wonder if I need to make a reservation?" he said out loud deadpan, starting towards the stone stairs to the ancient jetty.

§

As he awoke the next morning he paused by the mirror in his tower room as always.

Robots have kitchens and greenhouses and apparently toilets as well, he mused to himself walking to the small stone container, fully plumbed and water flushed, an automatic device that used sea water. He had not yet traced the path of the sewage pipe.

This will be my task today, to find out where the sewage goes.

He hesitated as he passed the mirror, and noticed he was free of the metallic alloy, pausing in amazement at his familiar but recently lost skinny legs reflected in the room. He approached the mirror and raised his leg, looking to see if the alloy was still there, but he could see no trace, just his skin which seemed unaffected. Turning his torso he inspected his body, the alloy had gone.

26

From the raft, the bank swept by surely and the canopy overhead cast light and alternating gloom as the craft flowed under the varying nettle cover. She made a sure, but nervous progress during the morning, crashing at one stage into a large flowing mass of caught logs and collected flotsam that she caught up to, and was unable to negotiate, the raft like a massive ship when turning, a slow lament.

Using the pole as a pike and moving the mass aside, the raft then picked up speed and she freed herself, leaving the first rubbish behemoth behind, the collection spinning and swirling in the raft's wake. Iris buzzed ahead, always updating her path and obstructions, the immortal flying fish at times jumping ahead of the raft like glistening bullets emerging from the swirling current as if they forgave her.

Every time they jump, I jump, they are beautiful though.

The river, Iris had told her would run through the forested section for another hundred miles or so, some of the forested channels were particularly dark and the twin suns were seemingly allowed to be shining, the cold clouds abated for the past few days with some green and blue sky she could see above at times through nettle canopy.

They selected a larger river bank grass area which came into view to stop for the night, the darkness descending quickly. She used the rudder pole to veer left to the bank gradually, the raft gently hitting the bank.

Securing the line and crawling up the embankment with her pack, making sure the pole and paddle were secured. The area was a flat stony area, some spiked rushes grew among the gaps in the rock. Before the forest trees proper large boulders lined the boundary and strange thin stalks of some plant rose in the gaps in the rock. Wary of her plant experience, she threw some small pebbles at the closest stalk, the plant seemingly inert, the pebbles scattering away with an echoed rattle.

She was delighted with the raft, but terrified of the icy water. In the current, if she fell it could be the end of her. *The raft is a good idea still.*

Noticing her legs were sore already, being on the water had been an exercise she wasn't used to, constantly bending to align the raft's weight. That early night the forest froze white a frost descended and she huddled under the terrain blanket in the warmth of the energy tent upon the rock shelf, outside she could hear cracks of wood and threshes of nettle in the increasing wind as if a front was passing.

Hearing also, what she thought were frogs calling during the late evening, a croaking sharp stretching sound but was unsure due to the wind gusting with a set tempo through the upper canopy; the gusts she could hear coming across the trees before reaching her like a giant using a leaf blower.

Ah, yes, leaf blowers, the scourge of suburbia, wheelie bin puppets and leaf blower trumpets..

§

The cold morning had a new chill as she emerged reluctantly from the energy tents' warm domain. The front had passed and left the air a colder tempest above, the river warmer sending a mist rising into the upper canopy. Iris had skirted as usual ahead.

"There are long hanging vines from the larger tree boughs ahead, they hang close to the water, just be careful they don't entangle you and pull you off the raft," the drone reported.

"Right," she replied thinking about the day ahead, finishing a clam breakfast.

The raft made good progress, up ahead she could see what Iris had seen, long thorny vines had descended from arching tree limbs across the river and were gently swaying across the river in a pendulum motion about a metre above the surface.

A section where she thought she could circumnavigate the tendrils, a gap close to the right hand bank of the river, where two vines seemed far apart. Starting her rudder shift early, she bent to the left, the raft obeying much like a super tanker; a slow turn as if reluctant at the request.

Heading was good as she checked the turn, as she did so, Iris buzzed past up above on a course through the gap she was navigating.

In an instant the drone seemed to collide with the nearest vine but then she realised that the tendrils had grasped the machine and were wrapping it up, Iris's rotors whirred a high pitched snap and two broke off falling into the river with a metallic plop.

"Iris!!," she shouted, still keeping the raft on course, knowing if she got too close her fate would be similar. "Fuck, shit, ohh, Iris can you hear me?," she inquired of the drone.

"Affirmative, stay clear!, they are meat eating vines, they seemed to mistake me for a flying fish, there are some carcasses in here with the tendrils," Iris exclaimed calmly.

The vines seemed incapable of moving far, they seemed to use the wind, Iris got a little too close. She passed in nervous terror between the two hanging vines, then felt relieved as she realised their tendrils were too far apart to bother her.

"Iris, what's happening?"

"I am afraid the vines are breaking my flight components, they are very strong when entwined around a victim, of which I am at the moment," Iris reported. She heard another crack and

another section of Iris fell from height and splashed into the river; she thought it might have been one of her rotor struts.

"Ok, Iris, I am going to moor the raft, hang on," she called out through the intercom.

"No, please don't, there is nothing you can do, the water is too cold for you to retrieve me, too dangerous to approach the vines, besides, what will you do?, swim in the freeze, then climb twenty metres while the plant strangles you to death?" Iris calmly stated. The drone continued,

"My responsibility is to preserve your life, not place you in danger"

At the last comment there was a grinding squeal of bent metal and Iris was flung out of the tendril mass, the plant seemingly unimpressed with the meal, the drone splashing into the river and sinking like a lead stone. She was still flowing downstream but was close to the right bank.

Ruddering against the bank, the flow was weak among the gathered detritus near the river side. 'Iris!,"she screamed, the drone was gone, submerged and lost, there was now no trace of the entry point into the river, the tendrils swayed as if they were harmless *old man's beards* in the wind.

"Iris, do you copy?"

"Affirmative, I am at the bottom of the river, I have no motor function, I have my primary casing intact and the fusion battery compartment attached, but that is all, my rotor struts have been ripped away. I am afraid down here I am not much use to you.

Nor the vine, I was a distasteful meal. I have a visual through your headset, I am glad you made it to the bank. I suggest you moor and do a careful recce down further before proceeding," Iris stated.

'How do we get you out of there? Are you moving with the flow?"she asked, upset and looking around across the river bank, her eyes level with the grass top.

"Not mobile, in fact I am sinking into deep mud, no visibility," Iris reported. "Fuck!," she shouted in frustration. She grabbed the bank and hauled herself up to the grass top, mooring the vine rope to a small sapling nearby. She reached down and grabbed her pack, then stayed kneeling on the frozen river bank, part stone, part odd looking lichen and moss cover, staring at where Iris had fallen about fifty metres downstream.

"Jessica, you must abandon any attempt at my rescue, this would be hazardous and dangerous, I have no way to grab any lowered object to haul me above. The river is flowing strongly down here, and you cannot dive this deep without equipment in zero visibility, and in addition it is far too cold for an attempt, besides...if you did manage to retrieve me, what use am I now?, " Iris stated calmly.

"Plenty of use," she replied, detecting an end game tone in Iris's voice, the drone was at the end of the road. "Oh, Iris," she lamented, "I am sorry, I can't help," she said, upset and looking down at the lichen surface of the rock as if the word *gone* was inscribed for her to see.

"I have to say it's quite unpleasant down here," Iris said in humour. *"Damage report states a breach in my kevlar hull, and this I am afraid will disable my fusion core by default shortly. I am sorry, I…"* The transmission ended suddenly. "Iris,...Iris," she tried to reach the stricken drone, the intercom was dead , she knew Iris was gone., the drone disabled.

She cried, Iris had become much more than a drone, her companion had gone, the AI had saved her life, she sat down on the cold stone, for a moment feeling she had had enough, the rivers washed Iris's watery grave, the current swirling under the vines like a water pyre memory.

The loss of Iris changes everything.

She lamented to herself,looked around, the riverbank wasn't ideal for a camp but the way she felt, returning to the raft seemed a poor choice.

The vines were visible downstream as well, she noticed, she would camp now and do a recce like Iris suggested, the drones last helping hand. She fastened the raft again to be sure and moved down the bank her pack secured, wiping her eyes of her drone sorrow.

Following the bank she climbed some fallen ancient logs, beyond another familiar flat stone area, the rushes, the tall stems swaying in the wind. The river winded left as far as she could see the vines extended down, in some places thick enough she estimated to be an uncomfortable journey, she would have to steer with precision if she continued sailing. The cold tempered her motivation and she decided then to set camp, the area around the raft good enough.

With Iris gone she would have to forage for food herself. *The sooner I learn, the sooner I will eat,* she thought gazing at the river flow thinking still of ways to save the drone.

My overwatch has gone, fuck, now I have to select carefully. she thought, Iris her sentry, and friend no longer with her.

§

The weather stayed clear and cold. She skirted the river bank on foot for two kilometres, the bank hard going, fallen trees, large boughs and washed detritus from previous flood blocked her way at intervals, she had to climb, squeeze and rappel at times to make her way.

The hanging strangling vines seemed to stop after the two thousand metres and she assumed their habitat had come to an end as the river trees subsided from the bank and the river started to exit out to the Western plain, where grass and spiked rushes grew and dominated. She turned around and decided to continue with the raft, returning to the camp.

§

The ancient forest's darkness subsided and the suns were above her as she ruddered the raft downstream. The water was still a constant flow, a meandering current, comfortable with the raft. She passed the last great tree, the boughs gave way to the sky like she was passing through a harbour exit gate.

The green and blue exosphere returned the light, the wind was freezing but light, the twin suns shining, but smaller in their elliptical revolution journey. After her last camp, where Iris had been lost, she had with glacial progress navigated the vine traps; two days she spent plotting her course.

Thankfully the masses of tendrils were too far apart and she was able with terrified steering to wind her way through, at any moment thinking she may have had to dive off the raft if off course and unable to steer away in time, the raft, like a large ship with a delay in turning ability.

As the great forest subsided and the land flattened she paddled her way through a rocky area where the river flowed a little stronger as if it had reached the upper limit of its slow flow and was moving with more gravity downwards towards the Western desert.

The river was still wide she noticed but flowed at a steadier pace through the basalt rocks and the eroded river gully of stone. She had to use the pole more than the rudder and poked her way at times through the course like a pinball game navigating the rocks and flow.

Halting for the day, after coursing through the basalt ridge and out to a billiard table terrain and with steaming pools of volcanic spring and a mat of spiky rush strewn dirt and mineral sand vista. The horizon was clear and a straight line and she could see the ground which stretched from the Eastern to the Western side of the earth; the change a contrast to the covered ancient forest.

The dusk was a red and green lament, the wind subsided and she could feel warm and cold air puffs like a season was changing in minutes. The rock river gorge ended at a large mini lake flat and with a grass dam wall before spilling again through a raised opening and surging again into the river banks awash across the sands and the plumes of hot pools.

I'm exhausted, this section is hard going.

She ruddered the raft through the surging rapids, thinking the wide river would correct her terrible steering and mostly she was proven correct, milling afterwards out the river proper, now surging and faster with the descent of the slope of the land down to the Western plain.

The raft moved steadily and she had only to make small rudder corrections. The morning already had been eventful, finding a dead enormous bird near the river bank, killed she thought overnight.

She surveyed around but there was no sign of the predator and she cut as much of the flesh off the creature as she could carry and stopped to cook a huge portion of meat on her stove which she ate like a salivating beast, the fat juice dripping down her cheeks with occasional starving sounds from her throat. The bird she estimated was at least five metres across and would have stood upright at the same height, the huge legs indicating a ground bird with considerable running power.

She finished her meal and then turned to descend down the river bank and wash her plate when the bird stirred.

"Oh, my, fuck!," she uttered in horror.

The bird she saw had opened its eyes and the clear green glassy cornea of the creature looked at her as though she was another bird.

"Oh, I am so sorry, you poor thing," she lamented trying to gauge what to do to help the beast. She looked around to see if there was anything to seal the gaping wound, finding little but grass and sand.

She shuffled down to the river and got some water in her pan and left it near the bird's massive beak resting in the mineralised sand.

A pitiful attempt, she thought.

The bird breathed with soaring inhalation like a giant vacuum cleaner, and she placed her hand on the beast's side, the feathers a soft beautiful gloss on her hand as they caressed her skin. She felt to see whether the creature's heart-beat could be felt through the massive pimply skin like a chicken leg.

Looking at the wound, she saw small shapes and realised that the healing bugs were coursing over the red and torn site and the creature's skin. In busy swathes the creatures milled around the sections where she had sliced the meat and the flesh started to reform before her eyes and the layers started to mould into the pimply skin of the animal that was the base for its feathers.

*Oh, my..*Transfixed, she watched scared to move.

The wounds started to change from trauma to preservation, and a shining new texture as the bug trail milled from the sand like an attacking cavalry army in full charge.

She cupped her mouth and watched as thousands of her cave companions that had healed her ankle dry cauterise the wound, sealing a repair, dancing in a thousand pairs like an ultimate ballroom display, then dancing in paired circles as one mass like an intricate clock mechanism then exiting the thigh along a straight trail under the bird's hock feathers and back into the sand, trailing down to a rock near the river edge.

The bird then on cue raised its head and shook its beak, back and forth and made a sound like a distant trumpet that some lost band member would play to attract attention in a city's urban maze.

It then raised from the ground, first rolling to a sitting laying position then raising its piston-like legs, the feathers stirring in the wind and raising its neck and head to full height above.

The creature shook itself at full magnificence and a mass of sand and dirt, and a mighty cloud of fine particles surrounded her and blew over to the river's flow. The dust blinded her and she sneezed and coughed and held her mouth as the dust settled on her ex-suit and finely ran in a sheet down her clothing.

Ohh!

She stood stunned, wanting to flee but the beautiful creature held her gaze and she stared transfixed.

The great avian beast rose and turned its head and lowered its beak and stared at her, edging the point of its mandible almost touching her nose. The full ten meter beast craned its neck to examine her.

She breathed in with terror and delight as the beak touched her lightly and she looked at the creature's eyes, both staring at her in a curious way. The two green and tan corneas were cross-eyed, staring across its nose, and glistening like unknown rare marbles.

The fine texture of the inner orb was a shattered fine lined master drawers sketch, star shaped, that seemingly moved behind the aqua colour and the fine dotted structures of the inner eye. Around the eyes and the great beak, finer hairs coloured orange and red surrounded the eye sockets and graduated up to the start of her head feathers.

Oh, hi, hi, don't worry I can't hurt you big one...

She felt the creature's bellowing breath course around her, the smell overwhelming and she wanted to cover her mouth but held her nerve and the creature turned its head and looked across the plain.

She saw the layers of coloured feathers that graduated through the bird's cover, a yellow down then green striated feathers with a purple stripe, blue hock feathers and an upper covering of light brown and grey spotted sheaths. The mighty legs were grey pillars of tree-ring looking skin and the texture of steel radial tyres ending in the three toed feet spanning at least three metres wide on each foot. The bird turned again and nudged her like an old friend; for its size a tender push, but enough to send her almost falling into the river.

Oh..

The behemoth looked at her then turned and walked away onto the Western plain, turned one last time then started to run and galloped away at a dust grinding speed and was gone. A dust cloud rose over the far river bank and she stood still and listened to the footfall of the creature thumping away.

She started to laugh with elation and walked up to see where the bird had *road-runned* away but the plain only revealed a small dust plume where the bird had run into the distance.

Watching as the disturbed dust descended higher with an updraught and she breathed in and closed her eyes and then opened them again and looked at the green sky, then back to the ground where the healing bugs were dancing in pairs beside her feet.

She sat down. The draining experience seemed not due to imminent death but more to the beauty of the beast.

Feeling weak, a sensation enveloped over her, she began to cry, she wasn't sure why, the tears falling down her cheeks in salt rivulets.

With an unfocused gaze she stared out to the Western plain to see if there was any trace of the bird but the wind blew softly and the table of sand was quiet and still. She sat in the sand and wiped her eyes and she noticed something in her hair and she reached up and pulled a small feather that had been caught and looked at the fluff, a slight reddish colour she could see through the fibres.

Calmness spread through her like a soft warm wind; the same wind that she remembered on a pier that jutted out to her parents lake on Earth, where she weaved dreams as a child, where frogs looked at her in the rain without fear.

She watched the river and felt the stone, while sobbing, the salt tears smattered on the rock and dissolved into the air.

She deduced then, that the childhood frogs knew so much more about the world than she, sitting in contentment, the water falling off their slippery skin in small droplets. She sobbed and was happy, the experience had shaken her and absorbed into her like part of the secrets of the planet had been revealed and the Universe had given her some important clue.

Feeling that even if she died soon, then she would have seen enough of the world. Pretending to wrap herself in the birds feathers and day dreamed that the bird would come to her when she lay as it had laid, and sit beside her and arch its wing over her while she lay on the sand if she was at the end of her life and wait till she passed back into the earth and the rocks and the sky.

She sat on the river bank in meditation and watched the raft swirl, anchored with her line to a small shrub on the pebble.

The river wash curled around the raft steeled in the small seeping inlet away from the harshness of the flow, and the water swirled away and she watched the eddies of the current curl from the raft edges and join the the flow as it winded now South West and towards the middle of the continent. She sat and her mind settled, and the quiet of the day enveloped her. She guiltily felt satiated from her live meal and wondered about the bird, and where it had gone.

Filtering the sand through her fingers, the grains fell onto the ground and a noise, like a motor, permeated the air. Startling herself out of her daydream she stood up to better listen to the mechanical din.

Epilogue

Silver weapons flew into the desert sky, as the armoured behemoth thumped and surged through the milling Androids who were chasing the vehicle as well, falling and striding over their broken comrades in a frenzy. Another rocket arced and swished at the vehicle just missing the top of the six wheeled monster, the spinning wheel beast surging in another wide sand churning turn. She watched as a circular serrated saw blade bizarrely spun in an arc high in the sky and then reentered the throng. Another rocket flew into the air the lighting the Androids around its burner like forge workers in the gloom, unguided and spun in a circle, she ducked instinctively then glimpsed, as it then returned to Earth and hit the mob to her far right and exploded sending several Androids flying into the air, and two Android arms spinning away and crashing down on the sand in an almost comical display of slap-stick theatre, one driving into the sand like a flag pole, the other striking a comrade and flattening the Android into the dust head first.

The vehicle roared again and drove a wedge through the rasping Androids, now a raging rasping torrent of mechanical rage, all were running fast and some had grasped the vehicle and were holding onto the sides, attempting to break the side window; one punching the glass which shattered but didn't break, like the plex-glass in Ate. One Android, she saw, held its ground in a foolish attempt to halt the vehicle standing with a chainsaw revving the spinning blade in seething high gain fury as the vehicle approached, standing like a bullfighter in an arena, but not turning at the last moment, the heavy vehicle flattening the Android with a krumping sound detaching the Android's upper body and legs, the two appendages whirling away on the sand, sending the chainsaw chassis spinning up in the air, the chain detaching from the guide bar and looping like a hula-hoop above, then hitting another Androids head on the path down attaching to its neck like a mechanical necklace.